Between one moment and the next, he was right there next to her, kneeling so they were face-to-face. She let out the air in her lungs in a rush, not sure of what she wanted to do or what he was planning to do. She parted her lips but didn't say anything, didn't want to put another question out there for him to address before he answered the one she really wanted to know.

Because she was hoping he was here for her—not for his childhood friend but for the very adult version of her who'd been waiting for him all this time.

Faster than she could react, his lips caught hers. The contact rushed through her in a lightning shot of surprise. Years of bottled-up frustration bubbled up and she leaned into him with a soft gasp.

And then he pulled back and she was left trying to catch her breath.

Slowly, carefully, he slid his arms around her back and under her knees. He cradled her against his chest and tucked her head under his chin. With her circled as she was in his embrace, he held her close. He pressed his lips against her hair.

"That was too close yesterday, Sophie." His voice was low and gruff and almost cracked with emotion. "The thought of losing you just about killed me."

Praise for Piper J. Drake's
True Heroes Series

EXTREME HONOR

"Drake's sharp storytelling shines with an engaging plot that's thick with tension and sizzling with David and Lyn's attraction."
—*RT Book Reviews*

ULTIMATE COURAGE

"If you're looking for something sexy, strong, yet sweet at the same time, then *Ultimate Courage* will not disappoint."
—*Heroes and Heartbreakers*

ABSOLUTE
TRUST

ABSOLUTE TRUST

PIPER J. DRAKE

FOREVER

NEW YORK   BOSTON

Copyright © 2016 by Piper J. Drake
Excerpt from *Ultimate Courage* copyright © 2016 by Piper J. Drake
Cover design by Elizabeth Turner
Cover copyright © 2016 by Hachette Book Group, Inc.

Forever
Hachette Book Group
1290 Avenue of the Americas
New York, NY 10104
forever-romance.com
twitter.com/foreverromance

Printed in the United States of America

First Edition: December 2016
10 9 8 7 6 5 4 3 2 1

OPM

Forever is an imprint of Grand Central Publishing.
The Forever name and logo are trademarks of Hachette Book Group, Inc.

The Hachette Speakers Bureau provides a wide range of authors for speaking events. To find out more, go to www.hachettespeakersbureau.com or call (866) 376-6591.

The publisher is not responsible for websites (or their content) that are not owned by the publisher.

ISBN 978-1-4555-3608-5 (mass market edition)
ISBN 978-1-4555-3607-8 (ebook edition)

This book is dedicated to Courtney Miller-Callihan,
who has kept me sane and protected me from myself,
who listened to me tell stories about my dogs
and the working dogs I'd met...
and said this, this is what I needed to write.
Thank you.

CHAPTER ONE

It was a quiet Tuesday afternoon in New Hope. Few people were out and about on the main street when it was this cold out, which was perfect for Brandon Forte. The jet-black German Shepherd Dog walking just ahead of him needed space for this excursion, a couple of things to look at but not too much to excite him. A few people to see was good for them both, too, so long as they weren't going to be overwhelmed with requests to pet or take pictures.

Besides, the bake shop all the way down on this end of town tended to have day-old baked goods at a discount, and the shop owner occasionally gave Forte a cupcake or cookie on the house along with special home-baked dog treats for whichever dog was with Forte. It gave the dogs and him something to look forward to on the walk.

Today, it was Haydn. Haydn was a seasoned veteran and one of the dogs Forte had trained on active duty for the Air Force. Now, Haydn had come to Hope's Crossing Kennels for a new kind of training. The black GSD had a lot of physical therapy ahead of him. He'd been fitted with a prosthetic to replace his front left leg prior to arriving, but it was up to Forte to help Haydn figure out how to use it. The big dog had walked the kennel grounds fine but was obviously getting bored. It happened with intelligent animals, the same way it could with people. Both of them were more than ready for a change of scenery and terrain.

Thus, the outing and the very slow walking.

Besides, it took skill to stuff a chocolate cupcake with cookie dough frosting dusted with sugar in one bite. A man needed to practice once in a while to make sure he could still manage it.

And it was a necessary skill, as far as Forte was concerned. Sophie tended to bring her own cooking and baked treats to Hope's Crossing Kennels every weekend. She was a close friend to everyone at the kennels, an integral part of what made the place home to each of them, and she was...more to him. If she caught him partaking of other sweets, she'd never let him hear the end of it.

Now if it was about dating, she never had a word to say about any of the women he saw or the one-night stands he indulged in now and then. He'd bumped into her once in a while in Philly on the weekends. They both dated, and it couldn't matter less to her who he chose to spend his time with, as far as he could tell. But take a taste of someone else's baking, and he was in for a world of hurt. Thus, the one-bite-and-inhale technique. Because she had a knack for popping up out of nowhere.

Which made it more fun when he took the risk and did it anyway.

Of course, he had a long history of crossing paths with Murphy's Law, and apparently, this was his day for it because who would be walking down the street but the very person he was thinking about?

Sophie Kim was five feet, two inches of nonstop energy, usually. Today, though, her shoulders were slumped and her steps lacked the brisk cadence he'd always associated with her. She was heading out of a small art gallery with a large paper shopping bag, and despite the difference in her body language, she was still alert. The woman had expansive peripheral vision and excellent spacial awareness.

Which meant she spotted him and changed course to head in his direction immediately.

Forte swallowed hard.

She must've come directly from work because under her very sleek black trench coat, she wore a matching pencil skirt. Three-inch red heels popped in contrast to the severe black of the rest of her outfit. Which did all sorts of things to him. Naughty things.

The kind of things that were so good, they were really bad. Especially when a woman was off limits.

"Hey! Is that the new guy?" Sophie slowed her approach, keeping her gaze locked on Forte's face.

She'd been around tiny dogs all her life, but she'd spent enough time at Hope's Crossing Kennels over the past couple of years to have learned how to meet the much bigger dogs in Forte's care. Training working dogs was his thing. Or in Haydn's case, *re*training.

Always a work in progress.

Sophie had been there when he'd come back from active duty, too battle weary to continue deploying. She'd helped him with the accounting when he'd established Hope's Crossing Kennels and had generally integrated herself into the private world he'd created for himself, Rojas, and Cruz while they all rebuilt lives for themselves.

Some people might've assumed he'd spent a lot of years running from New Hope between high school and now. He'd been away a long time, explored a lot of different places around the world. But there'd been no question about where he'd end up between deployments. He always came right back. And her friendship, her smile, had always been waiting for him.

Sophie's bright smile faded as she waited for him to answer. She always sensed when he got too caught up inside his own head.

"Yeah." Forte came to a halt and murmured the command for Haydn to sit.

Instant obedience. Despite his injury, surgery, and current need for recovery, the dog was as sharp as he'd been on active duty. The mind was eager, ready to work. The body, not so much.

Sophie's smile renewed, the brilliant expression stopping his heart, the way it had every time he'd seen her since they'd first met way back in high school. She came to a stop in front of them, barely within arm's reach. "He must be doing well if you've got him out here for some fieldwork."

Haydn remained at ease, unconcerned with her proximity, as Forte and Sophie stood there. Curious, even, if Forte was any judge of body language. And he was. For dogs, at least.

He shrugged. "Easy going with Haydn. He needs a lot of light walking, over different kinds of surfaces, to get a feel for his prosthetic. We're not out for too long. I don't want to tire him out or put too much strain on his legs."

Sophie nodded in understanding. "Glad to meet him, though. I thought I was going to have to wait until I stopped by this weekend."

While they spoke, Haydn watched them both. Then he

stretched his neck and sniffed the back of Sophie's hand, which she'd been holding conveniently within reach.

Introductions were simple with dogs. Stay relaxed, let the dog know the approaching person wasn't a threat via body language, and give the dog time to investigate on his own. Sophie's body language was naturally open and non-threatening. She had learned from Forte not to look his dogs in the eyes. The dogs he trained tended to be dominant and aggressive, and they required a more careful approach than the average pet on the street.

Usually, he preferred if a person asked to be introduced, but this was Sophie. If she'd approached anyone else, she'd have requested permission to say hi to the dog. But this was him and her. Between the two of them, everything was an exception. She spoke to him and took it on faith that he'd tell her if she needed to keep her distance. But then again, he also wouldn't bring a dog out in public that wasn't ready to be socialized.

It showed how well she'd come to know the way he worked in the past few years. He'd changed with every deployment. It happened. And she'd adjusted and accepted those changes in him without a word when he came back. She was the steadfast forever friend.

He'd never told her why he'd left in the first place or why he'd come back. She was so good at just accepting him that she might never know. And he was a coward for not telling her.

"What's your plan for him?" Sophie glanced down at the dog, now that he'd sniffed her hand. "Haydn, right?"

Forte gave her a slight nod, and she ruffled the fur around Haydn's ears. The big dog's eyes rolled up, and he leaned his head into her hand for more enthusiastic scratches.

Definitely no problems socializing. Then again, in Sophie's hands, most males turned to Silly Putty.

Or...he needed to stop thinking about what could happen to him in Sophie's hands.

"Yeah." Forte cleared his throat. "He's got a couple of weeks of physical therapy first. Then we need to coordinate with the Air Force on his adoption."

"Ah." Understanding in one syllable. She had the kind of caring heart to fill in the gaps when something went unsaid. "His handler didn't make it?"

Part of why Sophie was one of the only people Forte felt easy around was because she got it. Only needed to explain once. And she *listened* the first time. Sometimes no explanation was required at all.

Forte shook his head. "Same IED that injured Haydn took out his handler. The deceased's family has been contacted, and they'll have first choice to adopt. We haven't heard back yet on their decision, but those kinds of things can take some time coming through the communication channels."

Sophie nodded and looked down at Haydn. "We'll give you time to figure things out while all the paperwork goes through, huh? It's nice to meet you, Haydn."

The black GSD leaned into her, his tongue lolling out in response to the attention and the use of his name. Haydn knew when someone was talking to him and, apparently, he liked Sophie's voice.

Every bond between working dog and handler was unique. Haydn was dealing with the loss of his handler in his own way, mostly by being generally friendly with the trainers and those to whom he was introduced. But there was friendly and there was truly affectionate. A deeper level of affection was something Haydn seemed to be holding in reserve. This physical training period would give the dog the time he needed to be ready to bond with someone again, too.

If he decided to. It was always the dog's choice.

"Where's your car?" Forte was not going to stand around long enough to be jealous of a dog. Not at all. "We'll walk you."

"Right across the street." Sophie jerked her head in the direction of a small parking lot.

They headed over, Sophie falling into step next to Forte. She didn't try to take his hand or tuck her own around his arm. They weren't like that. Besides, she knew he didn't like to be all wound up with a person when walking out in the open. It was another way her understanding of him manifested. It was a regular reassurance. A comfort.

Better than free cupcakes.

"Has Haydn met Atlas?" Sophie asked casually.

The first rehabilitation case at Hope's Crossing Kennels had been Atlas, a dog suffering from PTSD after his handler had died. One of Forte's trainers and close friends, David Cruz, had worked with Atlas and still did now that the dog had become a permanent part of the kennels. But Atlas's challenges had been psychological. With the help of Lyn Jones's approach to working with dogs, Cruz had successfully brought Atlas back up to speed.

"Briefly." He glanced at Sophie and caught her making a face. "The dogs don't need group therapy sessions."

The psychology aspect of the rehabilitation was something Forte was willing to entertain only so far. Lyn got results with her work, yes, but he was not going to go all the way into the deep end with the dog whisperer approach.

He made a stupid face right back at Sophie. "You do not need to come over and sit Atlas and Haydn down to compare notes on what they've been through. Souze doesn't need counseling, either."

Souze was Rojas's partner, a former guard dog turned service dog helping Rojas face the challenges of reintegrating into civilian life.

Sophie was silent a moment, a sure sign his guess at her thought process was on target. "Well, they do need to play with each other sometimes, right?"

"Dogs are social creatures, and, yeah, some playtime is good if they can socialize with other dogs that way." He'd give her that. Forte made sure the dogs trained at Hope's Crossing Kennels could socialize well with both human handlers and other working dogs. "Haydn's the second military working dog to come to us for help after active duty, but his challenges are mostly physical. We have to watch him carefully with the prosthetic on until we all know what he can do with it, including him. But, yeah, he's gone out with Atlas and Souze on a couple of group walks without the prosthetic."

Honestly, Haydn was pretty spry even without the prosthetic. The dog just had better mobility with it.

"Okay." Sophie let it go. "I just think you and your working dogs could use a little more playtime in your lives. Like a doggie field day or something."

He snorted.

Sophie's car was a sensible sedan, the sort to blend into a lot of other normal, everyday cars. What made it easy to spot was the pile of cute stuffed animals across the back. Not just any stuffed animals—a gathering of cute Japanese and Korean plush characters from her favorite Asian cartoons.

As they approached, Sophie juggled her shopping bag to pull her keys out of her purse and triggered the trunk.

"Need help?" Forte came up alongside the car, scanning the area around the parking lot out of habit.

"No worries." Sophie lifted the trunk door and carefully placed her shopping bag inside the deep space, leaning in to move things around to where she wanted. "I need to make sure this is arranged so stuff doesn't shift. It's delicate!"

He was not going to admit to anyone, ever, how much he was willing to stretch his neck to catch sight of her backside while she was leaning over.

Haydn sniffed the side of the car. The big dog was very engaged, his relaxed attitude changing over to a sharper set of movements. Forte tore his attention from Sophie. Actually, the black dog was very interested in the car.

Forte tuned into the dog's body language, changing his own to match. He leaned forward a fraction, his balance over the balls of his feet. He kept his limbs loose, ready to respond to the unexpected. It didn't matter that they were in a sleepy town on the edge of a river in the middle of a peaceful country. It didn't matter that there shouldn't be any real danger there.

Haydn had detected something out of place. Something wrong. Forte's stomach tightened into a hard knot. Nothing wrong should be anywhere near his Sophie.

His attention centered on the sniffing dog. Whatever Haydn did next, Forte would act accordingly.

Haydn deliberately sat and looked up at Forte. It was a clear signal. One Haydn had been specifically trained to give as a military explosives-detection dog.

Shit.

"Sophie. Step away from your car." He'd explain later. Be afraid later. Rage. Worry.

Later.

She popped up from the trunk. "Huh?"

"Do it."

They had to move now.

Sophie always listened to him, Rojas, or Cruz when they were urgent. She complied, thank god. He gave Haydn a terse command and circled around to grab Sophie and get more distance. He steered her across the parking lot toward a big Dumpster. It'd serve as good cover. Then he reached for his smartphone.

They got a couple of yards away, and Sophie craned her neck to look back at her car, even as she kept moving with him. She always did as he asked immediately, but she had a brain, and she insisted on explanations after she complied. "What—?"

Behind them, the trunk hatch came down with a solid *thunk*.

Forte let out a curse and grabbed her, pulling them down to the ground and rolling for the cover of other cars as an explosion lifted the entire driver's side of her car.

*   *   *

Sophie screamed. Maybe. She was pretty sure she did, but wrapped in Brandon's arms and smooshed up against his chest, she wasn't sure if she'd gotten it out or if it'd only been in her head.

The explosion was crazy loud. The concussive force of it slammed into her and Brandon despite the shelter of the cars and the Dumpster he'd pulled them behind.

He covered most of her, one of his hands tucking her head protectively into his chest. His other arm was around her waist. They were horizontal.

Not the way she'd daydreamed this would happen.

After a long moment, all she could hear was the ringing in her ears. Her heart thundered in her chest. And she thought, maybe, Brandon's lips were pressed against her temple.

Or was it her imagination?

His weight lifted off her, and his hands started to roam over her, gentle but with purpose. Looking for injuries.

His voice started to penetrate the roaring sound filling her head. The words slowly started to make sense. "Are you hurt?"

"Haydn?" She sounded funny in her own mind, but Brandon met her gaze for a moment and jerked his chin to one side.

"Don't turn to look until I check to see if you hurt your neck or head." His admonishment came through sharp. It was the way he talked when he was worried. People thought it was meanness, but it wasn't. He was frightened. For her. "Haydn's right here. He's fine; a little shaken up by the blast, but his training will help him keep his shit together. He's fine."

As Brandon continued, a cold nose touched her cheek. Big ears came into view, and warm, not-so-sweet breath huffed across her face.

"I'm glad you're okay," she whispered. It was for both Brandon and the dog.

A brief whine answered her. Then a large, furry body lay down next to her, just barely touching her shoulder and side. A fine tremor passed through the big dog and then he pressed closer to her.

"He's going to stay here with you." Brandon rose. "Can you lay here until the ambulance comes, Sophie? Please? He'll be calmer if he has you to watch over."

Then she realized things hurt. Her right shoulder, her hip. Pain shot from her right ankle. Maybe the only thing that didn't hurt was her head. Brandon wasn't just worried about Haydn.

"Is it bad?" She stared up at Brandon as he lifted his smartphone to his ear. Sirens were already approaching.

Brandon held out his hand. "Give us space, please. Stay off the blacktop!"

People must have been gathering. He was stepping out to take command of the situation. He was walking away from her. Again.

"Don't leave me," she whispered. She always said it quietly. Because she didn't want him to actually hear her.

A soft *woof* answered her instead. Careful not to turn her head, because Brandon had asked her not to, she looked as far to her side as she could. There was Haydn lying next to her. His eyes were dark, almost as black as his fur. And his gaze was steady on hers. Calming. He wasn't going to leave her.

"Okay, Haydn," she whispered to her new friend. "We'll wait right here for him."

It was what she'd always done. And this time, she had company.

CHAPTER TWO

Forte leaned against the wall, keeping an eye on all approaches in the hospital corridors. From his vantage point, he could monitor the elevators to his right and the nurse reception area for the floor. To his left, the hallway stretched all the way down to the one emergency stairwell. If anyone odd showed up, he'd see them right away.

Haydn lay with his big head on his paw at Forte's feet, keeping him company. The dog appeared to be resting, but his ears were up and alert. They'd both been there for hours since Sophie had been brought in, assessed in the emergency room, and admitted for further observation. Haydn had accepted a bowl of water from the friendly nurses, but Forte hadn't taken them up on offers of food from the cafeteria or drink. His stomach was a tight knot of cold anger, pent up and controlled, waiting to hear more on Sophie's status.

Those hours had been long and filled with tension, but they had allowed both Haydn and Forte to assimilate the "normal" sounds on this particular hospital floor. Any time an unusual clang, ping, or voice broke that learned sound-track, Haydn's ears twitched and Forte searched for the source to assess the potential threat.

It might be overkill. Maybe. Forte was reasonably certain it wasn't. He'd wait until he could check in with Rojas and Cruz to be sure.

Officer Kymani Graves was in Sophie's room now, asking her about the explosion. In the absence of Sophie's direct family, Ky had arranged with the hospital to allow Forte to remain nearby. Which was good because nothing would've kept Forte from being as close to Sophie as possible. He'd almost lost her today, and his heart stopped every time he thought about it.

Forte had to respect the hospital staff, though. They'd been understanding and had given him space. Apparently, they'd gotten used to the vigilance of the Hope's Crossing Kennels trainers when one of their own was under medical care.

Back then, it'd been Alex Rojas keeping watch. Elisa had become the kennel's administrative assistant and an integral part of Rojas's happiness. When she'd been attacked by her stalker, Rojas and his dog, Souze, had intervened in the kidnapping. It'd been too close a thing for any of their peace of mind. But Elisa had only needed a few hours under observation to be sure she hadn't suffered any major injury from the harrowing ordeal.

Forte hadn't envied Rojas the worry, but he'd understood. Or thought he had. Now, when it was Sophie here, Forte wasn't sure how to keep the seething combination of rage and anxiety in his chest under control.

Sophie—*his* Sophie—had been hurt. There'd been a bomb in her car.

Until they all knew exactly how and why it'd happened,

there was no way he was leaving Sophie's safety to question. She wasn't just a childhood friend; she was his reason for breathing.

And he'd never said it to her out loud.

Haydn lifted his head, issued an almost inaudible whine, and came to his feet. Forte murmured quiet praise and reassurance, straightening away from the wall to stand and be ready for what might come next. The GSD wasn't his, specifically, but Haydn had been right there with him through the hours without a single complaint. This was work, and Haydn was a working dog at heart. It allowed the big dog to focus on the task at hand and get past the aftershock of having been near another explosion.

Ky emerged from Sophie's room, closing the door behind him quietly. The officer glanced down to the end of the hallway, then turned to find Forte and smiled. Relief flooded through Forte at the sight of Ky's brilliant white teeth contrasted against the backdrop of his dark skin. The man had a grin that could disarm an entire crowd.

"She's fallen asleep." Ky reached Forte in a few long strides, his uniquely resonant voice pitched low so it didn't travel too far down the corridors. "I asked her a few questions, but she wasn't able to answer in much detail. I'll be back in a few hours to question her again once the initial sedation has worn off. The doctor tells me she'll be more lucid after she's had a chance to rest and recover from the shock."

The doctor had grudgingly given Forte a more detailed catalog of Sophie's injuries. Superficial cuts and scrapes from the asphalt of the parking lot were the least of the worries, though the most visible at the moment. Mild tinnitus would mess with their hearing for a while longer but was likely temporary. The cars around them and the Dumpster had saved them from the shock wave of the explosion, thankfully. But contusions incurred from falling to the ground would start surfacing in a couple of days, and Sophie would be aching, sore, and in some pain from those. The biggest concern at the moment was her right ankle. She'd twisted it severely as they had gone down and they'd need X-rays to determine whether it was broken.

It could've been worse. Unspeakably worse.

Still, Forte considered every one of those injuries his fault. If he'd recognized Haydn's signal sooner, gotten her away from the car more quickly, she might not have been hurt as badly. He had his fair share of scrapes and bruises, too, especially across the outsides of his forearms, but he'd learned a long time ago how to fall and get to his feet ready to take action. Sophie had learned to land on mats at Revolution MMA in the women's self-defense workshops, not on hard asphalt with things blowing up around her. She'd stiffened up as they went to the ground and hadn't quite rolled with him as he'd tried to distribute their momentum. It'd been enough for her to come out the worse for wear between the two of them despite his attempt to protect her from flying shrapnel.

"I'll stay with her." Forte didn't expand on how long. It wasn't even a question. He'd watch over her while she needed him.

"Her family's out of town, from what I gathered?" Ky didn't pull out his notebook. The police officer had an excellent memory. Forte guessed he took notes only for the benefit of the people he interviewed.

"Yearly visit to South Korea." Forte considered the date. "They should be back just before Christmas, in about a month and a half."

He'd been considering how to reach out to them. He wasn't her father's favorite person in the world. Actually, the exact opposite. They hadn't spoken since Forte had graduated high school, and her father wouldn't be happy to speak to Forte now. The man had made it clear all those years ago that it didn't matter what kind of person Forte grew into being; Forte would never be a good enough person.

And her father was right. Forte was not a good man.

"Sophie didn't want them contacted." Ky grimaced.

Forte shared the man's frustration. Family should be contacted, but Sophie was an adult, and even if she was out of it currently due to medication, her life wasn't immediately in danger. At least not from her injuries.

"I'm betting she managed to mumble about being back on her feet by tomorrow and no need to freak everyone out. She tried to make you promise to let her family enjoy their vacation, didn't she?"

Even as Forte finished the thought, Ky sighed. "You know her better than anyone."

Yeah. He did. Forte chuckled. "I've known her a long time. Don't worry. I'll be here. Lyn and Elisa will probably be here as soon as the doctors say she can have visitors."

With Lyn Jones and Elisa Hall would come David Cruz and Alex Rojas, respectively. Sophie was a part of Hope's Crossing Kennels, even if she didn't work there. Oh, she kept the accounting on track, but in reality, she was the heart of Hope's Crossing Kennels. Her caring came in the form of home-baked rolls, pastries, and cupcakes. Her laughter filled the shared kitchen in the main house, and every dog had learned the sound of her footsteps on the grounds.

He wouldn't have it any other way.

"Blood is family." Ky paused. "Family can be more than blood. I'll have a word with the doctor about each of you."

"Thank you." Forte's throat closed some at the thought. Yes, the others from the kennels were Sophie's family, too.

What he felt for her was...a different kind of connection. "We'll keep watch while she's recovering."

And once she was discharged from the hospital, having him keeping watch nearby would liven up her apartment complex some.

Ky only nodded, his brows drawing together. "We're actively investigating the explosion. The forensics team is on site now and studying what they can of the car. There aren't any immediate answers. Let me ask her what happened when I get back. Until then, if she wakes up, keep conversation away from anything I'll need to ask her later. It'll be better if she answers me to the best of her memory, without the filter of anyone else's impressions on what happened."

Forte nodded. Sophie would be full of her own questions when she woke up. But he understood the implicit warning in Ky's words. With her at the center of an active investigation, it would be best if she didn't receive influence from anyone around her, accidental or not.

For his part, Forte raised his eyebrow at Ky. He couldn't ask Ky about an ongoing investigation, and Ky couldn't tell him anything anyway. Not directly.

Ky snorted. "It could still have been a random incident. A lot of people could've been caught in the explosion with it going off in a public place, and it was lucky no one else was hurt. It was good for every person in the general area that you and one of your dogs were present to call out the warning. Who is this, by the way?"

Haydn tipped his head and looked up at Ky as the officer gestured at the big dog. Innocuous as it was, it was still a motion in Haydn's direction, and the GSD was sensitive to it.

"*Zit.*" Haydn complied immediately, sitting at his side and turning his dark gaze up at Forte for the next command.

Satisfied, Forte returned his attention to Ky. "This is Haydn. He's joined us at Hope's Crossing for some physical therapy and advanced training with his new prosthetic."

"Fine dog. Never thought we'd need a military explosives-detection specialist here." Ky didn't crouch to pet Haydn. It was a silent acknowledgment that both Haydn and Forte were in working mode. "Well, I've got your statements on record already, and I'll arrange for you to be point of contact while her family is out of town. Your name was listed as emergency contact anyway, so it shouldn't take much convincing with the hospital staff. If I need to find you, I'm guessing I only have to come here for the time being."

Forte nodded. "You've got my number once Sophie's discharged. Or you can ask for me at the kennels."

He might not be there, depending on where Sophie decided to stay while she healed up, but his partners, David Cruz and Alex Rojas, would know where to find him. He planned to have eyes on Sophie until they were absolutely sure who had set the IED and why.

Ky nodded, his expression showing no sign of surprise. "I'm on this, Forte. We'll find out what's going on."

Forte nodded in return. Ky trained at Revolution MMA with Rojas and Forte. They had learned to spar together, run timing drills, and train in various forms of martial arts. This wasn't an official collaboration, but they were working together all the same. Ky was good people.

With a parting nod, Ky headed over to the nurses' reception desk. The tall, lean police officer paused to chat with the nurses. Forte envied Ky's ability to set civilians at ease, engage them, and foster an open channel of communication. Every nurse there had a bright, cheery expression for Ky. By the time he'd finished checking in with them, he'd probably heard all about their lives, from what they'd had for breakfast to where they went after their shifts were over. The useful part of the flow of information was the amount shared unintentionally. Nurses noticed everything. Ky would find out if there'd been anyone poking around on any of the hospital floors looking for a recently checked-in patient.

When Ky straightened and gave Forte another nod, Forte relaxed. No unusual visitors on the patient floors.

As Ky left, stepping into the elevator, Forte resumed his watch.

*   *   *

Something was beeping.

Sophie drew in a deep breath, slow and steady. The air had a tang of disinfectant. She opened her eyes, blinking rapidly. Waking up was a struggle, the way it could be when she'd napped too hard, too late in the afternoon. But it was well past afternoon based on the darkness outside the window, and there was only one sterile, white light behind her head.

Where was she?

The beeping picked up speed, and she took in the rest of the room in a rush. A chair in the corner, a tray stand. The bed she lay in had guardrails. Sheets layered with a tan blanket covered her. Her entire body ached in a dull throb, accentuated by a sharper pain in her right ankle and a few other places. Cuts and scrapes, maybe? Not the ankle. She tried to wiggle her toes through the pain.

A quiet knock came at the door.

Startled, Sophie tried to respond and croaked. Swallowing against the dryness in her throat, she tried again. "Come in."

The door opened slowly, and something below her line of

sight came in the room, panting. Then Brandon opened the door wider, holding a cup. "Thought you might be ready for a few sips of water."

Relief flooded through her. He was here. Hungrily, she took in the sight of him from head to toe, noting the scrapes on his muscular forearms and the torn state of his left sleeve. His dark hair was disheveled, the way Korean pop stars tended to wear their hair to look sexy. And on Brandon, it was a good look—even if she was sure he hadn't done it on purpose. How he managed to look so incredibly hot even banged up and the worse for wear was beyond her. The man cleaned up well, but parts of her still melted whenever she saw him rough and ready for action.

To be honest, she was melting now as his broad shoulders filled the doorway, and not in the delicate-flower kind of way. More likely, she was a hot mess.

Sophie made an effort to fix her gaze on the cup of water in his hand and nodded gratefully. "Is that Haydn with you?"

"Yeah." Brandon came to her and pressed a button on the side of the bed. The bed made a soft buzzing noise as it raised her upper body to something closer to a sitting position. "Did you want to see him?"

She tried to take the cup from him, but he didn't let it go. Instead, he held it to her lips. Heat warmed her cheeks as she gingerly placed her fingers over his to tip the cup and sip. Cool water slid over her tongue and eased the dry tightness in her throat even as electricity zinged through her fingertips from touching his skin. Another sip, and a third, then Brandon gently pulled the cup away.

"Let's take it a little at a time." His tone was gruff, but with the odd note of gentle amusement she hadn't ever heard him use for anyone else. "Haydn."

Brandon placed two fingers on the side of the bed. Haydn

reared up and placed his good right paw on the bed. He struggled with the prosthetic and missed the edge.

"Oh." Sophie started to lean forward, but Brandon touched her shoulder gently. She settled back.

"It's okay. He's still getting used to it, and this is the first time he's tried to do this on command." Brandon watched Haydn find a comfortable position standing.

For his part, after the initial awkward moment, Haydn seemed unfazed. He regarded Sophie with a doggie grin.

"I'm glad you're okay, too, Haydn." Sophie remembered the earlier part of the day, parts of it coming to her in bits and pieces. In particular, the feel of the asphalt pressing into her back. And the warmth of Haydn pressed to her side as they waited for Brandon and the EMTs to come to her. The big dog had made the fear less in sharing and she'd done her best to swallow the sadness of Brandon stepping away from her.

It was stupid. She always told herself it was because Brandon was a far-ranging spirit and she'd never wanted to try to hold him in place. His nature wouldn't change. It was why she'd spent so many years convincing herself he was better, safer, as a friend who came and went throughout life instead of hoping for other kinds of dreams.

And today, he'd stepped away because he was needed elsewhere. It made sense. It wasn't because he'd been trying to leave her. He'd been ensuring the safety of everyone in the area, including her.

She kept rationalizing it all to herself. It was only helping her feel a little bit better.

"How are you feeling?" Brandon's voice brought her back from the memory and her own tendency to chew on things.

Sophie blinked and looked up into those hazel eyes she'd known forever. They were more green than brown right now, because of the green in the shirt he wore. It was the same shirt he'd been wearing when she'd last seen him, so she couldn't have been asleep for too long. The ripped-up sleeve was beyond mending, though, so she made an extra effort to commit it to memory since he'd probably toss it in the rag pile later. "What time is it?"

He raised an eyebrow at her. "You first."

Oh. "Sorry. I'm fine."

A jumble of questions filled her brain, and she hadn't meant to ignore his.

"First of all, no need to be sorry. It's about twenty hundred hours. Elisa and Lyn are going to be here any minute so they can see you before visiting hours end for the night." Brandon turned his head and gave Haydn a quiet command. Haydn let his tongue loll out as he backed away from the side of the bed and dropped down to all fours again, disappearing out of sight. "Second, you have a habit of ignoring your body. You always say you're fine, and at least this evening, I'd like you to clarify."

Her mouth had fallen open midway through his second point. She realized it as her tongue started getting dry again. Closing her mouth and swallowing, she tried to give him a real answer. "My ankle hurts. I guess I got scraped up in a few other places. And I'm a little sore but not ready to cry or anything."

He nodded. "The doctor will probably be in soon. I let him know you were awake. Can you give him even more honest detail when he gets here?"

Of course she would. Well, okay, Brandon did know her. She preferred not to make a big fuss out of things. Being in a hospital at all was out of character for her, but even she couldn't argue the need for formal medical attention after being caught by an explosion.

Her body tensed at the memory of it. Startled, she drew in a quick breath and then forced herself to exhale slowly. She didn't want to think about it.

"How did you know I was awake if you only just came in?" She accepted another sip from the cup of water he offered. The monitor issued an irregular beep as her heart stuttered. Damn. She couldn't keep her cool around Brandon even for something as small as this. "And you could just give me the cup."

Brandon didn't give her the water, but at least he made no comment about the heart rate monitor. "Haydn got excited and started sniffing at the bottom of the door, so I figured it meant you were awake. Your eyes are pretty dilated, and you might be shakier than you think, so I'm making sure you don't accidentally dump it all over yourself."

Easy as that. Simple answers to her questions. Totally logical. That was Brandon's way. But something had changed about him. His gaze had weight to it, and his intensity was focused more directly on her than it'd been in a long time. But they weren't teenagers anymore, and the adult version of Brandon had a lot more impact than his teenage self had had.

Her nipples had gotten embarrassingly tight under her hospital gown.

Be that as it may, she was not going to let him start getting fussy over her. If she did with even this little thing, he'd get out of control. "I'd rather hold my own cup."

Silence.

Irked, she put more force into her words. "If I spill it, I'll take accountability for my own shaky hands. Give it."

Grinning, Brandon held up the cup for her. She took it from him carefully, determined not to let a single drop spill. He'd had a point, though; she was unsteady. But she wasn't going to let him be right. Besides, having his fingers so close to her mouth inspired too many interesting ideas. She took a long sip of water to prove she could without spilling and to clear her head of inappropriate thoughts.

Then again, most of what popped into her head when it came to Brandon was inappropriate.

Suddenly the room got crowded as the doctor and several of her friends all arrived at the same time, including Ky. Elisa and Lyn beat the doctor to Sophie's bedside while Brandon prudently stepped aside and closer to the head of her bed.

"How is she?" Elisa asked, the question directed at Brandon.

Brandon nodded to the doctor, behind Elisa and Lyn.

The doctor was the same one who'd taken care of Elisa a little more than a month ago. Sophie recognized him. "Miss Kim is going to be fine. Banged up and bruised with a few cuts and scrapes. We'll be taking her to radiology to get a few scans of her ankle. Once I see those, I'll be able to determine what the next steps for her right ankle will be."

"Why is Ky here?" Elisa asked.

Alex Rojas stood behind her and let her ask the questions, which were incidentally the same as some of the ones Sophie had herself. When great minds thought alike, it was easier if only one of them did the asking.

It was Brandon who answered Elisa, though. "There was an IED in Sophie's car. No one was hurt, luckily."

Elisa paused. "An IED?"

"Improvised explosive device." Alex gave her the terminology in grim tones.

Brandon, David, and Alex exchanged one of their serious looks.

"Lucky is right." Sophie shook her head slowly. "Someone could've been seriously hurt. What the hell was a bomb—IED or whatever—doing in the middle of suburban Pennsylvania? In my car?"

The doctor cleared his throat and glowered at all of them.

Brandon spoke smoothly beside her. "Officer Kymani Graves is in charge of the investigation. We don't know much of anything, but he's going to need to meet with Sophie and me to talk through what happened again."

That caught her by surprise. "Again?"

The doctor leveled a patient look at her. "Officer Graves spoke to you in the ER and while you were being admitted. Once you were transferred to this private room, I gave you a mild sedative to help you recover from the shock of the explosion. He did ask you a few questions at the time but has returned now to follow up if I deem you ready and able."

They all remained silent for a moment. Sophie absorbed the last bit and decided it wasn't up to the doctor, really. "I feel fine."

Brandon tapped her shoulder with a finger.

"Achy and bruised," she amended. "And my ankle does hurt. But I'm definitely able to talk with Ky. I have some questions for him, too."

The doctor grunted. "Let me check a few basics first."

The doctor made a shooing gesture to get Elisa and Lyn out of the way, and then he leaned in close to check Sophie's eyes. She wondered if they were really as dilated as Brandon had said.

"How long is Sophie's family out of town again?" Elisa continued discussion behind the doctor. "They went back to Korea for an extended holiday, so it's going to be a while. Will she need anyone to help her out at her apartment?"

Good point. But then, Elisa had a way of thinking through the practicalities of a situation quickly. The boys had been lucky the day Elisa had walked into Hope's Crossing Kennels. She'd done amazing things with the administrative side of the business once Alex had hired her. She'd become a major part of Alex's life, too, as well as a good friend to Sophie. Still, she'd start organizing the "get Sophie home" initiative without any input if Sophie let her keep going.

"No." They all leaned around the doctor to see Sophie. She set her jaw and got ready for a battle of wills. "I'll be totally fine on my own."

"I'll take you home." Brandon stepped into her peripheral vision on the other side of the bed. He must have slipped around behind the bed, still managing to be right at the head and within easy reach.

Sophie looked up at him and smiled. "I'm fine. You don't need to go through the trouble."

Honestly, having him take her home would've been wonderful if it'd been for other reasons. She might have a few choice daydreams about it, but she didn't want it to be because he felt obligated to take care of her.

His eyes narrowed, and a crease formed between his brows. "You're not. And it's not trouble. You help us out at the kennels all the time. Me taking you home is easy."

"It's not necessary," Sophie insisted. "I'm perfectly fine getting home on my own, and I don't want to make this into a big thing."

If it'd been Lyn, David would've been allowed to help. If it'd been Elisa, then Alex would've wrapped her in a hug and convinced her to let him help.

But this was Brandon. They weren't a thing. She wasn't going to let herself even start to believe his taking care of her was anything other than friendship.

Brandon Forte's friendship was important to her, and she wasn't going to let her bruised heart make this into anything more than what it was.

CHAPTER THREE

Forte stepped out of Sophie's hospital room, Haydn close at his heels. The hallway was clear. Cruz and Rojas sat waiting for him at the end where he'd stood watch earlier in the afternoon. This time, with his two partners there to help keep an eye on the approaches, he slouched into one of the armchairs in the small waiting area.

Damn. There'd been days when he'd been deployed where he'd gone out knowing he or any of his unit might not return to base. A day could start out peacefully and go to hell in a cascade of explosions and gunfire.

But today. Here. He'd almost lost her.

The relief of seeing her safe and whole, blinking those chocolate-brown eyes at him, was enough to leave him shaking. She just meant so damned much to him.

"Today was unexpected." He didn't need a response, but both men standing by grunted an agreement.

Rojas had Souze with him, the handsome black-and-tan German Shepherd Dog sitting next to his chair wearing a service dog vest. Souze had become Rojas's service dog, helping to control and ease Rojas's post-traumatic stress disorder symptoms. Cruz had Atlas with him almost as much but not today. Atlas was a working dog, not a service dog. They tried to respect the appropriate time and place for the dogs in public situations, no matter how well trained they were.

"Sophie didn't ask to see the boys?" Rojas sounded worried.

Normally, she would've asked after both dogs when she hadn't seen them. Rojas had ordered Souze to wait outside when it'd become clear the hospital room was going to be too crowded for two aggressive dogs, and Haydn had already been inside the room.

Forte shook his head. "She will the next time she sees one of us for sure. She's still shaking off the effects of the bomb."

Cruz grunted again, this time an angry sound. "Not something anyone just shakes off."

Forte nodded. Truth.

Finally seated, with people he trusted around him, Forte let some of the weariness take over. Aches and pains from his own exposure to the explosive shock wave throbbed in a dull, steady beat. They'd get worse over the next couple of days, but he'd deal. The doctor had given him a once-over, too.

The three of them might look calm, and they were maintaining the quiet, easy tones of a relaxed conversation, but every one of them was scanning their immediate area. A similar emotion to what Forte felt burned in Rojas's gaze and in the set of Cruz's jaw. They were all on edge, angry.

Even with the investigation led by Ky, there was no way any of them were going to sit around waiting to see if anything else happened. They were going to plan and execute on what they planned. It was just a question of what, when, and whether they could rest up enough to be prepared. Forte gave Haydn the command to lie down in a low voice, and the dog obeyed with a groan.

Rojas studied the dog. "Should we take him back to the kennels to get some down time?"

"Probably." The question had layers to it, the opening for deciding what the next steps were without being obvious to idle listeners that might walk by at a given moment. Forte didn't want to send Haydn away, though. He'd checked the big dog over, and Haydn had come out of the whole thing in better shape than he and Sophie.

"He's doing real well with this hospital environment, though. You might want to keep him with you if you're going to stay here." Cruz lifted his chin to indicate the whole building. Because there was a need. They all recognized it. An IED, a bomb, in a car wasn't a random act. Not here. Maybe if this had happened in DC or some other major city, but not in a riverside town with a big-city feel. "The other dogs in training aren't as seasoned. Haydn's your best partner for the moment."

Easy, relaxed. Yeah, Haydn was handling the surroundings well. And Forte would need a partner when more IEDs were possible. "He's amazingly steady since the explosion."

"Yeah?" Rojas let his hand fall to Souze's shoulders, his fingers burrowing into the thick fur there.

None of them were free of memories of IEDs. They'd all experienced their share from their multiple deployments. The when and where didn't matter. There'd been enough situations for multiple lifetimes. But Haydn's were the freshest, and he'd been exposed at close distance again today.

"Sophie asked for him and he settled in next to her. Pulled

himself together and kept her calm." Forte owed the dog for that alone, if there was any kind of way to repay the comfort Haydn had given Sophie. It wasn't something quantifiable. "Either way, Sophie woke up jittery, but seeing Haydn distracted her. I'd rather she stay distracted until Ky has a chance to ask all the questions he has for her."

The well-being of the dog should come first, and Haydn should have a chance to go back to his familiar kennel and get some rest. But if Haydn could be of help to Sophie, Forte was torn. Ky would share as much as he could with Forte, but the team at Hope's Crossing Kennels had crossed paths with shady groups twice in the past year now. Forte would not take the risk of assuming this was a freak coincidence.

"For now, I'll take off his prosthetic and let him rest." The other two waited while Forte followed his words with action. Once the prosthetic was removed, Forte checked Haydn over for bruises or sensitive spots. He'd left the prosthetic on for longer today than Haydn had worn it since he'd been fitted. No signs of overuse, but he'd keep an eye on Haydn. For the moment, the big dog was happy to remain lying on the cool floor of the waiting area. "I want eyes on Sophie around the clock."

Neither Cruz nor Rojas expressed argument.

"We can stretch to cover the lessons for the next day or two." Rojas took up the conversation again once Forte returned his attention to the humans of their group. "It'll free you up to get Sophie settled back at home."

"Think she should go home?" Cruz asked. "Lyn was asking whether Sophie should come to the kennels."

They all chewed on the suggestion for a minute. The kennel grounds were more secure. It would be easier to watch for the next move of an enemy they knew existed but hadn't yet identified. But they weren't active military or law enforcement. They couldn't just whisk Sophie away even if it was for her own good.

"Sophie wants to go to her home." Forte drew the sentence out. Something about it twisted him inside, but he respected the life Sophie had built for herself since they'd graduated high school. She had a career, an apartment of her own, friends and family. Most important, she'd put her life together the way she wanted it. "I'll take her there and make sure she's okay. Depending on what the doctor says, things could be simple and all she'll need is rest, or things could be complicated."

Whoever had set the bomb might come back to make sure their target was well and truly dead.

Cruz shrugged. "We can help with whatever."

"Whatever she lets us." Rojas grinned. "This is Sophie. She's got a mind of her own."

"We're going to make sure she's safe, regardless." Forte leaned forward, resting his elbows on his knees. "We need to look hard at the possibilities."

The other two men sat forward, grins gone.

"We crossed a couple of ex-SEALs and some still active duty when Atlas came to us." Cruz rubbed his chin. When Atlas's handler died under suspicious circumstances and Atlas had come to Hope's Crossing Kennels, there'd been multiple clashes with ex-military-gone-private-contract resources. "There's a possibility Lyn's father would have some insight. We'll reach out, see if there's activity in this area again. He's going to want to look into it if there is."

Forte nodded reluctantly. None of them wanted to lean on Lyn's father. He was still active military, high ranked, and involved in a very discreet investigation. The less to tie him to them, the better for all involved. But this was more about sharing information. Giving Lyn's father a heads-up could be good in the overall scheme of things.

Rojas sighed. "We didn't make friends with Corbin Jr., either. Either him or Daddy could be irritated with us."

"True." Forte was starting to fight off a headache.

Joseph Corbin Jr., Elisa's stalker, was awaiting trial for assault and attempted kidnapping. He and his father had the means to get him out on bail. In the meantime, they couldn't go after Elisa again, but they had the connections to go after someone close to Elisa.

Or someone who meant something to all the people who'd become a part of Hope's Crossing Kennels. Like Sophie.

"Either is a possibility, and there's a lot of potential threats from either direction." Forte clenched his jaw. "I don't plan to leave Sophie open to further 'accidents.' If we can convince her to leave town for a while, that'd be a good way to take her out of harm's way."

"She's not going to like that." Rojas sighed. "Not arguing with you. It's just that Sophie will listen and comply in an emergency. Now that there's time for her to make decisions, she's going to need to understand and agree with you before she decides to disappear, even if it's only temporary."

Forte nodded. "We'll make a case. In the meantime, we should probably talk to Elisa and Lyn."

"Or you could include us in your powwow." Lyn smiled to take the edge off her comment. Cruz leaned back in his chair and held his arm out. Lyn stepped into the curve of his arm and placed her own around his shoulders, leaning against his chair.

Elisa patted Forte's shoulder as she circled around him. "Your meeting should include us today."

She gave Souze a quick scratch at the base of his ears before she dropped a kiss on Rojas's cheek.

Forte wasn't going to argue. There would be times when he and Cruz and Rojas would need to speak privately, but this time it was more efficient to communicate with the ladies directly. They were all strong personalities, and he respected their judgment. Having their agreement would make protecting them much more effective.

"We're going to ask you ladies to take extra measures to ensure your personal safety." Or at least *he* was asking, though Cruz and Rojas nodded in time to his statement.

Both Lyn and Elisa were silent for a moment.

"I'm not going to ask the obvious." Elisa started to knead Rojas's shoulders. "But I do want to know what you think could happen and why."

Watching Rojas's guard ease at his lady's touch, Forte was just a little jealous. Then again, both Cruz and Rojas were incredibly happy with their ladies. They were like new men. Still the friends he'd come through hell and back again with, but they were whole. They carried the scars on their souls from the various horrors they'd each been through, but they had healed in a way.

It was like the *kintsugi* pottery Sophie loved at the museums. The pieces of pottery had broken, and instead of being trashed, they'd been repaired. Gold had been used to fuse the pieces back together and fill the cracks. The broken pottery was whole and had become something more for having been broken.

Forte considered the situation. "More explosives are a possibility. Sophie's car was parked in a public lot in broad daylight. It wasn't left overnight. Whoever did it had brass balls the size of Manhattan."

He bit down on the last comment. Shit, he tried to be more respectful around the ladies.

Lyn waved away his comment. "It's okay. You're worried

about Sophie, and I'm inclined to agree with you even if I don't know exactly what it would take to accomplish it. So what do you want us to do?"

Forte glanced at Cruz and Rojas. They both gave him a nod. They were taking his lead in this. If he proposed something they didn't agree with, they'd interject.

"Probably best if neither of you drive anywhere on your own, especially if you're going to leave your car parked for any length of time. Would you mind if one of us drove you, or if Gary and Greg brought you back and forth from Revolution?" It'd limit their outings for a while.

Forte looked at Elisa in particular. He hated to limit her freedom only a few months after she'd definitively broken free of her ex-boyfriend's influence.

"I assume Boom will be asked to do the same." Elisa looked from Forte to Rojas for confirmation. Rojas nodded. "That's fair. Makes it harder to target one of us with the same attack, right?"

Maybe the ladies were picking up too much vocabulary from them. Guilt pinged in Forte's chest and he struggled with it. He valued their presence at Hope's Crossing Kennels and what they did for his friends. He didn't want to be a darkening influence on their personalities. And he definitely didn't want to bring more danger into their lives by association.

Forte sighed. "Most likely, the next time will be different, but there's no need to leave any of you vulnerable to it. Atlas has some military explosives experience. Souze doesn't. His training is specifically *Schutzhund*—search and service oriented."

Atlas had been a military working dog for the Air Force. He and his handler had been assigned to various military units, including work with Navy SEALs. There weren't many dogs like Atlas, with multiple skill sets. As excellent as many working dogs were, they usually focused on a particular set of training. Scent dogs could specialize in explosives detection, live human search, narcotics, and more. Training them to recognize more than one category of scent and differentiate enough to know what they were actually being asked to find in a given situation wasn't standard procedure.

It was doable, though.

Haydn was specifically an explosives-detection dog.

"We've got one or two other dogs in training with an aptitude for explosives detection," Forte said finally. "We can make use of their training if we need to. In the meantime, we're asking you to limit how much you all go out, and when you do leave, check in with us often. Maybe every half hour?"

Lyn's eyebrows raised, but she didn't voice an objection.

Elisa nodded. "I can text. I don't think we need to make it a phone call every time, do we?"

Forte shook his head. "Couldn't hurt to call if you're gone a while, though."

"For now," Lyn agreed.

"So now that's settled." Alex pulled out his smartphone. "We've got at least one potential client coming on site tomorrow to stay in the guest cabin."

Forte groaned. He'd forgotten.

"Beckhorn sent him, saying he was good people," Cruz added.

Cruz's friend at Lackland Air Force Base didn't give his recommendation lightly. Beckhorn knew dogs and men. He was sending them a good potential owner for one of the dogs they'd trained up.

"He's staying about a week, right?" Forte struggled to remember the details. "Looking to bond with one of the GSDs for search and rescue, some specialized attack work."

It was a hard truth when it came to training dogs for military and law enforcement: These dogs would need to protect themselves and their handlers.

Cruz nodded. "I can meet with him and get him settled until we know more about Sophie's situation."

Forte sighed. "That'll do for the next twenty-four hours or so."

Rojas pitched in, too. "Once we know more, we'll plan accordingly."

* * *

Sophie looked around at her hospital room with its single chair, utilitarian tray table, and off-white micro-blinds. It could be so much more comforting with some sheer curtains and maybe a simple quilt.

Judicious attention to details could make a big difference. And right now, she could use those to cheer herself up.

Her car was blown to pieces. Literally. And she didn't have it in her modest budget to buy a new one unless she delved into the one special nest egg she'd promised herself she'd never touch. If she'd lived directly in Philly, the loss of her car might not have been as big an issue. Walking was absolutely feasible in the city. Or if she'd lived directly in New Hope, it would also have worked out somehow, because one could walk from end to end of the small town. But no, her apartment was in the middle of suburbia, where it took ten to twenty minutes to drive anywhere, much less walk there, and the commute to her job was a minimum of thirty minutes by car.

Now that she'd had her visit with the radiologist, she'd

had a good look at her ankle. Even if it wasn't broken, it'd be a while before she could do anything but hobble from point A to point B. Driving, even if she had a car, would've been insanely awkward.

Fantastic.

"Anyone hungry in here?" Brandon was back at her door.

Her heart skipped a beat the way it always did when she saw him. It didn't matter whether it'd been days since she'd seen him or minutes. The man had an impact on her, and she'd be damned if she let him know what he still did to her.

Brandon was a kind man, even if he had the hardened-soldier thing going on. He wouldn't let their friendship continue if he knew he broke her heart every time she saw him.

Ugh. Pull it together, Sophie. You're usually better than this.

Then again, she'd been blown up and rolled across asphalt, then poked and prodded at the hospital. Maybe she was entitled to a judicious amount of internal whining, so long as Brandon didn't know about it.

"You're still here?" She kept her words light, but hearing them, she clamped her mouth shut. They had come out sounding like she didn't want him there. And that was absolutely not the case.

Brandon entered the room anyway. Since she was still sitting up, she managed to glimpse Haydn trot into the room on three legs.

"Before you freak out and ask what happened to Haydn, he'd been wearing his prosthetic long enough. I decided to take it off before it rubbed him raw." Brandon skirted around the end of the bed and set a tray down on the table. Then he started to wrestle it into position closer to the bed so the tray was comfortably over her lap. "Standard chicken and veggies for dinner, but I managed to get you an extra helping of the red Jell-O."

Sophie leaned to one side to get a better look at Haydn. "He's okay on three legs, right? I've seen videos online of animals who can move around great on three legs, even two."

Brandon chuckled. "Figures you'd like those videos. Yes, Haydn can get around just fine on three legs in a lot of cases."

Haydn appeared at the side of the bed. Maybe she was projecting on the dog, but she sort of thought he looked happy to see her. She was definitely glad he was there.

Thinking about Haydn was a lot better than thinking about her current situation. "Then why does he need the prosthetic?"

"Will you promise to eat if I explain it to you?" Brandon sounded more amused than annoyed to her. But then again, it was Brandon. If he was too irritated, he'd just leave. He never did anything he truly didn't want to do.

She nodded solemnly.

He huffed out a laugh. Reaching across the bed to touch the edge nearest Haydn, he gave another quiet command. Haydn reared up and placed his good paw on the edge of the bed. His other front leg ended a couple of inches below the joint, the shorter fur covering most of the stump.

"Haydn has a partial amputation." Brandon gently touched the place where Haydn's leg ended. "If he was older and not as prone to the level of activity he's been used to, then he might have been fine without a prosthetic. He can move along for short distances easily in a limited amount of time."

Sophie tipped her head to one side. Haydn, watching her,

mirrored her. She couldn't help but smile. "He seems so energetic."

"He is." Brandon hesitated. "Haydn, *af*."

The big dog returned to the floor. His fur was so dark, he looked truly black in the hospital room lighting.

"The amount of weight he'd put on his good leg was a big deciding factor. The more he tries to do, the more stress will be on the good front leg. The prosthetic will help in turning or moving from side to side." Brandon tapped the tray.

Sophie picked up a spoon and started eating her Jell-O. He narrowed his eyes at her, so she widened hers in response. "What? There're two servings. I can have one before and one after the standard stuff."

He shook his head. "No matter what, it's important to make sure the prosthetic is a good fit or he'd try not to use the leg. Then it'd be dead weight."

"Huh." She didn't even worry about talking around a mouthful of sweet. "He can't go back to active duty, though, right?"

"Correct." Brandon's expression went neutral, which was his version of sadness. "But he can still be active. He lives to work. He wants to work. This is the closest I've seen him to his old self since he came back to Hope's Crossing, based on the videos they sent with him."

"But he doesn't have a forever home yet." She ached for him. "Poor pup."

"He is an adult working dog, Sophie."

She wrinkled her nose at Brandon. "He's lost probably the most important person in his world. And now, anyone he gets used to might be gone again in a few weeks. It's really tough for animals."

Her father would've said it was just a dog. But then, her father had spent most of his life in South Korea. Perspective on pets differed from culture to culture, and her opinions varied widely from her father's in a whole lot of ways. Brandon was another example.

She and her father had never been in agreement about Brandon.

"You both must be tired, though." Her thoughts were wandering down weird paths. The fatigue must be getting to her. Or the pain medication. "You two should go back to the kennels and get some rest."

The tray moved away, and she realized she'd managed to eat half the meal. "Don't eat my second Jell-O."

The bed started to collapse slowly behind her, lowering her back to a reclining position without laying her flat. It was much more comfortable.

"It's okay for you to rest, too." Brandon's voice came softly, right next to her ear.

She turned, found herself nose to nose with him. His eyes were still a deep green. "Why did you stay so long if you need to rest?"

"Because, Sophie," he whispered, "you hate hospitals. I'd never leave you here alone when you hate being here."

He remembered. But he was Brandon. He always remembered.

CHAPTER FOUR

Ready to go home?"

Sophie sat forward and immediately started to press buttons on the guardrail at the side of her hospital bed. "So ready! Tell me you brought pants."

"We did not bring pants." Lyn sounded way too cheerful about that.

"You're kidding, right? I can't wear the outfit I was wearing yesterday." The clothes in question were folded neatly in a plastic bag and sitting on the one chair in the room. Her very cute shoes were tucked away under the same chair. She wasn't going to be wearing those shoes any time soon, either; not with her right ankle and foot encased in a medical boot. "You know what? I don't care. I'll walk out of here with no pants on."

She struggled harder with the guardrail.

Lyn sighed, gesturing to the wheelchair behind her in the hallway. "You mean roll out of here."

Sophie didn't even respond. She just started to wrestle

with the damn thing, trying to lower it by brute force. Which she apparently didn't have a whole hell of a lot of today.

"Whoa, whoa. Let us help you with that." Elisa hurriedly set down the tote bag she'd had slung over her shoulder and crossed over to study the guardrail. "These things usually have a button to make it simple."

"That's the problem." Sophie blew out a breath in frustration. "This one's modern enough to have a lot of buttons. Every one of them does something nifty, but I'm too stir-crazy to sit here and figure out which button does the exact thing we want it to at this very moment."

Lyn laughed outright. "Patience is not one of your virtues."

Elisa snickered.

Sophie narrowed her eyes at both of her friends. "No, it's not. But normally I can at least pretend it is. I'm just so done with this place."

She'd slept in this morning. Something she never did. When she'd realized the time, she'd almost panicked. But when she'd called in to work, they had seemed surprised she'd called in at all. Her boss had told her to take the time she needed, of course, and that they'd talk when she returned to the office. She'd ended the call with a very bad feeling.

Yesterday had been an afternoon off at her boss's suggestion, one she'd started with an excursion for some retail therapy. She'd planned to splurge and binge on some sweets, then maybe go over to the kennels and indulge in a massive round of stress baking. All to avoid thinking about the recent change in climate at the office and her doubts about the career she'd chosen.

She'd only accomplished the one thing on her list, and even that was for naught. The tea set couldn't possibly have survived the explosion. Her day had been completely hijacked in a way no one could've anticipated.

Kind of like her life.

If she believed in signs—and she did to a certain extent—then she'd figure yesterday was a big one. Change. Things were changing in abrupt, hurtful ways, and she wasn't sure what she was supposed to do next.

At the moment, she had no desire to do anything but get home, curl up on her sofa, and sulk.

"Sophie? What's wrong?" Elisa had lowered the rail, and Sophie hadn't even noticed.

"Sorry." Sophie dredged up a small smile, not wanting to worry Elisa.

"Do you want to talk about it?" Elisa stepped to one side as Sophie carefully swung her legs over the side of the bed.

Elisa had escaped an abusive relationship. Her ex had not only been an intelligent, calculating person, he'd been a man of influence and financial means. It'd taken a combination of courage and wits to not only survive being with him but also to leave. As a result, Elisa was hypersensitive to changes in mood in the people around her. She could walk into any situation and immediately gauge the temperature of the personalities around her.

Sophie didn't try to hide her troubled thoughts. Elisa would only call her out on them. It was part of the reason Sophie valued her friendship.

"Did you all wonder why I was in New Hope yesterday, in the middle of the day on a workday?" Only Ky had asked her yesterday, in his capacity as a police officer. So he'd been the first person she'd told. Today, she needed to tell her friends and maybe some of the anxiety would give way so she could do something constructive about it.

Lyn pulled the wheelchair into the room and closed the door. "We figured you'd get around to telling us."

Now was a better time than later, then. They'd been wondering, and she really appreciated their consideration in not peppering her with questions yesterday when she'd been out of it.

"I was wondering, too." It'd been weird. A red flag. "My boss gave me the afternoon off, and I was wondering if there was something wrong at work. Maybe the company is going under."

Lyn sucked in a breath.

Elisa's eyes widened. "Do you think your job is in danger?"

Sophie pressed her lips together and shrugged. "I'm not sure. I'd gone through the morning tasks and prepped a couple of client folios for afternoon appointments. My boss called me into his office to comment on how hard I'd been working lately. Then he said I should take the afternoon off. Clear my head."

It'd been out of character for him. Since the day she'd started working with the small accounting firm, they'd always had the expectation that she be in early enough to set up and be working promptly at the start of the business day. Staying late was a given around tax season, but it happened heading into the fall, too, because a lot of small businesses set their budgets in the fall. There'd been a lot of work to do over the past week or so, and she'd put in long hours to keep them all from getting buried.

"Seems odd." Lyn owned her own dog training business, working with dogs with behavioral issues and their owners. She'd been successfully running her own business for years.

"It was, absolutely." Sophie tugged at a length of her hair. "And I was excited to take an afternoon away. It's been really uncomfortable at the office lately."

Elisa frowned. "How so?"

Sophie considered for a moment. "More tense than usual. Everyone's snapping at each other. I took the time to reconcile an extra few sets of client data in prep for their upcoming budget reviews, and my boss snapped at me for handling other people's client work."

Lyn raised an eyebrow. "Did he have a point?"

"Yeah." Sophie sighed. "I was doing the same for my own clients, so I figured it was just another set of things to do along the same lines, and I was already at the office late anyway. But I guess I may have stepped on a few toes."

"If it's interoffice territory, seems like something that could be cleared up with a frank discussion." Elisa's voice had taken on a more brisk tone. She'd worked for a few years in a corporate environment as a very capable project manager before she'd gotten involved with her ex. "Communication can resolve a lot of these situations."

Sophie nodded. "It was my boss's client, and I've taken on some of the overflow before, so I hadn't thought twice about doing it for this. But it's not just the one incident. Everyone has become more irritable, on edge. It's not a big office, and the environment has gotten stressful in general."

Elisa studied her. "You said you were excited to take the afternoon off."

Sophie nodded, a knot of tension in her chest loosening. This was the issue she'd been chewing on since yesterday. "It's one thing to be aware of the work environment and relations with coworkers. But something's wrong with me, too. Yesterday afternoon, I felt like I'd won the lottery. I couldn't wait to head out of there."

"Seems like a normal reaction," Lyn ventured.

"Only I've been considering taking a mental health day here and there for months now." Sophie looked up at the ceiling. "Once in a while is fine. We all need a break from what we do for a while to come back fresh. But I've been waking up almost every morning now having to convince myself to get up and go to work instead of calling in sick and taking a mental health day."

Both Lyn's eyebrows shot up this time. "Okay, yes. That's not a good sign."

Elisa retrieved her tote bag from where she'd set it against the wall. "Let me guess what's eating at you, then. You don't want to go to work. Then you feel guilty because you ought to go to work. Then you make yourself go to work and end up mentally, emotionally, and physically tired because you probably should've taken a break but feel guilty for wanting it."

"This is supposed to be the career I wanted." A hint of bitterness crossed Sophie's tongue. "I went to school for accounting, took internships to gain experience in it, and I'm lucky to have this job so soon in my career."

Or at least she knew she *should* feel lucky. She didn't. Accomplishing goals was rewarding, but actually doing her job? She gained more joy out of refining her recipe for strawberry sweet rolls with vanilla frosting to make Brandon's eyes roll into the back of his head.

"You've worked hard to advance this far in your career." Elisa's words were firm.

Sophie nodded. "So why do I hate the idea of being an accountant for the rest of my life? It's what I should want, but I don't. I just don't want to be practical Sophie anymore."

Elisa and Lyn smiled. Neither of them looked surprised or disappointed. There was none of the censure Sophie had been half-expecting.

"I think we need to get you freshened up and into the casual skirt I brought for you." Lyn's tone was brisk, almost cheerful. "Then all three of us are going to go back to your place and raid your tea stash to continue this discussion. I'm betting you have home-baked cookies at your place, too."

"Right now? We're going to put this on pause right here?" Sophie was miffed.

"Yup." Elisa was obviously backing up Lyn on this one. "Mostly because a whole lot of mental clarity can be found over a cup of tea and a few of your cookies. And somewhat because Brandon is going to stomp in here and try to help if we take too much longer."

"Why is Brandon still here if you two are taking me home? He has obedience classes to teach." She knew his kennel schedule by heart.

Both of her friends stared at her.

After a moment, Lyn cleared her throat. "This has been a long time coming, but I'd say you're going to be making a lot of life choices in the near future. We may need something stronger than tea and cookies."

Elisa snickered. "We could spike the tea with bourbon."

Sophie struggled to hustle into the clothes they'd brought for her. "You two just want to raid my cookies."

Lyn tipped her head to one side. "Valid assumption. We also want to get you settled and make sure you feel comfortable."

"I'm always comfortable in my own home." Sophie huffed in exasperation.

"Good." Elisa's voice took on a brisk tone. "Then let's see how comfortable you are with Brandon. In your home. Because we plan to leave him there with you."

* * *

Sophie had worked hard on this little apartment. She'd repainted the one bedroom, bathroom, kitchen, and living room herself. The floors were a light-colored hardwood, softened by a few thoughtfully placed rugs. She'd kept the furniture sparse to keep the feeling of wide-open space, even if her actual square footage was limited.

It was her cozy haven. One that currently had a man banging around in her tiny kitchen.

Sophie eyed Brandon's broad back as he moved around her stove and counter space like they were his. "You have classes to teach, dogs to train."

People to see, things to do. He'd built the equivalent of a small ecosystem on the acres of land he'd bought four years ago when he'd returned from deployment. It was a haven, in Sophie's mind. And it was unsettling to see him anywhere but there.

Instead, he was here. And this might be the first time he'd been here for longer than a few minutes. She didn't plan to ever admit to him how happy it made her.

Lyn and Elisa had been true to their word. They'd settled her on her couch and retrieved cookies from her kitchen plus tea spiked with bourbon. They'd taken up Brandon's offer to move around furniture to make it easier for Sophie to be comfortable. So she'd nibbled on a cookie, wide-eyed, as she watched him heft her solid wood breakfast table and move it within easy reach of her couch. Then Lyn and Elisa had brought the chairs over and sat with her for a quick chat.

In the end, they hadn't gotten around to talking about her career again. Brandon hovering nearby hadn't helped. She'd been distracted and pondering if there was some other heavy piece of furniture she could get him to move around for her. Besides, Lyn and Elisa each had to get back to Hope's Crossing Kennels and their respective responsibilities.

"You have nothing but cookies, brownies, cupcakes, and sweet rolls here." Brandon's observation was delivered in a neutral tone, over his shoulder. "I figure you've got at least one neighbor who'll show up with a casserole or their special lasagna. Until then, I figured I'd make a couple of easy-to-heat-up meals for you."

"It might've been easier to pick up a few frozen dinners." She fussed with the blanket he'd draped over her lap. It was one of several she had in easy reach, because she liked to make a nest for herself when she curled up to read. This place was where she could enjoy her quiet evenings without troubling anyone else.

"Picking up fresh stuff cost about the same, and it'll be healthier for you." He chopped vegetables while chicken breasts baked in her oven. Muscles twitched and rippled across his shoulders and back with the precise movements. She wondered if he could look any hotter. She leaned over to catch a glimpse of his rear around the edge of her newly relocated breakfast table.

"What are you making?" It did smell really good. Or maybe she was getting her appetite back.

"Simple, easy-to-spice-up dishes." Brandon was practical that way. His cooking was always straightforward, incorporating just a few ingredients, and comforting. He also handled a knife with flare. "Mostly chicken paired with veggies. I'm keeping it lean because I figure you're going to be snacking on all your baked sweets."

Her cheeks heated. Come to think of it, he'd been dropping comments ever since the hospital, reminders of how well he knew her and the people around her. Her neighbors were likely to bring dishes of easy-bake carbs, too. "You're probably right."

He lifted a shoulder in a shrug. "Seasoning is light because I don't know if your stomach might still get queasy with the pain meds. Just salt, pepper, and garlic."

She bit her lip as a warm happiness continued to spread

through her chest. He was always considerate, but this was a whole new level of thoughtful care. "I've got a jar of pesto in the fridge if I want to change it up."

She also had a variety of hot sauces and soy-based stuff.

"There's also a big container of kimchi in your fridge in case you really want a pop of flavor." Definite amusement in that statement.

She sighed. "Mom left it for me to make sure I didn't run out while she was gone."

There were containers of various other Korean dishes on the same shelf in her refrigerator, too. Her mom was an amazing cook, actually. Sophie just didn't eat Korean for every meal.

"The amount of food in there is enough to feed you awhile." Brandon started setting up small plastic containers in rows. "But it'll take some effort to pull all those containers out and set up a plate of what you want. Plus, those are served at all different temperatures. You'd end up on your feet for twenty minutes heating everything the way it should be served. That's a lot of effort. So the ones I'm putting together are an easy two or three minutes in the microwave and ready to eat."

She didn't know what to say. He was right about the Korean food she had on hand. It was all delicious, but she liked to put together plates for herself exactly the way he'd described. And there'd been more than one occasion when she'd skipped a meal because she'd been too into a book or too tired to fuss around with putting together her dinner.

There was something to be said about the food he was preparing, too. Especially because he was cooking for her. How many times had he heard her tell Boom how a person's love went into the food they made for someone else?

Every conversation, every meal at Hope's Crossing

Kennels, she'd enjoyed for the company of the people there. But also because Brandon had always been around at the periphery.

She sat up straighter as he took the chicken from the oven and let it rest on top of the stove. "After you're done, what are you going to do?"

He shrugged.

He hadn't joined her and Lyn and Elisa earlier. But then again, their chatter didn't seem to be something that interested him often. Even when she was visiting them at the kennels, Brandon didn't often directly join the chatter.

But come to think of it, this was familiar. He was generally on the edge of her conversations. And they rarely hung out, just the two of them. But here he was now. Aside from nattering at him about what he was cooking, she couldn't think of how to engage him in discussion. It was like they didn't have easy conversation between them anymore.

"I can't remember the last time we sat up and talked until dawn."

Brandon paused. "I can."

"Really?" The question came out softly. She didn't know why, only that she wasn't sure if this was exactly what she'd wanted to talk about either.

"It was before I left." Brandon transferred a chicken breast to a cutting board and began slicing it. "We were talking about all the places you wanted to travel after college."

Oh. Her cheeks heated at the memory. They'd talked and they'd done...other things. "You said I was weird because I didn't want to stay in big hotels or resorts. I wasn't interested in all the places our friends wanted to go for spring break."

His kisses had been intoxicating back then, and teasing. He'd drawn out her hopes and dreams in between stealing her breath away. Maybe those kisses had changed now, but she had no way of knowing. And inside her own head, watching him, she wondered whether they had.

"You wanted to explore Ireland by traveling from one bed-and-breakfast to the next." His voice took on an odd note. "You wanted to travel Japan by going from one *onsen* to the next."

She smiled. It was true. Especially the Japanese *onsens*, because who didn't want to slip into a hot spring and let all their tension soak away? She could use one now. "The places to stay and rest are as important as the destinations. I like the different ways someone can make a place a memory."

And back when she'd shared those dreams with him, she'd wanted to make those memories with him. Then, he'd left. It hadn't stopped her from dreaming, or traveling a bit, but on every trip she'd wondered what it would've been like to experience it with him there.

Maybe she should've been angry or bitter, but she'd burned all of that out of her system years ago. When he'd come back, she'd decided she wanted him in her life again, at least as a friend.

And that was all they were. Friends.

"You wanted to try the B-and-Bs on the Big Island in Hawaii and compare them to the places they have in the Caribbean islands." He'd finished assembling the small containers, snapping each closed and stacking them neatly in her refrigerator. His movements were careful and precise. He did that when he was feeling strongly about something. "You were going to move far away from here."

Well, that'd been the thought of the moment back then. He couldn't be agitated about things she'd decided not to do, could he? "I traveled, but I didn't want to move to any of those places. None of it was practical."

She'd gone directly into undergraduate school, living at home to save money. When she'd graduated, she'd taken on internships and worked to earn her MBA. It'd been sensible and she'd come out of it with some student loans but not nearly as much debt as could've accrued if she'd gone away to school.

"Practical is a good thing." Cooking utensils clanged as he made quick work of washing what he'd used. "Your knives need sharpening."

"I have a knife sharpener in the drawer to your left." She considered the dream she'd shared with him.

He didn't mention the way they'd planned to explore those faraway places together. They'd spent hours negotiating, prioritizing which of the places they'd visit first.

And then, one day he'd just gone. He'd enlisted. She'd asked his parents and they had only said he'd been very sure he wanted to go.

She'd never known why he left, and she hadn't asked when he'd come back to Pennsylvania.

Instead, she asked a different question. "Why are you here, Brandon?"

He stopped cleaning up. When he finally turned, his eyes were unreadable, the gold flecks showing against the backdrop of green and brown. She wasn't even sure how she could notice so much detail from all the way across the two rooms. She held her breath as he stared at her, unable to look away and only thinking he was on the edge of bursting somehow.

But he was crossing the distance between them. Between one moment and the next, he was right there next to her, kneeling so they were face-to-face. She let out the air in her lungs in a rush, not sure of what she wanted to do or what he was planning to do. She parted her lips but didn't say anything, didn't want to put another question out there for him to address before he answered the one she really wanted to know.

Because she was hoping he was here for her—not for his childhood friend but for the very adult version of her who'd been waiting for him all this time.

Faster than she could react, his lips caught hers. The contact rushed through her in a lightning shot of surprise. Years of bottled-up frustration bubbled up and she leaned into him with a soft gasp.

And then he pulled back and she was left trying to catch her breath.

Slowly, carefully, he slid his arms around her back and under her knees. He cradled her against his chest and tucked her head under his chin. With her circled as she was in his embrace, he held her close. He pressed his lips against her hair.

"That was too close yesterday, Sophie." His voice was low and gruff and almost cracked with emotion. "The thought of losing you just about killed me."

Trembling with reaction, and very much wanting him to kiss her again, Sophie buried her face in the hollow of his neck. "I'm here. I've always been here."

She'd stayed right where he left her, for the most part. Because this was where her family was and this was where she had her best memories to build on for the future. Maybe he'd come back knowing he'd find her here, too.

She had another question, but she wasn't willing to break the moment to ask it. Instead, she melted into his embrace and savored the heat of his touch. Later, she'd try to figure out what was supposed to happen next.

CHAPTER FIVE

Walking with a medical boot strapped to her right foot wasn't as doable as Sophie had thought. Lyn had come by to help Sophie that morning and given her a ride into Philly on the way to the airport and another West Coast consulting trip.

Sophie's ankle already throbbed, and she'd only just arrived at her office. Navigating the sidewalk, lobby, and elevator, then the long hallway to the cluster of offices on the corner had been draining.

She fumbled in her purse for the slim, white access card, but when she found it and pressed it to the sensor pad, it didn't work.

Weird.

Maybe it'd become demagnetized at the hospital or during the explosion. She'd have to ask Brandon if that sort of thing even happened. It was easy enough to have reset by building security, in any case.

Thinking of him set butterflies loose in her belly and she

bit her lip to hide the silly smile forming on her lips. She'd think more about what their kiss had meant after work, or at least when she was seated at her desk and not likely to trip over nothing.

She rang the doorbell.

Someone was in the office already. Her boss tended to come in early, around seven a.m. Some of the other accountants came in around the same time, too, so they could leave for home before the rush hour traffic got really bad.

The second time she rang the doorbell, she heard steps and could see the shadow of someone coming to the tiny reception area on the other side of the door.

Whew. Standing there was becoming a challenge. Her right ankle definitely wasn't up to taking her weight for too much longer. She'd have to find a way to prop it in her office. It should remain elevated.

"Sophie, you should have called ahead."

Sophie blinked, startled.

Her boss, Jeff Santos, stood in the doorway, holding the door partially ajar but standing directly in the opening. "We weren't sure if you were going to make it in today."

"I'm fine." The words fell out of her mouth with the ease of frequent use. It was her go-to phrase whenever there was too much to explain about her current state. And, honestly, there was no reason for her boss or anyone else she worked with to care so long as she could do her work well.

Jeff studied her, then stepped back and gave her enough space to hobble into the office. "Before you go to your office, please come to mine. We need to have a chat."

A mental alarm dinged, and she squashed the sudden surge of anxiety. Maybe he just wanted to discuss what work needed to be done to make up for her day out of the office. The afternoon prior to her sick day had been at his recommendation but there was always work to catch up on at their firm. Being out a day and a half meant there was plenty to do.

Their cluster of offices were split by two hallways extending from the reception area. The reception area itself was really only large enough to hold two chairs and an unmanned desk. Occasionally, they had an intern sitting there doing filing in the summer. But most of the time, there was no receptionist.

Her boss's office was down a different hallway from hers, and it was all the way at the end. He'd set a brisk pace she normally could've matched, but hobbling as she was, she struggled to keep up.

By the time they reached his office, she was doing her best not to let her discomfort show in her expression. Most of the other offices were glass from floor to ceiling. She'd thought it was a sleek, elegant layout at first. It definitely allowed for more natural light to filter into the interior of the office. But the glass also meant her office and the others were essentially fish bowls. Anyone could see what they were doing at any time of the day.

In contrast, her boss's office had frosted glass, completely opaque. It allowed Jeff—and any clients he had—privacy. His office was large, spacious, elegantly appointed with comfortable chairs for his clients, as well as a pair of armchairs to one side for more casual conversation. His desk was huge, made of dark wood with a glass panel set over the surface. And on top of his desk was a box.

Peeking out of the box were the corners of a few picture frames and the ear of her favorite stuffed animal—a German Shepherd Dog wearing a collar with a tag that read "Hope's Crossing Kennels."

"Have a seat, Sophie." Jeff's voice had turned grim.

This wasn't happening.

She sat in one of the chairs in front of the desk, staring at the box holding her personal items. They hadn't been packed with care if so many random corners were jutting out the top.

Jeff took his seat on the other side of the desk and sighed. "I would have liked to have been better prepared to have this conversation."

Funny. She couldn't decide if she would've wanted to be prepared or if she just wanted this over with now.

"The incident from the other day is not only all over the local news but has also gained coverage on national news channels." Jeff glowered at her. "Even though your name wasn't mentioned in the newscasts, someone who knows you would recognize your car."

"I haven't seen the newscasts." She really hadn't watched any television at all, either at the hospital or once she'd gotten home. She preferred to watch movies or TV series that'd already completed. Currently, she was rewatching a few favorite Korean dramas on her laptop as a comfort watch.

"We might be a small accounting group, Sophie, but we do have a certain reputation for respectability and reliability." Jeff grunted as he leaned to one side and pulled his smartphone from his pants pocket and placed the device on his desk.

"How does my being the victim of a random accident impact the company?" They couldn't possibly think she was involved in...

"Obviously you must be involved in questionable activities." Jeff dropped his hand flat on the desk surface in a show of temper. "Car bombings aren't like flat tires. They don't just happen randomly. You or someone associated with you has gotten tangled up in unsavory business."

Jeff's lips were pressed in a hard line, and his brows were

drawn together as he glowered at her. His focus was somewhere around her forehead; no direct eye contact.

He was really taking their discussion down this path, and
even he probably knew deep down that this was bullshit.

"I'm sure you know what comes next."

Oh, there was no reason to make this easy on him.

"I'd like to go over it in detail." She sat straight, her
shoulders back, the pain from her ankle suddenly incon-
sequential. She wouldn't give the man the gratification of
seeing her vulnerable or upset. "I'm sure you have the appropriate paperwork drawn up. I'd like to review it carefully
and understand the exact grounds of my termination."

"Sophie, really, just sign." Jeff pulled a packet of papers
out and placed them on the desk.

"I'll read everything first." She set her jaw and reached
for the paperwork. "Then I'll go clean out the rest of my office."

There'd been papers, desk accessories, an extra pair of
shoes tucked away in one drawer in case the weather got bad
and she couldn't wear her heels home.

"No need to clean out your office. We've collected all of
your personal effects here." Jeff stood, agitated. "Anything
else was generated on behalf of and is the property of this
company. Just read and sign. Then you can go home."

Bitterness welled up and spread across her tongue. She
swallowed the shame threatening to choke her. This was the
first time she'd ever been fired.

She hadn't done anything wrong. "Is there any question
regarding the quality of my work?"

"Excuse me?" Jeff's attention had strayed to something
on his smartphone.

"This termination is specifically due to my involvement
in the accident two days ago." She kept her tone carefully

calm. "Is there any concern about my ability to fulfill the responsibilities outlined in my job description or the quality of my work?"

It was important to clarify. She didn't want any nasty surprises if a future employer contacted this company to confirm her employment history. Besides, it mattered to her. She was a good accountant.

Jeff sighed. "The reason for your termination is stated in the paperwork. Just read and sign."

Sophie gritted her teeth and made a point of reading every line. He stood over her, but she remained seated and made sure she understood the exact terms for her termination. And honestly, she was a fast reader, but she took her time because he was trying to rush her.

Twenty minutes later, she was making her way down the long hallway back to the elevator. Jeff hadn't even offered to help her with her box to the front of the office, much less out the door and into the hallway. Now she'd be damned if she'd put this thing down before she got down the elevator and to the lobby.

Her ankle throbbed with every step, and her eyes burned with the effort to keep her tears from falling. This had been her dream job after finishing her MBA. Her father had been so proud when she'd gotten this position.

Worse, she was embarrassed. She shouldn't be. While they had the right to end her employment at will, the reasons provided were ridiculous. She knew that. But it'd been humiliating limping her way out.

She tried to maintain her indignation over their claims, letting it fuel her progress toward the exit, but she got to the lobby wrung out and exhausted. As she stepped out of the building, she thought of the comforting warmth of Brandon's strong arms around her.

Something between them had changed last evening and she wanted to see him, know that he was there. Beyond losing her job, fear was growing in her chest that her life was only going to get more insane. And the worst thing she could think of would be to find out he'd gone again.

So she called, and asked him to come for her.

*   *   *

As Forte pulled up to the front of the building where Sophie worked, he spotted her right away. She was standing out in the open and easily visible. Vulnerable.

Damn it. Something was wrong, but at least it wasn't of the life-threatening, immediate kind. It was broad daylight, and she wasn't standing near anything that might unexpectedly blow up... unless you counted the building behind her.

"Haydn, *blijf.*" The big, black dog remained obediently on his belly in the back of the SUV, safely kenneled in the custom-altered trunk area.

Satisfied that Haydn was good to wait in the vehicle, Forte exited and headed for Sophie.

"Put the box down. I'll get it." *Damn it.* She shouldn't be on her feet this much, and she especially shouldn't be carrying boxes around. *What the hell?*

Sophie regarded him with large, dark eyes glistening with tears on the verge of spilling over.

Shit.

Rage burned up from deep in his chest. Someone had made her cry. Suddenly, he had the urge to run past her into the building and tear the place to pieces for hurting her. But stronger than the destructive impulse was the need to wrap her in his arms and make her safe.

He'd compromise.

Taking the box from her, he herded her back to his SUV. Once he had her settled in the front passenger seat, he placed her box carefully in the seat behind her. Then he skirted around and got back behind the wheel. "Where to?"

"Huh?" Sophie's voice was strained.

"I'll take you home if you want to go home." He turned his upper body to face her and reached out to catch a tear as one finally fell down her cheek. "Or I can take you someplace else, anyplace. You pick."

At this moment, he ached for her. He could guess what the box meant. She worked so hard, with long hours, taking pride in her work the way so few did in whatever their jobs were. She wouldn't walk out with all her things like this unless she wasn't planning to come back.

His years in the military had taught him to be ready to move on. Assignments changed. He could be deployed, and those deployments could change in length of time or locale. He recognized the signs when plans changed without warning.

The career Sophie had built for herself was completely changing, and he wanted to help her keep her footing as her world shifted around her.

"Anywhere?" she asked. "I could ask you to keep driving until we hit the ocean or, say, Canada or Mexico."

He'd go anywhere if she asked. Leave everything behind if she needed him to. She just didn't know it.

He grinned at her. "Well, we'd get started and I figure we'd stop in about an hour when you realized you had to use the restroom."

She gasped and gave him a solid whack to his shoulder.

There. That was the spunky Sophie he liked to be around every day. "What? You have a bladder the size of a Cocker Spaniel's."

Sophie narrowed her eyes. "Ooh. Not nice, Brandon. My mother's Cocker Spaniel is high-strung."

He snickered. "Sure she is. She pees when she's gotta go. She pees when she's scared. She also pees when she's happy, or excited, or surprised. Generally, that dog drinks a lot of water and pees. Often."

Actually, he had nothing against Cocker Spaniels, but he was totally willing to tease the breed to keep that spark of Sophie's temper going.

Tears forgotten for the time being, Sophie was almost grinding her teeth. "I'd like to go home, please."

Of course. He'd figured. But maybe he'd take a small detour along the way.

Her decision made, she turned in her seat to look into the back of the vehicle. "Hey, Haydn. How are you?"

Haydn was still under the command to stay, but he stretched his neck just enough to pant happily in her direction.

"So do you want to talk about it?" He figured he knew the answer but decided to give her the opening anyway.

"Not really." Her words were short.

He waited. He wouldn't push her, but if she decided to uncork, it'd be better. He'd found that out with his own bad days. And if Sophie was having a bad day, it was serious.

"I got fired today." It hadn't taken her long. Her words were sort of strangled as she got them out. "Because they were sure I must be involved with unsavory persons to be mixed up with a car bombing. Like I'm involved with some sort of mafia."

Guilt stabbed him in the gut and twisted his innards. His worst nightmare was happening. He was becoming a blight on her life. "I'm—"

She held up a hand. "Don't. Don't you dare take the

blame. You and Haydn saved my life. Don't even think this is remotely related to you."

"But it could be," he snapped. He hadn't meant to. It took a minute to modulate his tone. "You're recovering and part of it is trying to leave the shock of the explosion behind, but you need to be careful. It might not have been an accident and you know we haven't been making new friends over the last several months."

"You all were helping Lyn and Elisa." Sophie had found her indignation. She paused for a moment, thinking. "And fine. If this wasn't an accident, I'm betting you asked both of them to be careful. It explains why you came home with me yesterday. I get it. But Ky is investigating. Do you really think there could be more?"

His chest squeezed tight in sympathy for her. The last question had come out quieter, with a hint of fear. And she needed it. He couldn't offer her comfort if it was going to make her less cautious. "There could be. You need to be careful."

I need to keep you safe.

Otherwise, he ought to take his shitty influence out of her life before he completely ruined it.

"Oh." The word came out small. "Is that the only reason why you stayed yesterday? You have the kennel to run. If there's danger, I could ask Ky for police protection."

"No." It came out fast and he didn't regret it one bit. "It's not the only reason. If you want to request additional protection, that's fine. But, Sophie, I'll be there, too."

She chewed on her lip and didn't say anything more. And damn, the silence was awkward. It took another minute for Sophie to realize he wasn't taking the direct route home.

"I thought you were going to take me where I wanted to go?" She sounded tired still and defeated.

Glad of the change in topic, he really hoped this was going to be a good idea. "We are. We're just making a stop first."

Speaking of which, he'd found a good parking place. He stepped out of the driver's side and jogged around to help Sophie out before she exited the vehicle on her own.

He scowled when he saw the way she stood. She'd been putting too much pressure on her ankle. He didn't have a wheelchair with him.

"What about Hayd—" Sophie let out a yelp as Forte scooped her up, cradling her in his arms as he walked the few steps to the front of the place.

"Trust me." He gripped Sophie tighter to him as he kicked the handicap button to trigger the automated door to open. "Haydn will be fine in the SUV for this quick visit. This time of year, it's cool enough outside for him to be completely safe. It'll be better for everyone involved."

He walked slowly down the corridor, trying to be careful of her foot and keep an eye on her expressions as they headed farther into the establishment. The corridor was lined with windows looking into a sweetly decorated lounge. The walls were painted in vertical stripes of cream and pink, accented by large cupcakes.

Incidentally, the large cupcakes were shelves—for cats.

They were scattered all around the room. Felines of all sizes and colors lay on the shelves, sat cleaning themselves in the windows, and took up positions of honor on the sofas. A few smaller kittens tumbled across the floor playing with some sort of automated fluffy toy.

"*Irasshai-mase!*" A young lady emerged from behind the hostess desk and rushed to Forte's side. "Oh! You're here to visit? Let's get you settled before we worry about any of the official stuff. Did you want cats or coffee first?"

Forte looked pointedly at Sophie.

Her attention was riveted on the windows into the cat lounge.

Sighing, he craned his neck to make eye contact with their hostess instead. "It's all about the cats." Though he could definitely do with a cup of coffee.

The hostess opened another door, gesturing for him to enter the lounge. "Welcome to our cat café. Please be gentle when playing with our feline friends and enjoy yourselves."

Forte walked in slowly, hoping any cats would avoid his boots until he had a chance to get Sophie situated. He set her down on a mint green couch, making sure her right foot remained elevated.

"Oh, here. Will this help?" The hostess offered him a felt pillow in the shape of a cheerful rice ball.

This was definitely Sophie's kind of cute immersion. "Sure. Thanks..."

"Kaseri. Most people call me Katherine if they can't manage the Japanese version." The hostess smiled. She had a nice face, round with dark eyes. Her hair was tied in twin ponytails at the base of her skull.

Cats were already starting to approach Sophie. She was completely gone, ignoring the other humans in the room. *Good.* This was the right place to bring her, then. Forte glanced down at the orange tabby winding its way between his boots. "Well, Kaseri, it's nice to meet you. How much for the coffee?"

"Five dollars. There're also toys you can buy for the cats."

He reached for his wallet and handed over the cash.

Kaseri took the money with a smile and glanced at Sophie's leg. "I'll be back with your receipt. In the meantime, take your time and enjoy. Don't worry about any time limits."

Forte nodded his thanks and turned his attention back to

Sophie. She was literally covered in cats. Apparently, they liked her. Carefully lifting his boot clear of the orange tabby, he stepped closer and kneeled down next to Sophie.

Her eyes shone with happiness again and her lips were curved in a bright smile. One cat had hopped onto the back of the couch and was rubbing its face into her hair while another had climbed up her chest to nuzzle her face. The others were making themselves comfortable on her lap and, hell, there was one play-attacking her medical boot.

"None of that now." He carefully got hold of the overly enthusiastic kitty by the scruff and lifted it away from her foot. He kicked a stuffed mouse so it bounced along the floor. "Here."

The enthusiastic kitty happily pounced on the mouse toy.

Sophie giggled. "I'm so used to seeing you around the big working dogs; being surrounded by cats is a change."

He glowered at her. Anyone else would've gotten nervous or backed away. Not her. She only laughed, cuddling as many cats as she could at a time.

"This definitely made this a better day. I didn't know they were open yet." Sophie nuzzled a particularly small, cute cat that had managed to perch on her shoulder.

He'd kept track ever since she'd mentioned a news article on the place. "It's an interesting business concept. I'm not sure if there's a potential for a dog version, though. Maybe."

Not that he had that sort of business in mind, but it was always an interesting mental exercise to consider possibilities.

"Oh!" Sophie was very enamored of the kitty on her shoulder. It was a soft cream color with darker fur on its nose, ear tips, and paws. "A dog café would totally be popular. German Shepherd Dogs, Belgian Malinois, and Labrador Retrievers can be warm and fuzzy snuggle buddies, too."

He snorted. He couldn't help it. "I'm not sure Atlas, Souze, Haydn, or any of the dogs would be immediately described as 'fuzzy snuggle buddies.'"

"They can be." Sophie had some of her steel back in her voice, too.

She had a caring heart and a fierceness to her when it came to any of his dogs. There'd been plenty of times when he'd first started the training school when it'd been Sophie's trust in his dogs that had shown others the intimidating canines could be friendly and sociable. She'd been a diplomat of sorts for his kennels in the first year or two.

"Here's your receipt." Kaseri was back. She bent to pet a few of the cats and caught sight of Sophie with her new cream-colored friend. "All of these cats are from a nearby shelter, by the way. They're fostered here, but they are available for adoption. That little girl was tossed in a Dumpster not too long ago, trapped in a trash bag."

"No!" Sophie cuddled the cat in question close.

Uh-oh.

CHAPTER SIX

Sophie clutched the handle of the brand-new cat carrier as Brandon set her down on the landing in front of her apartment. He needed to stop carrying her, especially there in front of her apartment where one of her neighbors would see. A long childhood of hearing "what will people think" made her extremely uncomfortable with exposing herself to the curiosity of the people in her family's social circle.

But she didn't say anything to him. Not after he'd done so much over the past couple of days, including helping her get through today.

"Doormat is in the right place. No marks on the door handle or doorjamb. Let me go in first and clear the apartment," Brandon murmured. "Come just inside the door behind me and stand in the corner, please."

She swallowed hard and nodded. His caution was frightening, but comforting, too. If he was this vigilant, then something bad couldn't happen again, could it?

She didn't ask. Instead, she prepared to look for anything

out of place once they were inside. The women's self-defense workshops at Revolution MMA taught awareness, perception. If she saw so much as one of her blankets moved or a blind bent, she'd be ready to let Brandon know.

He paused a foot away from the beginning edge of her apartment door's silhouette as he gently placed his knuckles on the doorknob. The memory of Sifu Gary's voice whispered in her head.

Is the door hot? Is there a zap of electricity? That might not be static. Try to notice anything unusual.

Less than second later Brandon tried the knob, silently turning it and pushing. The door was locked, as it should be. He inserted her key into the deadbolt and turned it, leaving the key there and turning the doorknob. As soon as the bolts were clear of the door frame, he forcefully slapped the door open hard. She couldn't help it; she jumped at the impact. And that was the point; it was supposed to startle anyone waiting directly inside her apartment.

Haydn had crowded forward at Brandon's heel, and Sophie did her best to do the same without actually touching either of them.

They waited there, silent, as a full heartbeat was allowed to pass.

No explosion. No shot rang out from an ambusher lying in wait. Just silence. Sophie's chest was tight with apprehension, almost wishing they'd found something. So they could relax.

Brandon murmured a command so quiet, she had no idea what he'd said. But Haydn had heard him and proceeded forward in a cautious crouch.

Brandon followed, springing around the doorjamb with his weapon up, walking heel-toe to keep the barrel level. Alex had demonstrated the technique once at Revolution

MMA. Brandon moved away from the hinges of the door, establishing his cone of fire from the far corner of Sophie's living room to the near wall.

She waited for them both by the still-open door, pressed into the corner and out of sight of anyone outside the apartment. She'd had workshops on this, seen the demonstrations, and committed to memory the reasons behind the procedures. It'd been fascinating, a glimpse into the life Brandon had led while he'd been away.

But the reality of being in the midst of it was terrifying. She balled her fists together and did her best to keep her eyes open, looking for anything out of place.

Brandon and Haydn worked as a cohesive team, systematically checking every nook and cranny of her home, even spaces no adult could fit into. She lost sight of them as they entered her bedroom, and there were more loud bangs as Brandon slammed open her closet and bathroom doors.

But there were no warning barks or snarls from Haydn. There was no shout or person charging out of some hiding place. In a few moments, Brandon was back with Haydn at his side. Without leaning out of the front door, Brandon moved to the left and right, looking as far down the entryway outside as he could. Then he retrieved her key, closed the door, and locked it.

"Clear." His voice was eerily calm and devoid of tone. A different man had spoken in that moment. A new facet of him she'd never encountered.

As he turned to her, she was caught in his gaze. His hazel eyes were tending toward deep green this evening. It dawned on her that he'd always spared her the direct intensity of his stare in the years since he'd returned and established Hope's Crossing Kennels. He'd been giving her space and letting her fall in at his side in their easygoing friendship.

But things were changing fast and it was coming from both of them.

When he came to a stop, it was way inside her personal space. The cat carrier bumped his legs, and he might've come closer if she hadn't had it in front of her. Instead, he braced one hand to the right of her head and leaned in until his forehead touched hers.

They stayed like that for a moment, and she let her lids close as she took in his proximity. He smelled like fabric softener and aftershave even after spending the afternoon out. Her heart rate was picking up, and butterflies were morphing into full-size mourning doves in her belly. If she listened hard enough, she thought she might be able to hear his heartbeat synching with hers.

When he pulled away, she leaned forward but he had retreated a step.

"You should ice your ankle, then get some sleep." His voice had turned gravelly.

She blinked and opened her mouth to say something, maybe not anything intelligent, but something. But nothing came out because she wasn't sure what she wanted to happen.

Brandon reached out and brushed a strand of hair from her cheek, turning the touch into a caress along the side of her face that ended with his thumb gently placed over her lips. "You've gone through insanity in the past couple of days. It's a lot to process. I can stay out here in the living room to watch over you, or I can be nearby. It's your choice."

But he hadn't given her the choice of addressing the chemistry sparking up between them. Frustration welled up inside her and she set her jaw.

But his gaze was gentle, caring, and earnest. "You ought to get rest, Sophie. Tomorrow's another day."

Ought to. Yes. Practical Sophie always did what she ought to do. The frustration fizzled out. He meant well. He had her well-being in mind. And if they pursued anything past that one kiss, they might not be able to be friends anymore.

The memory of their kiss burned on her lips, but right then, she really needed her best friend, Brandon, to face tomorrow.

She breathed out a sigh. "I think I need my apartment to myself tonight to get my head straight. I want to manage on my own, get myself the things I need, and just get a good night's sleep."

She needed to figure out what she wanted to do about her career, what she wanted in life. And she needed to do it before she pulled Brandon into the mix.

His acceptance was a simple nod. He backed away even farther and opened the door out of her apartment.

"Call me and I will be here." His promise resonated deep inside her chest. "Good night, Sophie."

*   *   *

"Forte." Rojas gave him a wave from beside his parked SUV.

Forte acknowledged Rojas with a lift of his chin, then headed in his direction. Along the way, he made a visual check of the parking lot and surrounding area. Rojas would've done the same. They weren't making an attempt to hide their presence, either. If this was a move to hurt the men of Hope's Crossing Kennels by targeting one of their own, Forte wanted their adversary to know Sophie wasn't an easy target simply because she didn't live on the kennel grounds.

Cruz had stayed behind to keep watch at the kennels, but

Rojas had brought their new client out to meet Forte face-to-face.

"Raul Sa, meet Brandon Forte, owner of Hope's Crossing Kennels." Rojas kept the introductions short. They'd all be doing plenty of talking later, focusing on what they really wanted to know about—dogs.

"Good to meet you." Sa offered his hand. "I hear good things about your dogs."

Forte nodded and extended his own hand. They shook and took each other's measure. Sa had a firm grip, not too forceful. Apparently, the man didn't feel he had something to prove. He had a calm demeanor, not reserved so much as peaceful. The shadows in the man's eyes and the tendency to set his jaw were subtle tells, though. Raul Sa might be carrying some internal baggage, but didn't they all? He kept it contained and projected quiet confidence.

Good signs in a dog handler. The dog picked up the mood of the handler. A nervous handler resulted in a nervous dog and a team that made mistakes. Calm confidence in the human gave a dog the reassurance needed to face any of the potential situations they might be headed into and inspired immediate response with any command. It was about absolute trust.

"Sa was Army. He's recently returned with an honorable discharge." Rojas continued to bring Forte up to speed. "He's entering the private sector and is looking for a new partner."

Sa nodded. "I was mostly stationed abroad contributing to combat operations by providing target odor detection."

"Explosives or narcotics?" Forte could train his dogs to detect either on command. The dogs were smart enough to learn to recognize the types of scents just fine, but it wasn't common to find a dog who could learn to differentiate what his handler *wanted* him to find. It required extra training for both the dog and the handler to develop the enhanced communication.

"Human. We specialized in high-value target location and acquisition." Which explained some of the shadows around Sa's eyes. Teams trained to track humans in those kinds of situations faced a lot of hard decisions. "My partner was retired when I was discharged, but she's too old for ongoing duty. My father's former military and adopted her, so she's still in the family and with people who understand her. She gets all the tennis balls she wants. She earned them."

Forte grunted. All lined up with what they'd figured from Beckhorn's recommendation. "How did you know Beckhorn?"

The corner of Sa's mouth lifted. "Met him during phasetwo training. Man knows his dogs."

Yeah, he did. Beckhorn was a key part of the training program at Lackland Air Force Base. There were instances when the various military branches came together or conducted cross-training. The program for military working dogs was one of them.

But Sa wasn't here on behalf of the U.S. military. Forte cocked his head to one side. "What skill sets are you looking for from one of our dogs?"

"I'm joining a private military contract organization. It was established years ago, but it's changing its base of operations to Hawaii and rebuilding. I did a couple of joint missions with their squad while I was still active duty." Sa rolled his shoulders. The memory of some of those missions might weigh heavier on the man than others. "This team specializes in search and extraction, VIP protection, and high-value target retrieval."

Forte raised his eyebrows. There weren't many private

teams like that. It was extremely specialized, even for his working dogs. But they could be the difference between the rescue of a hostage and that person disappearing from existence.

"Combat or stealth?" It may or may not matter when it came to the specific dog, but Forte wanted to know in general. Sometimes a client wanted a team to go in the front door and make a lot of noise while they were at it. Other times, the client needed a team to go in and get out without ever showing up in the public eye.

"Stealth, for the most part." Sa chuckled. "With private work, sometimes the missions turn out to be a little less defined, from what I hear."

Forte had considered private contracting. Hell, it was a valid career option after military service, to be sure. He'd made a different choice, but he did like to keep contacts out there with good people in the business. When it'd come down to it, he'd opted for the simpler way of life when it came to training dogs. Every day wasn't a balance of ethics and finance.

"Get settled tonight. Let's have you work with one of the dogs tomorrow and see if there's a connection." He had his impressions, and so far, Sa was a good candidate. Ultimately, though, Forte would let the dog judge the man. "Rojas will get you started and I'll be on site in the morning."

Sa looked around them. "You all seem to be somewhat stretched for resources."

Forte met the other man's steady gaze. There was nothing but professional interest. No malice. "We've got a situation in need of careful attention."

"Understood." Sa paused. "If I, or my team, can help, let me know."

Forte nodded. This wasn't just about the acquisition of a working dog. This was an offer of a business relationship. "Thanks."

Networking. Connections. Considering the suspicions Forte had about Sophie's safety, they could come in handy if they cleared Cruz's background checks.

CHAPTER SEVEN

Early-morning runs were always interesting with the way the seasons changed in Pennsylvania. Fall had come quickly and given them a good cold snap, but the past few days had been pleasantly mild. Still, the nights had been cold enough to create a thin layer of black ice on the asphalt until the sun came up and melted it away. It required a decent amount of attention to make sure he didn't wipe out on the street. Luckily, Haydn had experienced it once and developed a good eye for the stuff. As long as the two of them jogged together, Forte could rely on Haydn to let him know when a minor course change would be advisable.

Forte opened the back of his SUV. "Haydn, *over*."

Haydn obediently hopped into the back area of the vehicle. On the two nights since Sophie had returned from the hospital, it'd been Haydn's home away from home. Mostly because Forte wanted to keep watch and hadn't wanted to risk staying in Sophie's apartment while he did it. The parking lot was a better vantage point than the inside of her apartment in any case.

There was also too much temptation there. And until he, Rojas, and Cruz were sure the car bomb incident hadn't been targeted specifically at her, he was going to maintain vigilance.

She was in danger. Anyone after her was going to wait for the police interest to die down some and for her to relax before striking again. He planned to be there to catch them and track down the people responsible for giving the order to target her.

Forte closed the back and moved around to the side to pull out a set of wipes for a quick refresh and a clean set of clothing. Just as he was pulling a long-sleeved shirt over his head, an older woman left her ground-level apartment and started picking her way over the pavement toward Sophie's home.

Forte quickly finished up, stowed his crap, and grabbed Haydn's leash.

"Are you headed upstairs, ma'am?" Forte caught up with the lady, doing his best to make some noise so he didn't scare the bejeezus out of her. He'd seen her around the complex but hadn't ever met her directly. She was a friend of Sophie's family, and he tried to stay out of Sophie's family's way.

The woman looked to be in her late seventies, active but not as spry as she might have been once upon a time. Clutched in her hands, the knuckles swollen with arthritis, was a large casserole dish covered in foil.

"Oh! Do I know you?" Dark eyes were still bright with intelligence, her sharp gaze taking in all the details about him and lingering on Haydn's front leg. "You must be Sophie's dog friend."

Forte wasn't sure if the woman meant he was a dog or if she was addressing Haydn. "Yes, ma'am, we're friends of Sophie's. Could we give you an escort up to her apartment?"

The woman considered him for what seemed like a long while in the cold. A slight tremor had started in her hands, and he was afraid she might drop her dish. Suddenly, the woman smiled, laugh lines creasing the corners of her eyes. "This should be fun. Why not?"

Yeah, sure. Why not? It wasn't like he'd been waiting for just this opportunity to check in on Sophie in person or anything. The lady might see right through him, and he suspected she did, but he was still going to grab the opportunity with both hands.

She allowed him to carry the casserole dish—actually, a deep covered dish of heavy pottery—and took hold of his arm just inside the elbow. Haydn's presence didn't faze her at all. They took the stairs one at a time, at her pace.

Once they reached the landing of the second floor, the lady took her casserole back and pressed the doorbell, waited a few seconds, then pressed it again.

"Coming!" Sophie's voice came from inside.

Forte was glad to hear it. As much as he wanted to be right there for her last night, he'd also wanted her to gain back some control in what was going on around her. But he wasn't a saint—exactly the opposite—so if she'd asked him to stay he'd have given in to just how badly he wanted to kiss her again.

It wasn't the right thing to do. And damn it, he'd have done it anyway.

The door finally opened and Sophie peered out, taking note of her visitor and him. She was still pale, but the circles under her eyes had cleared and there was a hint of color to her cheeks. She'd rested. "Mrs. Seong, how nice to see you. I wasn't expecting you to bring more company."

Sophie glanced up at him and narrowed her eyes.

Hah. She knew exactly why he was there.

Mrs. Seong pressed her casserole dish into Sophie's hands. "Oh, I picked up a few strays on the stairs. Since you've just adopted a new cat, I thought you might like these boys, too."

Sophie looked at Forte, then Haydn. Haydn waved his tail side to side once. Forte just tried to look like there was nothing unusual about his showing up.

Sophie pressed her lips together.

Apparently, he'd failed.

"Well?" Mrs. Seong asked, a hint of a sharp expectation to the word.

"Oh, do you mind cats? I wouldn't want to trouble any allergies you might have. Thank you so much for the food." Sophie seemed to struggle with keeping her thoughts organized as she spoke to the senior woman.

"I love cats." Mrs. Seong bustled into the apartment without further invitation. "If the boys can't behave well around your new cat, they can leave."

Forte started forward. He'd take the opening provided and make a mental note. He owed Mrs. Seong a favor.

Sophie sputtered some, but she opened the door farther to let all of them into her home.

The cat was nowhere to be seen. Figured. It'd only been around overnight and it was probably still nervous from the move. Once it became obvious Sophie was really going to adopt the cat, Forte had invested in a cat carrier plus a starter kit of supplies. She'd apparently set up everything after he left.

And now he was back.

"Why don't I heat up some of this for the two of you to enjoy right away?" He took the casserole from Sophie's hands and headed for the kitchen, Haydn still on a leash at his side. He was going to keep Haydn with him until the cat made an appearance.

Mrs. Seong nodded. "I made *sundubu jjigae*, your favorite, Sophie. It has plenty of mussels and other seafoods in it, with lots of silken tofu. I still remember how you like it. The dish can be reheated on the stove. You can have some now and more later with rice."

Apparently, Sophie had decided she was going to have to just roll with the situation. She limped back over to the couch, inviting Mrs. Seong to sit at the breakfast table still in her living room.

He reined in the desire to help her onto the couch. Every step she took bothered the hell out of him while she was still limping. He'd take it away and bear it himself if it were possible, because it was definitely his fault she'd ended up injured in the first place. Hell, he was bad for Sophie. Real bad. And just like every time he'd come home after a deployment, he'd come back just to be near her. She was an addiction.

And it was only getting worse inside his head. The night had been too long.

Sophie and Mrs. Seong began a lively discussion. Or more accurately, Mrs. Seong proceeded with a precise interrogation regarding Sophie's harrowing experience with the exploding car.

Forte bit the inside of his cheek. He wasn't sure if he wanted to laugh or hate himself even more. Rojas and Cruz still had feelers out for information on the car bomb. Ky hadn't come back to him yet on the status of the investigation. But Forte's gut told him this entire situation was because of the people they'd crossed. A spot between his shoulder blades itched, and he was convinced he wasn't the only person keeping an eye on Sophie's apartment. He'd need to change surveillance points tonight to see if he could flush out the watcher.

For the moment, though, he placed the dish on the stove as instructed, removing the foil covering the top. It was a clever dish, complete with fitted lid. The stew inside was new to him, but it smelled interesting. Maybe Sophie would let him try it later. He made a mental note of the name. He'd let it heat with the lid on for the first few minutes, then remove the lid to make sure nothing boiled over by accident.

While the Korean-style stew heated, he grabbed two mugs and rummaged around until he found the tea stash. Sophie had one of those continuous hot water dispensers from Korea. It was so handy, he was considering getting one for the little coffee station they had in the main house back at the kennels.

With Haydn's leash still hooked over his wrist, he served the ladies the hastily prepared tea.

Mrs. Seong gave him another close-mouthed smile. "This one is very nice to look at, Sophie. You should let him visit you more often. He can find his way around a kitchen without too many questions or broken glasses. Are you dating him?"

Pink rose up on Sophie's cheeks. The pretty color made his groin tighten, and he was glad he'd pulled on jeans instead of coming up here in thinner running pants. Forte made sure her guest couldn't see his face as he raised an eyebrow at her. He was playing with fire here, but teasing Sophie was irresistible.

Sophie let out a scandalized laugh. "Mrs. Seong, I

haven't dated anyone for a while now, and Brandon has been a close friend for a very long time. Don't go telling stories."

And wasn't it good to know Sophie wasn't dating anyone currently? He'd deliberately tried not to know over the past year or two. But now, well, it was welcome information.

Even if he shouldn't do anything with it.

"You are grown; it's okay to date." Mrs. Seong lifted her chin in Forte's direction. "Test drive before you decide to lease the car, hmm? Nowadays, you don't even have to commit to buying. I go test driving all the time for fun."

Forte had been quietly chuckling through Mrs. Seong's commentary; then Sophie's mouth fell open and he choked. There were too many things he wanted to do with her very luscious mouth. He was going to hell.

"Mrs. Seong...," Sophie started to reply, but her new cat chose that moment to stroll into the living room from the bedroom.

"Ah, this is the new roommate? She is beautiful." Mrs. Seong clapped her hands in delight, but she did slide a sharp glance at Forte and Haydn.

Forte remained relaxed. "Haydn, *blijf.*"

Haydn obeyed, staying at his side, but vibrated with eagerness to investigate.

One of the key traits Forte looked for in the dogs he trained for service was a strong prey drive. Haydn had a fantastic drive, in fact, which could be an issue around smaller pets like cats, ferrets, rabbits, or hamsters. But Haydn was also extremely well disciplined. Forte had every confidence he could maintain control over the big dog.

The cat, on the other hand, was an uncontrolled variable.

Unconcerned, the feline made its way farther into the living room and came to a halt about a foot in front of Haydn. Then it...puffed.

That was the only way Forte could explain it. One minute, the cat had been a sleek, pale, furred being. Elegant and aloof, the rescue brought on images of cats in ancient Egypt and Asia. The next minute, it was almost double its size in fur, as if it'd been struck by lightning.

Haydn's lip lifted to reveal an impressive set of canines.

"Haydn, *los*." Forte put some force behind the command. He wanted to be sure Haydn understood the importance of this one.

The big dog relaxed his muzzle and lip, no longer revealing his teeth. His body language was still on guard, but he wasn't wound up and ready to lunge at the cat. Instead, he watched it.

For the cat's part, it moved past Haydn on stiff legs, then jumped onto the couch. Once it was safely on Sophie's shoulder, it curled up and resumed its normal size. Sophie immediately gave it loving scratches.

Haydn let loose a very faint whine.

Mrs. Seong cackled. "Yes, you should have these boys over more often. It'll liven up your days. You spend too much time up here, tucked away with your books."

Sophie sighed, petting her new cat. "I like my books and this apartment. It's very relaxing to have time to myself."

"Sometimes. Not too much time." Mrs. Seong waved a finger at Sophie. "Have you named your new friend?"

Sophie nuzzled the cat. "Not yet. The right name will come to me and she'll let me know if she likes it."

Of course it was a female.

*   *   *

A savory, spicy smell was starting to come from the kitchen, and Sophie's stomach growled. Mrs. Seong's *sundubu jjigae* was simmering. Before Sophie could mention it, Brandon dropped Haydn's leash and headed for the kitchen. The black dog remained where he was on the command to stay.

Mrs. Seong watched Brandon go, then turned toward Sophie. The senior raised her eyebrows, and her lips formed an *O* of delight.

Great. Just great. The minute Sophie's family returned from their visit to South Korea, they'd hear from Mrs. Seong about Brandon in Sophie's apartment.

Oh, her parents already knew Brandon from Sophie's high school days. Her father hadn't liked him then, but her father hadn't liked anyone. Aside from mentioning Brandon's return and establishment of Hope's Crossing Kennels, her family hadn't discussed him at all. If her parents were aware of how much time she spent at the kennels, they didn't mention it, and she wasn't particularly inclined to discuss it. Most of her discussion with family centered on her career and nice Korean boys her mother wanted to introduce her to from their local community center.

"This one is good, Sophie." Mrs. Seong's idea of a whisper was distinctly audible. Brandon could definitely hear her from the kitchen. "Those other boys your parents try to show you, no. Not good. All of them lazy. They make their mothers work hard to feed them and do their laundry, even now when they are finished college. This one, he has the dog farm for the military, yes?"

In the kitchen, Brandon froze. He lowered his head and the muscles in his back started to twitch.

Someone save her.

"He doesn't grow the dogs like vegetables, Mrs. Seong." Sophie glanced at Haydn and his prosthetic. "Brandon trains the dogs to be working dogs for military or law enforcement."

"Yes, yes. That." Mrs. Seong waved away silly semantics.

"He does good things for the military, then. This one, this one is very polite even though he is a tripod."

There was a clatter from the kitchen.

Mrs. Seong turned. "Careful when it is hot. If you burn yourself, you will have to go home to take care of it. Sophie should concentrate on healing herself. Oh, good! You know to serve the *sundubu* in bowls. Perfect."

Brandon returned and set a bowl in front of Mrs. Seong, accompanied by one of the long handled, Korean-style spoons Sophie had in her utensil drawer. Good guess. She was pretty sure Brandon didn't eat Korean much—there wasn't a Korean place that delivered near the kennels—but he'd matched the utensil to the dish well. His expression was decidedly blank.

Either he was angry or he was trying really hard not to laugh.

"I'll be right back with yours, Sophie." His voice rolled over her, darker than his normal conversational tone and full of secrets.

Mrs. Seong's eyebrows rose another quarter of an inch at least.

As he returned to the kitchen, Mrs. Seong leaned closer. "He does good things. He makes enough money if he owns his business, yes? He is probably skilled in bed, too. Soldiers are trained in many things. He will treat you well, Sophie. Make sure he comes back!"

Sophie didn't dare look in Brandon's direction. Heat burned her face, and if it weren't for the cat purring against her ear, she might try to get up off the couch and make a break for it. She wouldn't get very far with her ankle, though. And Haydn was between her and her bedroom any-way. Knowing her luck, Haydn would stay right where he was supposed to be until she tripped over him.

A warm, soft hand patted the back of her own. Amusement sparkled in Mrs. Seong's eyes. "I only tease, Sophie, because it is good to see you happy after such an accident. You deserve to be happy."

Tears pricked in Sophie's eyes as she met Mrs. Seong's kind gaze. She was a longtime friend of the family and had known Sophie since she'd been a baby. When Sophie had wanted to move out on her own and become financially independent, Mrs. Seong had spoken in her favor. It was good for a young woman to want to take the burden from her family by going out on her own, Mrs. Seong had argued when her parents had been concerned. Sophie's parents had conceded when Sophie chose an apartment so close to Mrs. Seong. It was not only proven a safe area, but there was a chaperone nearby for all intents and purposes.

But Mrs. Seong had let Sophie have her privacy. She checked in only when Sophie was particularly sick.

"Careful. It's hot." Brandon was there with the tray she kept on top of her refrigerator. He set it carefully in her lap, then placed her bowl of *sundubu jjigae* on it, accompanied by another spoon.

"Thank you." She smiled up at Brandon and then over to Mrs. Seong. "Thank you for everything."

Mrs. Seong gave her a serene smile in return. "If this boy goes fishing and brings back good fish, I will fry them and make this again. *Sundubu jjigae* is good with a bowl of rice and a whole fried fish."

Brandon chuckled. "I could go fishing."

Sophie choked on a spoonful of her *sundubu*.

CHAPTER EIGHT

Sophie, what are you doing on your feet, and what is that amazing smell?"

Sophie laughed as Lyn entered the kitchen area in the main house of Hope's Crossing Kennels. She was glad to see Lyn back from her latest business trip so soon. "My ankle is feeling a lot better. I can stand for a while as long as I'm wearing the medical boot for support. And this is avocado and fried egg on toast."

As she spoke, she took a nicely toasted slice of rye bread and spread a spoon of fresh avocado mixed with crumbled goat cheese across it in a generous layer. She sprinkled a touch of sea salt over it, then used a grinder to add a hint of black pepper. Then she carefully slid one of the sunny-side-up eggs from her pan onto the avocado. She finished it off with a spoonful of fresh diced tomato tossed with shredded basil.

It wasn't summer yet, but Mrs. Seong had a good eye for produce and had dropped off some for Sophie last night.

Rather than have Brandon pretend he just happened to be in the neighborhood again that morning, Sophie had called him to ask if he could pick her up so she could hang out at the kennels. At least that way, he wouldn't be torn from his responsibilities at the kennels just to babysit her. Besides, it gave her people to feed the excellent produce to, and cooking made her happy.

"Don't tell me you baked the bread yourself?" Elisa arrived and hooked the leg of a stool, taking a seat at the breakfast bar. "Boom will be along in a second. She had to run back to the house to grab something she forgot in her room."

"Gotcha. I'll have her breakfast ready in a sec." Sophie placed a serving in front of Lyn and another for Elisa. "I didn't bake this bread, but maybe I will next time. This loaf was dropped off by a neighbor, and I couldn't finish it before it went stale, so I decided to bring it along to share."

"Always enjoy your cooking, Sophie." Lyn got started on her portion.

"Good. I love cooking for all of you." Sophie usually only got to bake or cook on the weekends. As she thought about it, she cracked an egg and accidentally let a piece of eggshell fall into the pan with it. She muttered a curse as she fished it out.

"While we benefit from your habit of baking or cooking when you're stressed, why don't you talk to us about the reason for it?" Elisa suggested. "Also, don't worry about breaking the yolk. Boom likes her eggs over hard lately."

Sophie huffed out a half-hearted laugh. "It's fun trying to keep up with the way her tastes change. Is it because of tween taste buds?"

Elisa rolled her eyes. "I don't even know."

They all shared a chuckle over that.

"Well, I haven't come up with any epiphanies when it comes to my next steps in job hunting," Sophie admitted as she plated another serving for Boom. "I've thought about it more, and while accounting is still something I like, it's not what I want to do for the rest of my life."

Lyn nodded. "That's fair. You like variety in your life. It follows that you might want a career that offers a broader spectrum of tasks to challenge you."

"What makes you happy?" Elisa asked.

What, indeed?

Sophie sighed. "This. The cooking and caring for a lot of people. Adjusting to changing tastes is challenging, too, and I love surprising you all with new recipes. But I don't want just this. I take care of the finances for the kennels because I like the change of pace. If I could find a job that combined all my hobbies, I'd be incredibly happy. I just don't think there is one out there. I thought I could do the most sensible thing as my career and just have the rest in my free time as hobbies, but...it wasn't right. I don't know what is."

Lyn chewed slowly and swallowed. "That's an unusual set of things to look for in a job working for someone else. Small businesses or companies generally have the opportunity to fill multiple roles, but your interests are an unusual combination."

"Yeah." Sophie sighed. "And it's not like I could take it all and turn it into my own business."

But she'd dreamed of it.

"But you have a concept in mind." Lyn sounded like she was about to spring a trap.

Sophie eyed her warily. "Maybe. I love bed-and-breakfasts. Everything about them. Running one would hit all those things and a lot of things I bet I haven't even thought of yet."

There. It was out in the open. She'd been reluctant to say it out loud because it was a wild idea. Not practical at all.

"It's not something I should do." She set Boom's plate up on the breakfast counter next to Elisa.

"Why not?" Elisa asked, stabbing the air in front of Sophie with a fork.

Sophie blinked.

"Lyn runs her own consulting business. Why can't you run your own B&B?" Elisa continued with inexorable logic. "You know the business. You've definitely visited enough of them. And this is a good area for them."

"You cook. You make amazing things." Lyn waved her fork over the remaining half of her fried egg and avocado on toast. Then she jumped on the idea and apparently decided to take it for a run. "You could incorporate your hobbies, like you said. No one has a better eye than you do for decorating a place to make it feel like a sanctuary. Maybe make it something of a yoga retreat and get certified to teach yoga classes, too. That'd differentiate it from the other bed-and-breakfasts in the area. You also feel passionate about mentoring the local high school kids. They'd be cheap labor to help you with cleaning and housekeeping if you're willing to mentor them. Some of those kids you tutor for next to nothing would do anything for you, and they're eager to make some extra pocket change."

"Having them do simple mail sorting or answering phones is great experience for a first-time job. It's something to get a résumé started," Elisa added. "I wouldn't mind helping set up a bookkeeping system for you."

Wow.

Sophie stared at her two friends, people who'd walked into her life in just the past year. They understood her, supported her, in ways she'd never experienced in anyone except Brandon. And she'd met them through him.

"I've been saving, hoping I could open a B-and-B of my own someday." Admitting her hope was harder than she'd thought it'd be. The words came out soft, barely more than a whisper. She was cringing, expecting some sharp, practical commentary on how she could better invest that seed money.

Instead, both Elisa and Lyn sat up with excitement.

"We could…"

"When…"

Sophie held up her hands to halt the enthusiastic start of a crazy discussion she wasn't ready to let happen. "It's not enough. I need the perfect property with a decent fixer-upper building or two. I need to budget for the renovation costs and startup costs. There's a whole lot of administrative and business expenses, plus whatever it'll take to set it up as a business. It's not enough for all that. I need a job to keep saving, keep planning."

She'd thought about all of it over a lot longer time than she planned to admit. And she'd fiddled around with the numbers while she'd been stuck on her couch over the past couple of days.

This just wasn't the right time.

Lynn studied her. After a long minute, she opened her mouth. "I…"

Sophie shook her head with a gentle smile to take the edge off the denial. "I won't take money from friends. Not as a gift, not even as a loan. It's not the way to keep a friendship. And your friendships mean so much to me."

She reached out and took each of their hands.

"I'll make this happen. I will. I just don't know how or when." She swallowed hard because for a second there, she'd been excited right there with them. "It's not going to be now."

They all shared one of those moments where words weren't needed. Then Sophie became aware of Boom standing in the entryway.

"What's up, Boom?" Sophie watched the young girl fidget for a bit before coming into the kitchen. "Breakfast here. Don't you need to get to school soon?"

The girl was a tween now, and sometimes she was the cute kid who'd arrived with Alex a little more than a year ago and sometimes she was a teenager. All of them were scrambling to keep up with the split-second changes.

Right now, Boom was a tween. And she was peering over her shoulder to make sure none of the men were in the room.

"You're all here. I thought I'd have to wait until Sunday. I'm really glad you're okay, Sophie. But I have something I need to talk to all of you about." Boom took a deep breath. "My birthday is coming up."

Sophie nodded. So did Elisa and Lyn. None of them would've forgotten, but just in case, every one of them had Boom's birthday in their day planners. She was family.

"Dad was asking if I wanted a laser tag party or a roller-skating-rink party or what." Boom shuffled her feet under the table. "And those are cool and all, but they're things everyone at the martial arts school does. All the guys."

Ah. Danger. Red flag. Sophie exchanged knowing looks with Elisa and Lyn.

"Would you like to invite girls from the martial arts school or from your middle school classes, too?" Elisa was a brave woman. But then, she lived with Boom now and had the best feel for Boom's mercurial phases.

"Yeah. We do every year. Dad wouldn't ever leave them

out." Loyal as ever to her dad, Boom nodded with each sentence to make her point.

"Okay." Sophie said it slowly, opening the door wide open to invite Boom to get to her point before one of the men actually did come wandering into this conversation.

Boom took a deep breath. "I wanted something different this year. Still fun, with lots of games and stuff. But... different."

Lyn nodded encouragement. "Sounds great."

Elisa and Sophie joined with the nodding. Nodding was good.

Boom's gaze locked onto Sophie's day planner where it lay on the kitchen table. Sophie had been adjusting her week plans because she didn't have a job to go to anymore, so she'd been trying to cheer herself up with pretty wash tape and stickers. Boom reached out and fiddled with a roll of cherry blossom wash tape.

"It's fun to have active stuff to do. I want this to be fun." Reiteration was apparently a way to find one's direction in a conversation when it came to Boom. "But for the food, I really like the stuff you bring from Sunday brunches, Sophie."

Ah. "Whatever you'd like for your birthday, Boom. I'd be happy to make anything."

A flush came to Boom's cheeks, a happy one. "And, well, Elisa, the pictures you showed me of all those tea parties you and Sophie and Lyn go to. I really like those."

They were making afternoon tea a regular thing. And Elisa had a passion for taking pictures of all the food with her smartphone. Sophie laughed. "Elisa can make anything look super tasty when she takes a picture of it. I don't blame you. I was there, and I look back at those pictures and want to go again."

Boom nodded. "Me too."

Oh. Sophie immediately tried to figure out how to yank her foot out of her mouth. They hadn't meant to leave Boom out of those trips. But usually, she was at the mixed martial arts school. Sophie mentally kicked herself for never having thought to invite the tween.

Obviously, Elisa and Lyn had come to the same conclusion. Lyn even dropped her forehead into her palm. "I can't believe we've never taken you out with us."

Elisa added quietly, "You are always welcome. It'd be fun to have you join us."

Boom smiled. She was a generous soul. "Thanks. I'd like to. And for my birthday, I'd like to have a tea party. An *Alice in Wonderland*–themed one. The kind where any of the guests can come and try any of the foods."

She tipped her head to the side and quickly added, "Not so much the sit-there-and-be-super-polite kind of tea party."

Sophie grinned. "We can set up a big table with chairs on one side so guests can sit if they want or just come up and take a few bites to try out in between games. We'll make it easy to choose."

Elisa nodded. "I can make fun Drink Me and Eat Me tags for whatever food Sophie makes."

"I can help with the table setting and stuff, too," Lyn added.

They were presented with a relieved, happy-looking Boom. "Awesome. That way Dad can set up a bunch of video and tabletop games and stuff for us inside, maybe some outside stuff if it snows. And we can enjoy all the delicious food, too. It'll be awesome."

Sophie immediately started jotting down ideas on a notepad she had on the counter. "I'll come up with a bunch of choices and you can pick. If there's anything you want, just let me know."

Boom nodded and bolted down the hallway. "Thanks!"

Lyn was staring at Sophie.

Elisa looked from Lyn to Sophie, and apparently there was a psychic moment Sophie was left out of because both Lyn and Elisa had their gazes locked on her, and she wondered if she should run.

Sophie leaned back on her chair. "What?"

"If you owned a B-and-B, you could definitely host parties," Lyn pointed out.

Elisa tapped her plate with her fork. "Afternoon tea, cocktail parties, you name it. You could host it."

"You guys are incorrigible." Sophie put down her pen with a snap. But they weren't wrong.

She could. If she had the place.

*   *   *

Forte heard the feminine laughter and made a quick decision to head out a side door into the kennel area rather than interrupt the fun the ladies were having in the kitchen. As much as he wanted to make sure Sophie wasn't on her feet too much, he also didn't want to cut short any fun they were all having. Besides, Lyn and Elisa would watch out for Sophie. Even Boom had been developing a knack for nudging someone into taking care of themselves when they might otherwise forget.

It was something friends did for one another. Exactly what he hadn't had when he'd first come off of active duty and searched for what to do with himself next.

His smartphone rang, flashing a familiar name on the screen.

"Forte." He kept walking toward the kennels as he answered. He wanted distance between himself and the ladies for this call, but he didn't want to cut past them to get into his office. Along the way, he'd make a visual check of the dogs in the kennels.

"Beckhorn here. I read the latest update on Haydn's progress. Good work." The man kept in touch when Hope's Crossing Kennels had one of his dogs on site. "I hear Sa is on site, too."

"Yeah. We're having him run through the training courses with a couple of the dogs, see which is the strongest match." This latest set of dogs had a lot of potential. Every one of them was sharp, eager to work. All of them had come through the initial phases of training with flying colors. The next deciding factor would be when they were paired with a potential handler or when they were evaluated by a military trainer for acquisition. Usually, Forte gave his military contacts first pick. Today was an exception.

"I appreciate you making him a priority." Beckhorn didn't ask for favors often.

"Not a problem." Forte paused. "I may need a little help, too, actually."

"Yeah?" Beckhorn had done some digging for them in the past. He could be another angle besides Ky's police investigation or Captain Jones's covert operation.

"I need to know about any new private contract organizations taking on domestic contracts." Forte followed a leap of intuition. "They might be looking into training facilities like mine."

There was a pause. Beckhorn cleared his throat. "We interested in working with them?"

"Unknown." Forte set his jaw as his temper smoldered. The memory of Sophie lying pale and still in the hospital bed floated across his vision. "Not likely. I'm looking for connections to people or places in the area here, searches and inquiries. I want to know who's out there."

"Your timing is creepy as hell." Beckhorn didn't spook easily. "There's at least two private contract organizations growing a name for themselves. One is the team Sa is joining. The other one has a more corporate structure to it. All about the bottom line and too many redacted files in the background checks."

"What's the name?" Forte could work with Rojas and Cruz to start their own searches.

"Labs-Anders Corporation." Beckhorn's tone turned grim. "Started by a recently retired Navy officer and a group of ex-SEALs. They're actively recruiting currently."

And Cruz had crossed a few former SEALs within the past year. Small world.

"I'd proceed with caution." Beckhorn's warning came out with an edge. "Part of the reason I work with you is because you manage to stay clear of the shady shit."

"Yeah. That's the way I'd like to keep it." Forte hadn't built Hope's Crossing Kennels to get tangled up with any organization that'd force him to make the best bad decision in a shit situation again. "But someone close to us might have a target on her back."

She wasn't just close; she was everything to him.

The sound of typing keys came across the line. "I'll do some discreet digging. File should be available to you in the next twenty-four hours."

"Appreciated." And Forte would do some discrete research of his own.

"If you're talking about the food, I don't believe you because you haven't even tasted it yet." Sophie stood at the edge of the dog runs holding a covered dish.

Forte ended his call and turned his attention to her. "You shouldn't be walking around so much."

She huffed out a laugh. "I'm getting to the end of my tolerance with people telling me what I shouldn't be doing."

He crossed the distance between them before she tried to start limping toward him. "Sorry. Thanks for saving some for me."

Sophie gave him a smile. "Well, the others all came through and had some. I didn't want you to skip breakfast."

He tried not to herd her back into the kitchen. Honestly, he tried. But they did end up back inside and sitting at the kitchen table.

Sophie gave him a pointed look and sat with her right leg hoisted onto a chair next to her. "Okay. I'm off my ankle. Eat."

He chuckled and complied.

"You know, everything was fine last night." Sophie played with a napkin. "Maybe you can just drop me off at home this afternoon."

He swallowed too fast and had to breathe through his nose as the too-large bulk of toast and egg and avocado stuck in his throat on the way down.

"I mean, I have to update my résumé and figure out what I'm going to do about a job." Sophie's words started coming out in a rush. "I've got savings set aside, but I'd rather not dig into them if I can help it."

"Sophie." He waited until she met his gaze. "There was a bomb in your car a couple of days ago."

He'd been impressed with how functional she'd been, how well she'd been dealing with it over the past couple of days. He hadn't realized until now that she had just pushed past it.

"Ky said it might've been random. A coincidence." Sophie didn't look away, but there was a pleading note in her quiet tone. "It could've happened to anyone's car."

Ah, hell. "I don't think so."

Her shoulders slumped slightly. "Why?"

He hadn't wanted to say this out loud. Not ever. But it was the truth and maybe they both needed to hear it. "I'm a negative influence in your life, Sophie. There hasn't been anything about me in your days that made your life better."

"That's not true." And there was the snap, the hard edge, the defensive tone she always took on his behalf. She'd done it since high school, even to her father.

"It's very possible that your association to Hope's Crossing Kennels, to me and Rojas and Cruz, made you a target." There it was. He hated even mentioning Rojas or Cruz in that statement because the kennels and everything that happened in conjunction with them were his accountability. But Rojas and Cruz had been neck-deep in the altercations over the last year and they took the onus of the situation as a team. "You're an integral part of this place and the most accessible."

"So someone is trying to get to you through me. Possibly." There was a bitterness in her tone. "Don't you think Ky will track them down? Or maybe the one thing with my car was a warning and there isn't more coming. Nothing happened last night. You stomped through my house and scared me out of my mind while you did it and there was no one there."

He couldn't believe what he was hearing. Sophie hadn't ever doubted him before, not ever. He'd been an idiot not to recognize the strain she'd been under after the explosion and then losing her job. Sophie's way of handling adversity was to push forward, head down, and keep going until she came out on the other end.

He couldn't let her do that this time.

"We need to be careful. This isn't the sort of situation where reacting will be enough." Forte hardened his tone. "If we let down our guard, the next time something happens, we won't be able to save you."

"I don't need saving." Sophie shot the denial back. "My entire life is in limbo. I can't stay like this, not doing anything but waiting to see if *maybe* something will happen to me. I have bills to pay and I'm supposed to have a career to continue. I need to—"

"Stop and think about whether you want to keep going with blinders on." He figured now was a better time than any to talk about her life. "Don't think I haven't noticed over the last couple of years. I've watched you go along with what you should do and then save your spare time for the real things that make you smile. Those things don't have to be just hobbies. If you were so happy with your career and doing everything your family said you should do, why were you always here? You're so good at helping other people realize their dreams. You're allowed to make some of your own happen."

She was staring at him, her lips parted. She'd probably been ready to fire back some hot retort. But instead, tears were welling up in her eyes and her lower lip had a barely perceptible tremor.

Shit.

He shot out of his chair as she struggled to get her leg under her. Coming around the table he wrapped his arms around her. "No, Sophie, I'm sorry."

She shook her head but didn't try to break free. She slumped into his hold instead, soundlessly sobbing.

He sat down in the chair she'd been using, pulling her across his lap. Once she was balanced, he tucked her head under his chin. "Just hang in there with me a little longer. Let me make sure there really isn't any more danger, then you can do what you need to do. I'll help you if you let me."

But wasn't this what she was refusing in the first place? She didn't want his help, especially when it involved saving her when she didn't believe she needed saving.

"I just keep thinking it's a bad nightmare, that there's some mistake," Sophie whispered against his throat.

He tightened his arms around her. He was going to hell in a hand basket because having her in his arms felt too damned good. He wanted to make everything better, kiss away her tears, and drive every fear out of her head in ways he absolutely shouldn't be thinking about doing.

"I need you to recognize the very real danger, Sophie." He craned his neck so he could see her face. Her cheeks were flushed and wet with tears. It tore up the inside of his chest. "Help me keep you safe so you have a life to go on with after this is over."

She didn't say anything immediately. There was a despair in her dark chocolate eyes he'd do anything to banish. He didn't know how. He only knew he needed to keep her alive so she could decide what happiness was for her.

After a moment her gaze dropped to his lips and a different, darker blush colored her cheeks as she turned her face away. "I'll get some work done updating my résumé in your office while you handle classes today."

There she went, taking refuge in practical next steps. He didn't argue.

"Can I ask a favor?" Her voice was soft, and she shifted her weight in her lap.

He did his best to keep his hands in safe places, but his response to her was becoming obvious even through his jeans. So he let his arms fall away so she could get to her feet. "Ask."

"Can Haydn hang out with me while you're teaching the classes?"

He chuckled and stood. "Yeah, I'll bring him in for you."

She and Haydn could rest together and keep each other company. He was glad she'd have the big dog's presence through the day. In a way, she'd be safer with Haydn than she would be with him.

Because he shouldn't want Sophie the way he did. But hell, he'd never listened to what he should and shouldn't do.

CHAPTER NINE

Let me down!" Sophie's whisper was actually pretty loud. "Brandon Forte, you let me down. What do you think my neighbors are going to tell my family when they get back? Because they are so going to see this."

Good. Forte grinned. Okay, so maybe insisting on carrying Sophie up the stairs to her apartment wasn't the most conventional way to do things. But he liked the feel of her in his arms, and this was one of the least dangerous ways he could indulge in having her close.

He pitched his voice a bit louder than conversational tone. "They're going to say your apartment complex doesn't have elevators and you live on the second floor. No one wants you putting more stress on your ankle trying to limp up the stairs, and you don't want people to see you sit on the steps and slide your butt up one step at a time."

That earned him a light *thwack* across the shoulder, but Sophie quit squirming.

It'd been a long afternoon, and Forte had been in a fairly

good mood. Raul Sa had turned out to be a dog handler on par with some of the better men Forte had worked with in the past. The man had gotten along well with two of the dogs, though Forte had a feeling one was a better match than the other. They'd have Sa take each of the dogs out again tomorrow for separate working sessions to confirm.

Forte had found Sophie cooking dinner, on her feet again, though she'd sworn she'd been sitting just before he'd arrived. He was going to need to think about a supplemental grocery run if Sophie was going to be hanging out at the kennels more in the next few days. They usually did a lot of ordering out for delivery.

Of course, he wasn't going to say no to homemade meals by Sophie more often. He just might need to increase his cardio. Portion control was harder with her cooking than it was with delivery.

Once he reached the landing, he set Sophie down slowly so she had time to establish her balance. She was light in his arms, supple. And the warmth of her lingered on his hands.

"We are going to need to come to an agreement as to when my ankle is healed enough to take the stairs myself." Sophie pulled her keys out of her pocket. They were attached to a Revolution lanyard. One thing Gary and Greg taught in their self-defense classes was to make sure house keys were easily accessible. A person was vulnerable if their attention was centered on rooting around in a purse or backpack for keys. "You can't keep picking me up whenever you feel I can't make it on my own."

"Oh, but I plan to anyway." She'd done it for him, figuratively speaking, more times than he could count, and she might not even know it.

Color rushed into Sophie's cheeks. It'd been happening

more frequently recently, and he was ridiculously proud to have caused it most of those times.

She handed him her keys and stood aside. He gave her a smile, glad she was acknowledging his caution, even if she still wasn't sold on the necessity. Then he turned his attention to her entryway and started the process of clearing her apartment. As soon as he opened the door, they both turned serious. Her apartment was freezing, and the opening of the front door created a cross breeze, meaning there was another aperture open somewhere in the apartment.

A deadly kind of calm fell over Forte as he gave Haydn the order to proceed, then followed with his firearm ready. Adrenaline flowed through him, and long years of training and combat experience kicked in. He extended his senses to catch any hint of danger. It was about more than sight. Scent, sound, vibrations coming from the floor up through the soles of his feet, and more could tell him what he needed to make sure they all survived. Gently, he guided Sophie into the "safe" corner. There was definitely something wrong, and he wouldn't leave her vulnerable in the entryway.

Sophie's new cat came out from under the breakfast table. It was fluffed back up to twice its size, walking on stiff legs with its fur standing on end like it was hooked up permanently to a Van de Graaff generator. It stared at Forte, then Haydn, for a second before rushing directly past them to climb up Sophie's jeans.

Haydn took a few steps forward and froze, his stance rigid and his head up. His weight was balanced forward evenly on both his good leg and the prosthetic. His ears had swiveled forward to catch every sound, and his attention was on the bedroom.

There was someone in the apartment.

Whoever it was remained out of sight. For the moment.

Walking into an ambush situation was never advisable. But Forte needed to determine whether it was one or more, then flush the bastard—or bastards—out.

If it'd been Sophie coming home by herself, they'd have been ready to catch her in the parking lot if she'd backed out of the apartment and run. Or they'd planned to be certain they caught her in here, before she had a chance to get away.

The thought of her coming home alone to this made his gut twist and burn. How dare they violate her home?

Forte considered his options. Sending Haydn in ahead was safer, but Haydn was still learning to use his prosthetic. None of his physical therapy had included any of the standard bite work or attack exercises. Haydn had no way of knowing yet how his lack of a left forepaw was going to change the way he could move in those instances. If they were armed, and Forte assumed they were, they'd shoot Haydn in a moment of lost momentum.

Could he risk his partner's life that way?

It was a reality of working dogs.

But Forte wouldn't send a soldier unprepared, and he wouldn't send in Haydn, either.

"Bewaken." He indicated Sophie with his left hand, fully extended, and issued the command so softly it was practically subvocal. But Haydn would hear him and guard Sophie while he advanced.

Keeping his firearm up, Forte established his cone of fire and advanced on the bedroom door. He walked heel-toe to keep the barrel level and kept his movement smooth, even, and as quiet as possible. Anyone hiding would strain to assess his position by sound at the least. His approach took him in an arching path to give him as much sight into the room as possible.

Suddenly, gunfire rang out in the silence. One shot.

Forte dove for the nearest cover at the corner of Sophie's couch. "Sophie, get down! Call nine-one-one!"

A figure dressed in dark clothes darted from one side of Sophie's room to her window. The man turned and took another shot, forcing Forte back to cover, and then he was out.

Forte almost lunged but checked his forward motion. He risked a glance back to make sure Sophie was okay. She was crouching exactly where he'd left her, and Haydn was still on guard. Then he approached the door at an angle to see as much of the room as possible. There could be a second person waiting in the room.

He entered cautiously and cleared Sophie's bedroom first, wincing at the way her belongings had been tossed. The floor was covered in her clothes and stuff from her dresser.

By the time he got to the window, there was no sign of her intruder. He'd figured he'd be too late, but it would've been potentially deadly if he'd gone straight after the man. Too many times, a fellow soldier or dog had gotten overexcited in the chase and gone into a room after a target before clearing the room. When a second or third hostile proved to be in the room, waiting, the result had been tragic.

And if Forte were taken down, who would protect Sophie?

Speaking of Sophie, he could hear her on the phone, giving her name and address. The police would be on-site soon.

Forte picked his way carefully through Sophie's bedroom, back to the door. Sophie had shrunken as far as she could into the corner, her face pale and eyes wide. She had her phone clutched in her hand like a lifeline but otherwise looked to be keeping her shit together. He gave her a nod and the tension eased through her shoulders.

It was the best he could do in the moment.

Haydn watched him, intense and ready to respond. Forte left him where he was for the time being and instead looked at the cat.

The thing was curled up on Sophie's shoulder, sleek and normal looking. No puffed fur.

Wasn't that interesting?

Cat and dog notwithstanding, Forte took the time to clear the bathroom and the rest of the apartment for nasty surprises before returning to the front door to stand with Sophie. She'd calmed and regained some normal tone in her complexion, standing just inside the door enough so she wasn't exposed to any additional threats coming up from outside. But her eyes were still wild and her knuckles were showing white as she continued to grip her phone.

"Whoever it was is gone now. The apartment is clear." He watched her carefully to be sure she heard him.

Sophie met his gaze, eyes wide, and nodded once. "You were right."

"Yes." It wasn't an I-told-you-so. It was just the state of things. His suspicions were confirmed. "Thank you for believing in me long enough to be sure this didn't go as badly as it could've."

She paled again, and he cursed himself. He was going to win the Asshole of the Year award for his conversational skills.

"The point is, it didn't happen. They didn't get you." He tried to put every ounce of reassurance he could manage into his words. "And I'm going to be with you until we make sure whoever it is can't come close to you ever again."

"Promise." The word came out in a whisper so low he almost didn't hear her.

"I promise, Sophie. I'll be with you."

Sirens came into hearing range, slowly getting louder as

they approached. *Good.* If the hostile had remained in the vicinity, he might leave the area completely. As much as Forte wanted to chase him down, Sophie was his first priority, and he wasn't leaving her until the police arrived. He'd just promised her.

"I wanted it to be an accident. Random. Some insane mistake." Sophie was cuddling her new cat, and the little beast didn't look like it planned to go anywhere.

No time like the present to test the cat to see if it could handle proximity.

Forte left the door open, but closed the distance between him and Sophie. The cat watched him with bright blue eyes and hissed when he approached. But then it held on to Sophie's shoulder for dear life as Sophie rushed Forte, wrapping her arms around his torso.

Her slight form was nothing to take into his arms, but the impact of her trust in him rocked him back on his heels. His chest expanded painfully as he held her to him, indescribably grateful she was okay.

Every *what if* and *what could have been* flashed through his brain in a split second. None of them were fit for civilized people. But then, he couldn't be considered civilized. Not really. Not anymore. Sophie, warm and alive in his arms, was his final reminder of the good things in this world.

"Shh. It's okay. I'm here." He hoped those were the right words to say. Mostly, he hoped he was giving her the comfort she needed because he could not tell her she was safe yet. Instead, he settled his arms around her, cat and all.

Sophie continued to hug him, her hands taking up handfuls of his shirt. She buried her face in his chest and shuddered. "What was he going to do with me if I'd come home alone?"

"Don't know." And he'd already thought of any number

of things. Every one of those possibilities burned a new whole in his chest as his rage built. "But this isn't good. We're going to have to take steps."

The sirens had come to a stop. Footsteps approached.

When Ky hit the landing at a run, Forte acknowledged him with a lift of his chin. Ky took in the open door and Sophie clinging to Forte, then turned to signal to his partner.

"Anyone hurt?" Ky asked as he approached, scanning the interior of the apartment.

"Not to my knowledge." Forte hadn't tracked where the one bullet had landed. He only knew it hadn't hit any of them. "Two shots fired. I did not discharge my weapon."

After retiring from active duty, he hadn't given up old habits. He did carry concealed, and he had a license to carry firearms in the state of Pennsylvania to do it legally. All the trainers at Hope's Crossing Kennels did.

Ky nodded in response. "You want to call in your dog?"

Forte complied. Haydn returned to his side readily.

Ky and his partner followed their own procedure, clearing the apartment and assessing the situation. Finally, Ky let Forte move Sophie farther into the apartment. Once he had Sophie settled on the couch with her foot elevated and a mug of tea in her hands, Forte stepped outside to have a chat with Ky.

"We've got questions for the both of you." Ky's expression was somber, his tone brisk.

Forte nodded. "First the explosion, then this. I'm not leaving her vulnerable to a third hostile act."

"We're continuing this police investigation. I'd prefer to have your cooperation." There was a warning note in those words.

"You've had it." Forte bit out the words. "Two shots fired and neither of them was meant for me. Sophie was the target, and she was supposed to end up dead. This isn't enough to keep her safe."

An investigation only went into what had happened and maybe who had done it.

"We can't have you or your colleagues interfering." Ky was all police officer at the moment, their friendship taking a second position to doing the right thing from his perspective. "We can't have you taking things into your own hands."

Forte held up his hands spread wide, palms out. "Go ahead with your investigation. None of us will get in the way. But we'll take steps to establish better security for Sophie."

Ky narrowed his eyes. "What did you have in mind?"

At least the officer was willing to listen.

Forte eased back from his anger a little. "I think it'd be best if she left town after tonight. Get her out of harm's way."

Ky studied him. "I can't detain her. She's the victim in this situation, and we can't stop her from leaving, but I'd prefer if she stayed to provide any additional information to help the investigation."

Forte set his jaw but didn't say anything.

After a moment, Ky sighed. "I'd appreciate it if you maintained contact. Off the record, what did you see when you looked into her room?"

Ah, Ky. Good man.

"Whoever it was, they tossed her room. They weren't looking for anything, and if they took anything, it was probably just to make it look like a robbery. But her most valuable belongings are in the kitchen." Forte glanced through the door at Sophie, her new cat now curled in her lap. "But they went through her bedroom like a hurricane. They went out of their way to break picture frames and anything that looked like a keepsake. They wanted to upset her. Make her afraid."

"Our forensics team will need to come and investigate the apartment." Ky straightened and spoke at a normal volume. "It'd be good if Ms. Kim had someplace to stay for the next few nights until we can finish looking into this."

At least the next few nights, maybe longer. Forte had the feeling this hostile was going to be somewhat harder to track down than the average thief. The local law enforcement was excellent, with good resources. But they weren't equipped to handle the kind of people Forte, Cruz, and Rojas may have pissed off in the past year.

Forte would rather plan for the worst.

"Ask your questions." He gestured toward the apartment and Sophie. "After tonight, she'll be out of reach."

* * *

Sophie's tea had gone cold. It didn't matter; she still kept her fingers wrapped around the mug. It gave her something to hold onto so her hands didn't shake. She was honestly afraid she'd crush her new cat if she tried to hug the sweet feline at the moment.

The initial scare had been the worst. There'd been someone in her home, waiting for her. Panic had stabbed her heart, and her lungs had contracted hard, making it impossible for her to get any air.

But Brandon had been there, gently moving her to the side and putting himself between her and her potential attacker. He'd gone to face whoever it was. And he hadn't even let Haydn go ahead of him. Watching, unable to call out or argue with him, her initial panic turned to fear for him.

And that was Brandon, damn it. He was the one to go head on into whatever was in front of him. He didn't let anyone face those challenges with him. She was going to ask, because she wanted to understand, but right now she wanted to be mad at him.

Mad was so much better than scared. For him. For herself.

Whatever this was, it was about her and she had no idea why. The police had asked. She didn't have any new information to give Ky. And no matter how comforting his bright smile was, she didn't feel it.

There was something about having your home invaded. Your belongings pawed and pried into. It was going to take her a long time to go through what was in her bedroom once the police let her in there.

"Here's a fresh mug of tea." Brandon gently pulled the cold mug from her hands and pressed a new one into her grasp. "I brewed the tea strong, then cooled it down with a splash of cold water. It should be drinkable."

She looked up at him. "I picked a second-floor apartment because it was supposed to be safer. Less likely to be a target for robberies because it'd be harder to get in the windows."

The invader had gone out the window in her bedroom. Two stories hadn't been any kind of deterrent.

Brandon set the mug on the breakfast table and kneeled down next to her. "It was a good decision. Your reasoning is sound in most cases."

She laughed. The brittle bitterness sounded harsh even to her ears. "Most cases. But not this one."

Brandon smoothed her hair away from her face. "No. Not this one."

She leaned into his palm, drawing as much comfort from his steady touch as she could. His hands were rough from the work he did, but his touch was gentle, for her. "Thank you for being here."

Even after she hadn't believed him. Even after she'd hidden from the reality he'd wanted to prepare her for. Someone else might've left her to her fate.

Not Brandon.

"I'm glad I was here." His voice had turned gruff, and there was that odd note of emotion.

She closed her eyes and tried to draw in air past the knot in her chest. It was a swirling, ever-changing mass of fear and anxiety, relief and joy in his presence. She might be going insane because the joy rose to the fore. He was here, with her, when her life depended on it. It buoyed her for a whole moment before the fear set claws into her and dragged her back into the thoughts of what could have happened.

"I'm cold, Brandon," she whispered. "I can't get warm. I can't get the feeling of that moment out of my mind, when I realized someone was here. He planned to ki—"

Lips pressed over hers, muffling the rest of her confession. Words scattered as the heat of his breath mingled with hers pressed back the cold. Brandon's hand curved around to support the back of her neck as he continued to kiss her. She tilted her head up, still leaning into the warmth of his palm.

This wasn't a quick, startling action. There and then gone. No. This time Brandon kissed her with intent, and he knew exactly what he was doing. Unhurried, deliberate, he sucked at her lower lip and coaxed her to open for him.

When she did, his tongue swept inside to taste her, tease her. Her trembling fear washed away in the heat of the hunger Brandon awoke in her. He smelled of clean cotton and tea tree. He tasted of coffee and something more.

Her thoughts scattered, even the concept of words, and all she wanted to do was savor this connection between them. She clutched at his shirt, pulling him as close as possible. His kiss sent her drowning in years of wanting, finally tasting like reality, and she wanted to savor it.

A hundred daydreams featuring Brandon flickered through her mind. Her nipples tightened and her lower body clenched as she tried to pull together her thoughts long enough to figure out how to follow this through to the next step.

Because she wanted to, very much.

But Brandon drew back until she opened her eyes. His gaze caught hers and held it. "Sophie, come home with me."

CHAPTER TEN

Rojas, Cruz, we've got a thing." Forte strode toward the kennel area where the other two trainers were standing with their client, Raul Sa. "Excuse me."

Sa nodded. "No worries. We were just finishing up here. I can head back to the guest house."

"Actually, would you mind waiting?" Forte had a wild idea, and all the status updates from Rojas indicated Sa was good people. "We've got a situation that might be outside our scope of current resources."

Sa's posture changed minutely. The man didn't turn closer toward Forte, but he was listening attentively. He'd offered, after all.

Forte filled them in on the break-in at Sophie's apartment.

"Shit. You brought her back here, right?" Cruz was working to rein in his temper, and the question came out harshly.

Forte nodded. "Left her in Rojas's living room with Lyn and Elisa. They're trying to make sure Sophie's got everything she needs packed in a go bag."

It was one of the things they'd managed to talk all the ladies into having: a duffel bag packed with all the necessities for a few days. Clothes, undergarments, first aid supplies, and even limited nonperishable food like protein bars were in each of the go bags. Even Boom had one.

"How long are you disappearing?" Rojas pulled out his smartphone and pulled up a calendar app.

Forte shook his head. "Ky is leading the police investigation. With forensics involved, it could take some time. He has to wait for results to come back."

Rojas sighed. "Elisa texted and wants to know if this is going to be for two days or 'unknown,' because a girl can only pack so much underwear."

There was a hesitation, then Sa said, "If she needs more, she can just buy some at Wal—"

"No." Cruz, Rojas, and Forte said it at the same time.

Sa fell silent.

Cruz and Rojas shook their heads to emphasize the point.

"Shirts, pants, socks, they'll make do." Rojas cut the air with the flat of his hand to define each type of clothing. "But underwear is a *thing*."

"I have no answer," Forte admitted.

They all stared at Rojas's phone.

Forte imagined Sophie's underwear, then tried to erase the images from his mind. In high school, Sophie had loved to wear cute panties with a cartoon animal printed across the behind. She had also loved to wear skirts. Add in her tendency to trip and he was very glad he'd been around to catch a glimpse when her skirt flipped up. It'd happened only a couple of times before she started wearing shorts under her skirts.

Still, it was enough to make a memory, and damn if he hadn't found those panties insanely tempting. Sophie's ass was tight, prettily curved, and led him to thinking about her shapely thighs. He even thought her calves were sexy as hell. Her feet were downright tiny next to his, and these days, the biggest tease was when she was wearing work clothes and heels. Especially when he could see the arch of her foot in the shoe.

"Earth to Forte, come in." Cruz's voice cut into Forte's thoughts.

"Shit. It's been a long couple of days." Forte grinned in apology and tried not to adjust his pants.

Rojas studied him. "Uh-huh. You've been sleeping in your SUV for the last couple of nights. Are you good to travel right now?"

It was a fair question. Forte would be watching over Sophie alone when they headed out, and he needed to be alert. "I'll catch ninety minutes of sleep before we head out."

It'd be enough to recharge him. Cruz, Rojas, and even Sa nodded in understanding.

"It's going to be tough for you to get her out of town if there are eyes on her," Sa ventured slowly. "You have anyone who can play decoy?"

Forte stared at Sa. "All of our contacts in the area are civilians."

"The person of interest is the young Asian lady in the kitchen earlier today, right?" Sa's tone was matter of fact. "I saw her come out a couple of times."

"Okay." Forte squelched his irritation for a moment to hear Sa out. The man was former military, and if it'd been any of the men of Hope's Crossing, they'd have taken notice of everyone moving around the immediate vicinity in the same way.

"I have a colleague in my new squad," Sa continued, pulling out his smartphone. "She's also Asian, not the same

region, but close enough to pass with makeup. Similar
height, basically same hair color and style. She's got the experience to watch out for herself and avoid potential issues.
It'd be safer to have her act as decoy than trying to involve
another civilian."

The man had a point there. It hadn't even been an option
in Forte's mind to endanger another civilian. Though hiring
an actor to pose as Sophie and lead whoever was after her
away was a good plan.

Forte rubbed his jaw, considering. "Having a skilled resource as a decoy makes the idea much more feasible. If the
opportunity arises—and I hope it doesn't—maybe your resource could gain additional intelligence if a hostile makes
contact with her."

Sa shrugged noncommittally. "Hard to say. She's sharp,
and she'll pass on any information worth sharing."

But they had no idea whether she'd be contacted at all before the hostiles made a move.

"Full disclosure, the first incident was a car bomb." Forte
wanted to be sure Sa and his teammate were making an in-
formed decision. "The apartment incursion was the second.
Based on what we've seen, they don't plan to acquire their
target. They plan to eliminate her. Tossing the apartment was
just for shock factor, maybe to make it look like an interrupted robbery."

Sa nodded. "I appreciate the clarification. I can relay the
proposal to Arin and see what she has to say. We'll need to
take a couple of current pictures of your friend, though."

Sa had paused on the word "friend." Forte half started to
correct him, but what could any of them call her? Sophie
was…Sophie. He'd never put a definition on what she was
to him because she'd simply been a singular part of his consciousness. What he'd done over the years and why he'd

done anything could be attributed to the thought of her if not directly to something she'd said. Forte wouldn't hold Sophie accountable for who he was or the things he'd done. That was a fool's mistake. He'd own his decisions and the actions resulting from them himself. But he wasn't going to deny the influence she had on how he reacted to the world.

"We'll take a few pictures tonight and get Arin a passport." Forte added those tasks to his mental list.

Cruz sighed. "This will work better if I work some magic with the passports. If we finalize this agreement, I'll need a current photo of your teammate."

They weren't going to clarify what sort of magic. It wasn't exactly legal, what they were about to do. Call it a gray area.

"Is there anything else the team can help you with?" Sa was texting on his smartphone.

Cruz crossed his arms. "Your team in a lull for contracts?"

Forte had been wondering the same thing. "How many people in your organization?"

Sa held up his hands. "It's a small organization, just our squad. We've got half a dozen permanent resources, and I'm the newest to the team. A couple of us are still in the DC area for the immediate future before we fly out to Oahu. We're willing to help and, to be honest, you all are valuable contacts. My team lead asked me to build connections where I could here. This seems like an excellent situation for that sort of thing."

True. Forte, Cruz, and Rojas were retired. They were done with the action. But they'd been finding themselves neck-deep in odd circumstances. It was advisable to keep a live network in place in case life continued to be as interesting as it had been over the past year.

"We're in between contracts for the next couple of weeks, but we won't be for much longer." Sa sounded confident. "Mostly, they took some time off to settle in at the new headquarters and integrate me into the team. Part of that is going to be a new canine if we finalize an agreement here. The situation you've got is one where we can provide support."

Well, Sa was decent about representing his team's services, at the very least. Plus, he was a capable dog handler. And when they got right down to it, the man hadn't been wrong yet in this conversation.

"Our finances aren't limitless." Forte hated putting a price to Sophie's safety. But private military contract organizations were ruled by the bottom line. It was why their employers were usually organizations or government sources, not individuals. "I need to see a price proposal before we finalize any deal."

Sa grinned. "Team lead is pulling it together now for an informal request for proposal. He likes to make sure agreements are clear for all parties."

More power to the man. Forte hated paperwork. But a situation like this couldn't be handled with a simple verbal agreement. There were too many variables that needed to be defined to keep them all in good standing with each other.

"Let's wait for him to get that finalized." Forte dragged his fingers through his hair. "And let's see you with Taz and Dodger. I want to get you paired with the best candidate before I leave, so you can complete your training with Rojas and Cruz."

*   *   *

"They didn't answer my text about the underwear." Elisa sighed and placed her smartphone down on the coffee table.

Sophie and Lyn sat on the couch with her, and the three of them stared at the go bag. It was a decent size. Boom could probably curl into it when it was empty. Currently, it held a whole bunch of practical items. Next to it on the coffee table was a cat carrier, containing Sophie's new cat.

The cat seemed unfazed about the sudden change of location. She wasn't at all upset about being in the carrier, either. She'd apparently decided now was the time for a nap.

"I packed this for a natural disaster or zombie apocalypse." Sophie poked the go bag with a finger. "I didn't think this was what I'd be taking with me on a trip with Brandon."

Though, it would be very likely in the event of an emergency that she'd have done her best to meet up with Brandon and the people from Hope's Crossing Kennels. Or she might've gone with family. Sitting there, faced with the bag right in front of her, the choices seemed a lot more real than when she'd initially packed it.

"Technically, this *is* an unforeseen circumstance. There's no telling what could happen." Lyn sounded thoughtful. "I may have to rethink my go bag."

"Me too." Elisa sighed. "Of course, Brandon might not realize the implications of telling you he was taking you away somewhere. Do you think either David or Alex might clue him in?"

Maybe? Hard to tell what those men communicated with one another. They were, by habit, concise. There'd been times when Sophie had seen them have an entire conversation in a series of head nods and hand signals. She was fairly certain none of them had done it intentionally, either. They'd just all been focused on getting work done and had fallen back on old habits.

Lyn shook her head. "I'd say it's not likely. They stay out of each other's romantic shenanigans."

Sophie groaned and let herself fall backward into the couch cushions. "This is absolutely true. But he *kissed* me."

Lyn grinned. "He did."

"Yup, he did." Elisa joined in with a grin of her own.

The memory of his lips against hers. Oh, they'd kissed in high school and she had those memories, but they were sweet and a little awkward. The way Brandon kissed now was a completely new, hotter-than-wow experience. She couldn't stop remembering. Not just the memory in her mind, but the heat of it on her lips. Sophie clamped her hands over her mouth.

This was crazy. And was this finally going to happen?

She so definitely wanted this to happen.

"I am tired of being the girl down the street." Technically. The girl next door to Brandon's house had been a cheerleader. He hadn't interacted with that girl, and Sophie truly couldn't even recall her name. No. Sophie had lived down the street from him, and he'd begun walking her home from the bus stop back in high school. It'd been a different time, and life was so much different now. "We know he hasn't seriously dated someone since he got back from active duty. Maybe he's not looking to make this a thing."

And part of the reason Sophie hadn't tried to let Brandon know how much she wanted him before now had been precisely because she didn't want to be one of those one-night wonders.

Lyn pursed her lips. "He might not be out there dating as much as it looks like he is. And you've dated, too, but it's been clear, at least to me, that your attention is focused on him specifically."

Elisa nodded. "Really, the only people not aware of what's between the two of you... are the two of you."

Sophie shook her head. She could believe them. She'd

watched both of them struggle through the madness when they'd begun their relationships with David and Alex.

"Don't worry." Lyn chuckled. "It's hard to see what's going on when you're in the center of it all. What you need to do is keep in mind what's right for you. He'll fumble around on his own and it'll be a mess. Don't let it push you away."

It didn't sound like fun. Yet another reason why she'd never broached the careful balance of friendship she and Brandon had. She'd been so happy he'd come back; she'd thought that was enough.

And, suddenly, it wasn't. At least, not for her.

Sophie sighed. "It is, without a doubt, a whole lot easier to watch it all happen. I remember the both of you while you were figuring out your relationships with David and Alex."

It'd been fun to meet Lyn and Elisa. Sophie wouldn't give up their friendships for the world. But it'd also been frustrating. She'd watched them fall in love, and there had been Brandon, showing no signs whatsoever of catching the love bug.

"Is this a good thing for us?" A sliver of fear stubbed the fluttering excitement in her chest. "Having his friendship, being able to come here and spend time with all of you, it could all get seriously screwed up if this isn't the right thing. I don't want to lose any of you."

And it would be awkward. Brandon owned Hope's Crossing Kennels. If they had a falling-out or if she pushed for a relationship he didn't actually want, she'd be mortified by his rejection. She'd also be broken. She'd picked up the pieces of her heart after he'd disappeared the first time. There was no guarantee she'd recover a second time.

"Sophie, honey, this is a good thing. It's okay to get excited. Enjoy it." Elisa paused. "Unless he's not a good kisser. That could be problematic."

Lyn stared at her.

Sophie bit her lip. Nope. No kiss and tell, just the memory of those firm lips on hers teasing her into opening for him and...

Lyn laughed. "Oh, that look is enough. If you were any happier with the way he kissed you, your nipples would be poking their way through your shirt right about now."

"Oh my god!" Sophie gasped and crossed her arms over her chest.

Elisa howled, laughing so hard she tipped off the side of the couch. That tipped Lyn off the edge and onto the floor, too, and Sophie doubled over laughing. Every time they subsided into giggles, one of them would make eye contact with the others and they'd launch into a fresh wave of laughter.

Finally, they were all lying on their backs wherever they'd landed, sucking in air and exhaling exhausted giggles.

"Wow, I needed that. I love you ladies." Sophie wiped tears from her eyes. It'd been an incredible relief after the insanity of the past couple of days.

"Right back at you, darling." Lyn pulled herself back up onto the couch.

"So the question is, are you going to be the girl from down the street and wait for him to figure this out, or are you going to take matters into your own hands?" Elisa sat up but didn't bother to get back up on the couch. Instead, she patted the side of the go bag.

Sophie shrugged. "Most of my everyday clothing was torn up and tossed all over my bedroom floor."

It'd hurt to see it. The intruder had deliberately shredded her clothing, and looking at any single garment brought up thoughts of what could've been done to her. After she'd picked up two or three garments all treated that way, Brandon had stopped her and just grabbed her go bag.

"This calls for something other than everyday wear, anyway." Lyn patted Sophie's knee, bringing her back from the memory of earlier in the day.

"She's going to have to be unorthodox, too." Elisa rose. "The minute he sees lace or gauzy anything, he's going to try to wrap her in a robe. Then he'll try to take a walk or something."

Yup. Sophie had tried the more obvious technique once or twice and Brandon had a way of pretending he saw nothing.

"So we need for me to be me, only irresistible." Sophie fought the heavy weight in her belly. "That's not exactly something I can do."

"Sure it is." Elisa pulled a sleep shirt out of the go bag. "It's just going to take a few creative adjustments to your sleep T-shirts and maybe one or two of your sweatshirts. Lounge wear can be incredibly suggestive when it fits just right."

CHAPTER ELEVEN

You rented a car for this?"

Forte glanced up into the rearview mirror to check Sophie's expression before he answered. "It's too easy to track me via my vehicle and plates. If we're going to take you off the grid, it makes sense to do it in a car that isn't connected to me. I didn't rent this vehicle, though."

"Brandon, this looks and smells like a rental vehicle. It's got the 'I was just detailed' smell to it." She wasn't challenging him, even if it sounded like it. Or maybe she was and he didn't mind.

He'd made a comfortable space for her in the backseat so she could keep her right ankle elevated. From his point of view, she looked damned cute in the nest of blankets and extra pillows.

Cute in a very adult, very irresistible way.

"It'd also defeat the purpose of being unpredictable if I was the one who rented the vehicle." He kept his eyes on the dark roads, watchful for deer.

Pennsylvania had deer problems all year round, and the last thing they needed was to bump into one. Literally. He'd seen a deer get up and walk away from a collision that'd left the car completely undrivable. It would be very bad for him to get too distracted by her reflection in the rearview.

"Ah." She sounded more satisfied with that answer. Blankets rustled as she stirred. "So who did you get to rent this car, then? And I guess it's just a detail that you're not listed as a driver?"

He clicked his tongue. "*Tch*. Such a lawfully obedient lady."

She sighed. "I shouldn't ask about the details."

No. She probably shouldn't. He'd explain to her if he had to, though. It was a part of the trust they'd built in the more recent years after he'd started the kennels. They had a deal. When it mattered, she'd do as he directed immediately with no questions asked. Later, after the initial threat had been addressed, he'd answer all her questions. She'd been careful to specify, because if they'd only agreed for him to explain things, she'd get a much shorter "need to know" version of the situation.

Originally, he hadn't thought it would ever come up in anything more serious than a dog training moment. Once in a while, a pair of new dogs could get into it with each other, and he'd wanted to be able to tell Sophie to get clear while he dealt with it. But in the past year, the scenarios had been more serious and nothing he could've anticipated.

If he was going to keep her whole and healthy, the trust between them was going to need to stay every bit as solid as it had been to date.

"One of the students at Revolution MMA owed us a favor. We worked it out for this trip, and there'll be no worries about consequences for him. Cruz and Rojas are keeping an eye out just to be sure." He might sound unusually cheerful about it, but he was actually looking forward to this road trip. It was a change of pace, got Sophie out of harm's way, and offered an opportunity to travel with her.

A whole lot of win as far as he was concerned, so long as he could keep her safe.

He drew in a deep breath and caught a more pleasant smell than the remnants of detailing. She'd showered before leaving, and the scent of her mint and rosemary shampoo was a light tease in the closed space of the SUV. It was just as well she was behind him and not sitting within easy reach. He might not be able to resist reaching out to tug a stray bit of her hair.

"Leaving in the middle of the night makes sense." She punctuated that statement with a yawn. "But I feel bad being back here instead of sitting up with you to help keep you company."

He smiled. She always thought about other people. Her warm consideration was something that'd never changed, or if it did, it'd only grown in her capacity to care for people. "Go to sleep. I tucked you back there so you could get some real rest."

She could sleep snug while he had driving to keep him busy. The memory of her in his arms, the softness of her lips as he'd kissed her . . . yeah, it was a really good thing for him to be busy driving for the next few hours.

"It's been a long day." She yawned again. "I'm glad you decided to bring Haydn."

The big dog lifted his head from the back of the rented SUV at the sound of his name. He whined briefly, then dropped back below line of sight. They couldn't install a kennel in the back of the SUV the way Forte's had been out-fitted, but they'd put in canvas to make riding in the back safer for him.

Forte could've brought one of the other dogs in training. But Taz was working with Raul Sa, and either Rojas or Cruz could oversee any of the other dogs currently at the kennels. Haydn required special physical therapy and attention. Plus, Sophie was comfortable with Haydn.

Besides, Haydn had at least met the lightning puff cat on board.

"Is your new friend doing okay back there?" He was amazed at her cat. It had the most laid-back attitude toward being in a cat carrier. Luckily, it also didn't get car sick. A carsick animal was never a fun time on a road trip, and he was going to be driving for a decent number of hours.

"I think so." More blankets rustled as Sophie leaned to check on the cat carrier nestled into the footwell of the backseat.

Forte heard a faint meow.

"She's fine." Sophie's voice warmed with affection. "I need to give her a name, though. I might be the worst owner in the world, not giving her a name by now."

Forte chuckled. "Oh yeah. You are the worst. How could you not give your new cat a name?"

There was silence in the back of the car.

Shit. She was too easy to tease right now and probably half-convinced he was being serious. Oy.

He continued in the same dry tone, "You've only been blown up, stuck in the hospital, fired from your job, and had your home invaded. That's not a lot to have going on in your life."

More silence.

Wow. He was batting a thousand.

"Sophie?" He glanced up into the rearview to check on her. She was sitting with her head leaning against the back of the seat. Her eyes were open. "You know I was kidding, right? You gave that cat a home. I think it can be patient about having a name as long as it has food and water and all the petting you give it."

Still no answer. He started looking for a spot along the highway with a shoulder large enough to pull over and safely get out.

"I'm trying to think of a name." Sophie's voice reached him just before he turned on his hazard lights and actually pulled off the road. "Something related to all the things going on right now. When you said it like you did, I realized it was a lot. And not a single one of those things is inspiring a good name for her in my head."

He had not anticipated or followed her line of thought. Not at all.

"Well, 'Boomer' might be cute." There, he could be helpful.

Sophie giggled. "Maybe, but not for this little girl. It's more fitting for one of your dogs."

"Well, there's Fluffy and Fifi, Snowball or Snowflake. Smokey. Precious. Ash. Angel. Lily." He was starting to run out, especially of ideas for cute names.

Thing was, he was used to naming dogs. Normally, he worked with German Shepherd Dogs, Belgian Malinois, and the occasional Labrador Retriever. He didn't tend to work with smaller animals unless they were attending some of the obedience classes he held at the kennels for the general public. All of the animals he was responsible for were working dogs, not pets. He'd always sent them out into the world to support either the military or law enforcement. Or, in some rare cases, private military contractors like Raul Sa.

"Nah. Thank you, but I don't think any of those are a fit, either." Sophie's voice was fading, the words tripping off her tongue.

He figured she'd be fully asleep in the next few minutes. He might be able to concentrate better on the road trip ahead or he might end up caught up in his own thoughts. It was a tough balance.

"The right name will come to you. Sleep on it for now." He wanted to be back there with her, cradling her and tucking her comfortably in against his side. They'd never done that before, but he wanted to. Wanted to hold her and make things right in her world.

He thought she had fallen asleep.

"Brandon? This isn't going to be just a getaway weekend, is it?" Sophie's voice was subdued. "You haven't told me how long we'll be away."

"As long as it takes." He tried to be honest with her. "We're planning a day at a time for right now and keeping things as flexible as possible. We're going to let Ky do his job. And once we know more, we'll make decisions on what to do next."

This was a feasible short-term solution until the threat to Sophie's well-being was resolved somehow. It wasn't something that could go on forever. He just didn't have the answers right now.

They were also taking a few risks, planning for a variety of eventualities. In a way, taking Sophie away like this was a lure. If their adversaries moved to locate and follow, they'd give themselves away. It was a possibility, and Forte planned to be ready to act if it happened.

"I hope Mrs. Seong doesn't come looking for me." When he had the chance to glance in the rearview at her, she was worrying at the corner of a blanket, tying it into a knot and untying it in turn. "And I haven't told my parents anything at all."

"For now, it's fine." Honestly, the less any of them knew,

the better. "If this goes on for more than a few days, we'll talk about how you can contact them and check in, if you still want to."

Sophie's family ties were strong. He'd envied that about her family. She'd grown up loved and surrounded by a mix of culture. She'd been cherished all her life. And he hadn't been the only person attracted to her bright personality back in their high school days.

To be honest, he'd thought she'd move away after she'd gone through college. She'd had so many dreams of travel. But between each deployment, he'd check back to see how she was doing and she'd been right where he'd left her, in the suburbs of Philadelphia. Her ties to family had been stronger than her wanderlust.

"Why me?"

He almost missed her question between his thoughts and the general noise of a few eighteen-wheelers driving past him on the highway. "What do you mean?"

She wasn't the type to whine. The question had sounded odd coming from her.

"I'm trying to figure out what it is about me. Why is this much attention on me?" She wasn't wallowing in fear the way a lot of people would be. No. Instead, she sounded logical, almost morbidly curious.

He paused to consider. In all of the events this week, he'd been reacting so far. He'd taken steps to try to get ahead of whatever it was, but he'd also been respecting Ky's jurisdiction on the investigation. When it came to keeping Sophie alive, Forte needed to ask the same questions she just had.

"Ky asked you questions after the bomb and after the break-in." He wanted to prompt her, see if something new came out. And if it did, they'd contact Ky and share it with him.

"Yes. Mostly what I was doing just before each of those things happened. We also talked about whether there was any way someone might want to hurt me." Her voice was steady for the most part, but she tripped up on the last two words.

"Problem is, none of us can think of anyone who'd be out to seriously do you harm." Forte had thought long and hard about the possibilities. "You haven't been dating anyone recently, so no spurned boyfriends. Your relationship with immediate and extended family is good. Your neighbors love you."

"You've been paying attention to who I'm dating?" Sophie's tone turned sharp.

Oops. "Well, you're at the kennels on a weekly basis. And you talk to all of us. It's not like you keep your dating habits a secret."

"I also don't kiss and tell. It's not like I'm waving my dating status around like a flag, either." She was definitely sounding unhappy.

"No." He'd acknowledge it. "You don't."

"Then why—"

Forte's phone rang.

*   *   *

"Hey, Forte, am I on speakerphone?" Ky came across the speakers via the rental car's Bluetooth connection crystal clear.

"Yeah." Brandon didn't mention Sophie's presence in the car.

Sophie considered speaking up but decided not to. Maybe Brandon had a reason for not using her name. She was fairly certain Ky knew Brandon was taking her away somewhere and obviously the two of them were in touch. But she had no idea how possible it was for someone to intercept the conversation or otherwise listen in to their discussion.

"We had our K9 unit search the area." Ky was all business on this call, his enunciation and cadence brisk. "They picked up a trail and followed it through a few of the neighboring apartment buildings, but the trail doubled back on itself. The perpetrator could be hiding out in any of those buildings or might have gotten into a vehicle and left the vicinity entirely. We're not sure at this time."

Sophie drew her good leg up to her chest and wrapped her arms around it. The person who broke into her home was still out there. And the person probably wanted to hurt her, if not kill her. Since a bomb in her car was definitive, she really needed to get used to the idea that someone was trying to kill her.

Brandon gripped the steering wheel, and even from the backseat, she could see his knuckles turning white. "So that lead isn't going to turn up new information for you."

"Not at this time." Ky sounded equally unhappy. "We've got descriptions on basic body build and height, but since he was wearing dark gear and had a hat on, there's not a lot of chance we'll catch up with him. We've done a door-to-door asking if anyone's seen anything, and there are no hits. Whoever it was might even have changed clothes once he was out of sight. He managed to go unnoticed by every nosy neighbor in the complex."

Wow. Sophie wasn't sure if even Brandon could manage that. Mrs. Seong had sharp hearing, and the elderly neighbor had called nine-one-one almost at the same time as Sophie because of the gunfire.

"We did locate the bullet in the wall of Sophie's apartment. That's a priority with ballistics, and we'll run it to see if there are any matches against any other crimes in the databases." Ky let out a sigh. Sophie wondered if he'd been working around the clock on this. "We're going to investigate Sophie's former employer, too. I'll let you know if we have anything new for you as soon as I can."

"Copy." Brandon ended the call.

"That's it?" Sophie was startled. No questions?

Then Brandon hit the button to roll down the driver's-side window. Cold air rushed through the SUV and the air pressure buffeted Sophie's ears. He tossed the phone out the window.

"What are you doing?" Sophie sat forward and craned her neck to see where the phone landed. She thought she might be able to see it lying in the middle of the highway.

"It was a disposable." Brandon rolled up the window. "Or are you upset about me littering?"

His eyes were framed by the rearview mirror, more brown than green in the dark of the night and barely discernable unless there was another car on the road to add their headlights to the reflection from the mirror. He'd been looking up into the rearview once in a while, and she was sure he was checking on her as often as he was checking for what was behind them on the highway.

"At first, I was freaked because I thought it was your phone." She pressed her lips together. "And I guess it makes sense to use a disposable. But I'm wondering how Ky knew to call you on the disposable number and how he's going to call you in the future."

"What do you think?" Mild amusement tinged his voice.

"I think you've got more than one disposable phone on you and Ky's going to know the numbers of those the same way he knew the other one." She considered for a moment. "How you coordinated the numbers and got them to him could be through too many possible methods for me to guess, but you can't have bought that many disposable phones."

He didn't answer.

Miffed, she continued. "So if I go with my extensive knowledge gained by watching the occasional police procedural show, the disposable phones are to prevent anyone tracing our location with the GPS. Which is why you had me leave my smartphone back at Hope's Crossing Kennels."

Brandon nodded, his gaze on the road ahead of them. "Exactly. And, granted, tossing the disposable phone out the window was on the dramatic side, but I did toss it hard enough to break it when it hit the asphalt. With any luck, somebody will run it over, too. I've got enough to cover us for the next few days. So we won't be completely unreachable but a lot harder to track down."

Sophie leaned her chin on her knee. "And, yes, I'm somewhat concerned about you littering."

He chuckled. "I'll arrange some community service to help clean up a park in penance after we get through all of this."

"Do you think I will?" Listening to Ky, the progress on the investigation didn't sound encouraging. What if they never found the man who was trying to kill her? Mrs. Seong had told her about a new crime show on television that covered stalkers and the way those people hunted down the focus of their obsession until they eventually killed them.

It was possible she had a stalker. Elisa had been able to get free of one only a few months ago.

"We'll take things one day at a time." It was strangely comforting the way Brandon didn't give her reassurances. Maybe other people would've wanted to hear that it would be all right. Or some ladies might want to hear Brandon tell them he'd keep them safe. His quiet, solemn voice colored with dark secrets and tempered with sincerity was certainly everything any romantic hero should have. But she didn't want him to over promise or, worse, lie. "You should get some rest. Sleep, Sophie. I'm here."

CHAPTER TWELVE

We're here." Brandon put the SUV into park and slid out the driver's side. "Hang tight while I see if they can accommodate an early check-in."

He walked around the side of the SUV and let Haydn out. He walked Haydn around the SUV once and left the dog sitting next to it with a single command: *"Bewaken."*

They'd driven through the night. Sophie had napped on and off along the way, tired but too wound up to sleep for long. Every time she'd awakened, though, there'd been Brandon driving. She'd asked a few times if he was okay, and each time he'd reassured her he was awake and fine to keep going.

They stopped twice at rest stops.

He'd walked her to the rest stop with Haydn at his side, then he and the German Shepherd Dog had checked over the SUV before letting her in again. Her new cat had protested once or twice along the way. Brandon had even experimentally taken her out of the carrier at a rest stop with a makeshift leash for her collar.

She hadn't run, thank goodness, and she had taken the opportunity to actually do her business. It'd surprised both Sophie and Brandon.

Super convenient.

At this point, though, it'd been a while since the last rest stop, and Sophie was ready to get out. Her stomach turned, queasy. Normally motion sickness wasn't an issue, but sitting sideways across the backseat on the winding roads they'd driven in the past hour getting to wherever they were had been rough.

The back of the SUV opened. She hadn't even seen Brandon return, but it had to be him. No one else would've gotten past Haydn without a huge fight. And Sophie had seen Brandon's dogs, dogs meant to serve as military working dogs. They could put up a real defense.

"Haydn, *over*." Brandon gave her a grin as she craned her neck to see him over the back of the seat. "Just another couple of minutes while we head to the cabin."

He closed the back and came around to the driver's side. Seated, he started up the SUV again and put it into drive.

"Our cabin has privacy, about a quarter of a mile away from the main house. There's a lot of heavy woods in between, but it's walkable along this road." Brandon was in a good mood. "I think you'll like it."

From the smooth ride, she was guessing the road was paved as opposed to the possible gravel or dirt. The woods they were passing were a mix of bare trees and evergreens. It made for a bare sort of beauty. A quarter of a mile wasn't far, either. She could walk it if she took her time and wrapped her medical boot up with some plastic to keep it from getting dirty or wet.

"I've asked them to deliver a late breakfast in about thirty minutes." Brandon put the SUV into park. "It'd be best if you don't go up to the main house unless absolutely necessary. They're very friendly people, but they like to talk up their clients a little too much. It could get awkward, and I don't want you to feel uncomfortable."

Okay, so maybe she wouldn't be walking the path for pleasure. He left Haydn to guard the car again while he went into the cabin. She guessed he was going room to room, clearing the entire building before letting her enter. Which was fine so long as he did it quickly because she had to pee.

Brandon was there in minutes, though, opening the side door opposite her. "Ready?"

She gave him a relieved smile. "So ready."

He tipped his head to one side. "You'd get inside and into your room faster if you let me carry you. If you walk, it'll just take that much longer before you can pee."

When he put it that way, she could hold it a few minutes more.

She set her jaw. "I can walk."

Amusement sparkled in his hazel eyes. He'd been teasing her again. She needed to work on not being such an easy target.

She scooted her butt to the end of the seat and got out of the SUV carefully. It would've been worse if she'd tripped on her way out because he was still standing right there, ready to catch her. And he was justified; she'd done it in the past on two good ankles.

With that in mind, she did place her hand in his to steady herself. His palm was warm and ignited tiny sparks under her skin, waking up the proverbial butterflies in her stomach.

The air was still cold, but the humidity had the hint of lingering autumn in it. She smelled the faint aroma of apples baking mixed in with the rich tang of evergreen and the earthier scent of fallen leaves beginning to break down on the forest floor.

These weren't Pennsylvania woods. They'd driven south for too many hours to still be in the same state, but the trees here weren't too much different.

"This place is nice." She wasn't certain what Brandon was excited about, but he definitely had a smug look about him with a hint of a smile playing around the corners of his mouth. "You like cabins where there's a clearing, right? So you can see what's coming from far away?"

Brandon placed a hand on the small of her back and encouraged her to start moving into the cabin. His fingertips rested against the curve of her spine and triggered more tickling sparks up her back and down her tailbone. "Yeah. This cabin sits in the middle of this clearing, so there's the same space all the way around. Makes it harder to sneak up on the building. I've got a few Bluetooth cameras with me from Cruz so I can set up some surveillance."

As he'd been talking, he'd been herding her toward the front door without actually rushing her. She took it at her pace but she didn't drag her feet, either, since he was so excited. The outside of the cabin was a lovely wood finish. From the windows, she'd guess it was more of a one-story rancher.

"I'll bring in your cat once you're settled. I want to set up a cat litter for her before I bring her in because she's going to want to go somewhere." Brandon continued to talk about unpacking the SUV, but Sophie was distracted from the minute she stepped inside.

The cabin or rancher or whatever it was called was huge on the inside, much roomier than the impression she'd gotten seeing the front. The foyer floor was set with cool, flat, walking stones leading in a curving path toward the back of the house and a large kitchen with an open layout. To her immediate right was a sitting area equipped with a settee and chairs arranged around a low coffee table. To her left was a living room with a couch and a pair of armchairs arranged facing a large stone fireplace. There was even a stack of real wood on the hearth, ready for a fire to be started in the fireplace.

"Rooms this way." Brandon urged her forward and farther into the rancher, past the living room area and down a small hallway. There were four doors, and she sort of wanted to open each one individually. But he coaxed her past the first set of doors. "Half bath and a linen closet."

Okay, fine, maybe not as interesting, but she still planned to come back and poke her head in when she had time to explore the place at her own pace. The last two doors were both open, looking into two rooms.

Their floor plans were mirrored in design, big enough to each have a king-size bed and...

"Do these rooms share a bathroom?"

Brandon sighed. "Yes, but you'll have your private space."

Because there were two bedrooms.

"Which one would you like?" Brandon asked.

He wasn't planning to share a bedroom with her.

All that planning with Lyn and Elisa was going to be for nothing. Those kisses, the way he'd coaxed her into melting under his mouth; they were just supposed to be ignored.

Seriously?

Like hell.

She stepped away from him without entering either of the rooms. Turning to face him, she folded her arms across her chest and prepared to break open the topic. If she didn't, she was going to let it slide for the rest of the trip, and if she let this go now, she'd regret it.

"Did you kiss me the other night?"

Brandon's expression immediately went blank, but he didn't look away. "Yes."

"Did you intend to?" This was an opportunity for an out if he wanted to take it. She'd be irritated and hurt, but it was a salvageable moment.

"Yes." There was an intensity in his voice, one that was new to her.

She kept her own tone calm even though the answer to her next question was one she was afraid to hear out loud. "Do you regret it?"

"No."

Relief flooded through her, but her belly was still wound up tight. There were still more questions, more things to straighten out, and some of them had waited since the day of high school graduation to be answered. She'd planned to see him in the evening after the ceremonies, waited for him to come to her house. And when he hadn't shown up, she'd gone looking for him, starting with their favorite meeting place along the route to their bus stop. Finally, she'd gone directly to his house, only to discover that he'd already left for basic. He'd had to have known in advance and he hadn't told her he was leaving. He hadn't said good-bye.

But she'd start simple and get to those when she was ready to reopen those old hurts. "So why? Why are we sleeping in separate rooms?"

Brandon dragged his hand through his hair, a sure sign he was frustrated and unsure. "Because you've been through a lot this week. And I want you to rest, heal, recover. All those things are going to happen faster if you have your own space. You should take the time."

Oh no. There were a lot of things she should do, ought to do, like call her family. But she hadn't for the first time in her memory. She'd placed her trust in Brandon. And now she was so frustrated she could hardly breathe.

She choked out a laugh. "You're so damned good at giving all the orders. Telling other people what to do. I've done exactly what you thought was best, and now I'm standing right here. Well, here's some instructions for you. Step up or get out of the way."

He frowned at her. "What do you mean?"

Here she was, in a romantic cabin tucked into the woods with him and he'd just told her to choose her own room. *What the hell?*

"You've been trying so hard to keep us in stasis. Friends. And you care about your friends, protect them. That's just great, Brandon. But you're a colossal cock block, too. Either step up and address this thing between us. Say it out loud. Acknowledge how much I've loved you since we were in freaking high school!" She sucked in a deep breath and gave him a hard stare. "Or get out of the way and let me figure out if I can possibly deal with the idea of finding happy with another man."

Somehow, the words had been different inside her head, but what came out felt more true to her heart. She'd spent a lot of years not even considering other men because he was the focus of her heart and mind. He'd been everything to her.

"Is that what you want? Me to get out of your life?" His brows drew together, and his face had flushed. His hands balled into fists.

He wouldn't hit her. He'd do damage to himself before ever coming close to hurting her. But he trusted her enough to let her see his temper rising. Trusted her to be around him.

And there was still a damned wall of friendship between

them. If he wasn't attracted to her in that way, she could've understood. But his kiss hadn't been chaste and hadn't been uninterested. There'd been hunger to match hers, and she needed him to acknowledge it or tell her she was wrong. She needed it to be spoken, even if it wasn't what she wanted to hear.

She shook her head, angry tears beginning to burn her eyes. "No, I don't want you out of my life. Not ever! But this pretending to just be friends is killing me. It's dooming us both to a lifetime of the friend zone, and I sure as hell don't want to live the rest of my life celibate—not with you around, doing insane things to my libido just by standing there. And I can't even stand the idea of you touching another woman..."

He grabbed her then, crushed her to him. "Never again. I won't ever again. Can't."

She turned her face up to him and a tear fell from the corner of her eye. She struggled to keep her brain working, and she leveled a sharp, pointed look at him. "Then why the hell are we being celibate? Because I, for one, am not into this kind of torture. Go find a waterfall to train under instead."

* * *

He'd held back for so long. Having Sophie challenge him like this drove him out of his mind. He bent his head and kissed her before she managed to say something they'd both regret.

She met him with a matching ferocity that caught him by surprise. She'd always been sweet, sunny, light. But this hunger of hers met him halfway and pushed him past any reason he'd ever managed to think of for why they would be better off with distance between them.

"It's a good thing you packed a go bag," he murmured against her lips.

"Mmm?" She nipped the corner of his mouth. "Why are we using words right now?"

He chuckled, and she stilled in his arms, wary. "It means you have extra clothes."

He gripped the fabric of her shirt and found her gaze, made sure her wide brown eyes were locked on him. Fabric tore. Fell to the ground around her. She gasped. Her pupils dilated. And everything in him roared up in a wave of desire. Holding her gaze, he stripped out of his own clothes, enjoying the hunger growing in her expression.

He bent then, wrapping his arms around her thighs, and lifted her. She held on to his shoulders as he carried her back into the bedroom she'd come out of and dropped her on the bed, enjoying the way her pert breasts bounced as she landed.

"Pretty. Very pretty." He leaned over her, placing a hand on either side of her hips.

She lay back as he climbed onto the bed with her, sighing and tugging at his shoulders. He pressed a kiss low on her abdomen, and then another one just above her navel. The next kiss was higher, but he opened his mouth to suck because he needed to taste her. Her skin was cool against his tongue, fresh and tasting of a hint of salt.

Her eyes fluttered shut, and she pressed her head back as he nuzzled the underside of her breasts through her bra. He grinned up at her. "Blue lace suits you. I like lace."

She let out a breathless laugh. "I know."

He continued to nuzzle and nudge the undersides of her breasts through the lace, enjoying the texture of the soft fabric and the give of her flesh. He caught the edge of the fabric over the curve of her breast and tugged with his teeth.

Her fingers tightened on his shoulders, and her thighs rose on either side of him as she squirmed under him. "Don't rip this one. I don't have that many with me, and I need my bras."

He wanted to argue. The idea of Sophie walking around the cabin for the next couple of days with no bras was very fun. It'd come up while he'd been driving, and he'd struggled to banish it to the back of his mind. Now, well, it was very enticing.

Instead, he licked the curve of her breast above the lace. Then he gently caught the edge of the fabric in his teeth again and tugged it down. Her already taut nipple popped free, and he grinned.

She gasped. "You have a very naughty expression right now, like a kid about to steal a piece of ca—"

He closed his mouth over her nipple and sucked. Hard.

She called out and arched against him. Her thighs closed on his and squeezed. He held her steady under him all the while, enjoying the feel of her nipple against his tongue. After a long moment, he eased back and laved her nipple in long licks.

She blinked her eyes and opened her mouth to speak, but he switched to lick and tease at her other nipple. Her lids shuttered closed again.

"Mmm." He tickled her nipple with short, firm strokes of the tip of his tongue. "I think your left nipple is more sensitive than your right. I'm intrigued."

"You're mean." She gritted her teeth and buried her fingers into his hair.

He chuckled.

This time, he suckled one while he played with her other between his thumb and forefinger. Every flick of his tongue, every tug of his fingers, made her writhe more under him.

"Touch me." Her command was desperate, not a request.

He paused, struggled to keep enough control to listen to what she wanted. "Where?"

"Everywhere!"

He liked a challenge. He rose up off her then and pulled her up to kneel on the bed with him. He gave her a long, lingering kiss, then coaxed her to turn until she was facing the headboard of the bed.

Behind her, he curved his hands around her ribs. "Trust me."

She let her head fall back against his shoulder.

He pressed a kiss against her jaw and let his hands begin to roam. Across her shoulders and along her arms, back to her torso and over the curve of her back. He reveled in the softness of her skin and the slight curves of her body. He pressed against her back, maximizing the points of contact.

It took a minute to help her get her medical boot off, then her pants. "You still wear the cute ones with the cartoon on the back."

Her skin flushed. "Yes."

Today was a bunny. Her tight butt was covered in the cutest cartoon of a bunny he'd ever laid eyes on.

He grazed the shell of her ear with his teeth. She shuddered in pleasure. "I like it."

He helped her out of those, too, and then she was naked. Kneeling and holding the headboard, trembling at his every touch.

Wow.

He spread his hands on the backs of her thighs, cupping below her bottom. When he squeezed, she trembled more and whimpered. "You like this?"

She only nodded.

He pulled her hips back, helping her adjust her stance

wider. He needed access. He used one hand to caress her, gliding over her side and under to her belly, then up to grasp one of her breasts. Then he teased the insides of her thighs with his other hand, exploring with gentle fingertips until he stroked one finger along her crease. She moaned.

His Sophie was wet for him.

He slid his finger inside of her, needing to be sure she was ready to take him. Her inner muscles were tight, and she gasped for breath as he slowly pumped his finger in and out, teasing her opening. Damn, he needed to take care of her first because he definitely wasn't going to last long inside her, not with her as tight as this.

He continued to knead and massage her breast with his other hand. The multitasking helped him keep his own need under control. His erection throbbed, and even the act of rubbing himself against the curve of her butt drove him wild.

She rocked her hips back against him, and he made an inarticulate sound of frustration.

She was going to push him too fast. He set his teeth against her shoulder and slipped a second finger inside her. She cried out and shuddered against him, but he didn't pull back.

"Come for me." He whispered the encouragement into her ear. "It's okay. Let me take care of you. Come for me."

Her next cry was desperate, and her hands clenched on the headboard as her inner muscles convulsed around his fingers. He held her against him, stroking her through and lengthening her orgasm.

She collapsed forward against the headboard at the end of it and presented her rear, and he couldn't wait anymore. He placed a hand on either side of her hips and positioned himself until the head of his cock pressed against her entrance.

"Please, Sophie?"

She nodded. "Yes. Please. Yes."

The request accompanying her permission undid everything inside him, made this more than sex. This was everything he'd dreamed about when he'd been away. This was his Sophie.

When he started to push into her, another groan escaped her throat, and she brought a finger to her mouth, biting it to try to keep quiet. The sight only turned him on more. Slow and incredibly good, he filled her, and she stretched to accommodate him until he was balls deep.

Oh yes.

He withdrew slowly, and her tightness almost wouldn't let him go. He breathed deep, hoping he could continue a little longer. Pressing back into her, he leaned over her until the length of her back pressed against his torso. He ran his hands over her, sliding up from her thighs and over her belly to caress her breasts.

And as he did, he pumped inside her.

She leaned her head back to the curve of his shoulder again, only capable of tiny gasps with every thrust.

"Is this everywhere?" he asked her.

She whimpered, and her insides tightened on the length of his shaft. She was almost ready again.

He straightened and gripped her waist. Gritting his teeth, he began thrusting harder. She leaned forward, bracing herself against the headboard and arching her back as he pulled almost completely out and then slid back into her in strong, firm strokes. Every one of them drove him closer and closer to insanity.

"Brandon." She gasped out his name, and it undid him.

His balls tightened, and he had only one more chance to pull out and thrust back into her. She cried out, her orgasm dragging him with her, and he shouted as he came with her.

CHAPTER THIRTEEN

I've got an idea."

Forte pressed his lips against Sophie's bare shoulder, enjoying the silken smoothness of her. He could hardly believe this wasn't a hallucination. He liked curling around her in bed. She'd commandeered his arm as a pillow, and she was lightly tracing random patterns along the inside of his forearm. Her featherlight touch didn't tickle so much as send tiny hints of electricity across his skin. "What's your idea?"

"Let's use this room for fun times and use the other room to sleep in." She yawned. "That way, neither of us has to sleep in a wet spot."

He chuckled. "Sounds like a plan. Speaking of sleeping…"

She squeaked when he pulled the sheet off them both. Rolling off the bed, he grabbed a lightweight blanket from the chest at the foot of the bed and tossed it over her, then scooped her up in his arms.

"You should take a nap while I go out and rescue the animals from boredom out by the car." Haydn could easily stay on guard for hours, even in the current temperatures. His thick coat would protect and insulate him with no problem. And the cat was still in a carrier inside the SUV, protected from the cold. But Sophie would want them seen to, and he planned to do everything in his power to eliminate any stress for her while she was with him. "I'll bring them both inside and get them set up with food and water."

The smile she gave him was unbelievably sweet and hit him directly in the chest with how good it made him feel.

He carried her into the next room, careful not to hit her head or her booted foot on a door frame. As they entered, Sophie perked up, taking in the decor of the room.

"Ooh, I like this. It's all cool blues and creams. Really relaxing." She remained sitting up when he set her on the bed.

Her gaze swept through the room, and he figured she'd wake up too much to get back to a nap. So he lunged.

She squeaked. Forte grinned, holding himself over her and looking down into her dark brown eyes. "You don't look tired enough for a nap. Maybe I need to work harder?"

Her eyes widened. "Oh. Yes, but Haydn and my cat. I—"

He kissed her very cute nose. "Should nap before I'm tempted to really start something up again. I'll wrangle the beasts."

Rising from the bed, he tucked her in to his satisfaction. "Nap. Food should be here by the time you wake up."

He closed the door behind him as he left the room. This was a good way to start. Once she woke up recharged, he'd take her through his security precautions and give her instructions for worst-case scenarios.

And there were several, all equally serious.

Haydn was right where Forte had left him. The big dog was alert but unconcerned. For now, at least, there was no detectable threat in the area.

Forte left him on guard and set about bringing their two bags into the cabin, then the box containing the various animal supplies. He found a small laundry room and set up the cat's litter box in there for the time being. He wanted it someplace accessible but out of the way. Hopefully, the cat would agree on his placement.

He'd never been a cat person. But he could see the benefit of having one or two on the Hope's Crossing Kennels property. Otherwise, mice had to be tracked down in the storage shed they used to store the dog food.

But the idea of an indoor cat hadn't ever been something he'd considered.

Forte decided to set Sophie's cat carrier down in the laundry room so the first thing the feline would see was where its litter box was located. The cat came out of its carrier at a leisurely stroll and sniffed the air for a moment. Then it headed directly to the litter box and started to make a deposit, looking straight up at him.

"Sorry," he muttered, and exited the room to give kitty her privacy.

He strode outside and closed up the SUV, then released Haydn from guard duty and led the big dog inside.

Forte's phone rang as Haydn made a beeline for the laundry room.

Shit.

"This is Forte." He might've sounded pissed, but he wasn't going to miss this call. At the same time, he needed to monitor this meeting of furry minds, too, or blood could be drawn.

"Rojas here."

Haydn stood just in the doorway to the laundry room, staring at what had become a lightning-struck cat puff in the litter box.

"*Los.*" Forte kept some force in the command. Responsive as Haydn was, he needed to understand this cat was consistently off limits.

"Who, me?" Rojas asked. He sounded like he was amused, though.

"Sorry, man. I'm handling Haydn and Sophie's new cat." The cat in question had begun to let its fur smooth down. It stepped off the litter box with a delicate shake of its paws and hopped up onto the laundry machine. It then sat and deliberately started to clean its lady bits right there in front of both him and Haydn, lifting one hind leg in a distinct demonstration of flexibility.

"How's that going for you?" Rojas seemed mildly curious.

"I've just been given the cat finger."

Rojas barked out a laugh. "What?"

"Never mind. I'll take a picture for you if it happens again." Forte would've had to fish out an actual digital camera from his bag because he'd left his smartphone behind at the kennels, too. "Trust me, you'll know it when you see it."

"Okay, then." And there was a story for Rojas to pass on to Lyn and Elisa when they badgered him about how Sophie was doing. "All's well here at the kennels. Sa is really working well with Taz. I think we've got a match."

"Good." Forte was pleased. The working dogs could usually transition to more than one partner in their lifetimes, but he and his trainers did their best to pair them in a strong bond at the outset. It made a smart dog and handler into a formidable working pair.

"Ky checked in, too." Rojas's cadence remained concise, friendly. Someone only partially listening in wouldn't be alerted to the more serious topic by a change in tone or volume. He just carried on like they were still chatting about cat fingers and dog training. "The current person of interest appears to be clean on the surface, but Ky's gut says there's something shady. He wants to dig, but it'd help if our lady friend can remember exactly which files she worked with in the last few days."

They weren't mentioning Sophie's name specifically. Someone monitoring the conversation directly would be able to figure out what they were talking about, but they were avoiding key words like names to circumvent software monitoring any number of conversations at a time "fishing" to find theirs.

"I'll ask and send a follow-up." Forte could access a virtual private network and send a secure update once he'd prompted Sophie to see what she could remember. Most likely, she'd be able to recall the exact names.

"Copy." Rojas paused. "The cat have a name yet?"

"No." Forte watched as the feline in question finally finished her grooming for the time being and hopped down off the laundry machine. "But we're going to need to come up with one soon."

The cat approached Haydn slowly, wary but not electrified for the moment. Her steps were fluid as opposed to the stiff-legged way she'd walked past him on their first meeting. Inch by inch, she approached until she was almost nose to nose with the dog.

Haydn, for his part, had stood his ground and allowed the feline to approach. Presented with the current challenge, he lowered his nose for a sniff.

"It looks like there's an understanding between the feline and canine elements." Forte chuckled. He'd have worked with them until there'd at least been a truce in which Haydn would leave the cat alone, but it would be better if they could get along. Sophie would enjoy the stay more if there was goodwill among furry things.

Rojas grunted. "Oh boy. We'll have to see if the new cat can make friends with Souze and Atlas, too. It might be a regular visitor."

Having fully sniffed Haydn over, the cat wandered out of the laundry room to explore the rest of the cabin. Haydn looked up at Forte once, then followed after the feline.

"Cat certainly handles big dogs well." Forte turned to watch the pair methodically explore their new domain. "It's got a healthy fear of them in the beginning, but then it figures out which ones will or won't present a threat."

"Is it fully clawed?" Rojas asked.

"Yeah." Forte had checked back at the cat café when Sophie had made the decision to adopt it. "Spayed, but all claws are intact."

Rojas grunted. "It can give out its own warning if it has to, then. We'll just have to make sure it isn't enough of a brawler to take out a dog's eye."

Atlas and Souze were each well-trained and exceptionally good at their work. They, like Haydn, would leave something alone no matter how tempting it was if commanded to leave it. So then it was on the handlers to make sure the cat didn't take advantage of the situation and permanently harm one of the dogs.

"I'll keep watch on things here." Forte acknowledged the caution. It was worth keeping in mind.

"Sounds good." Rojas sighed. "I can think of a certain child who will most definitely want to go to the same place and adopt a cat, too, if this works out."

Ah. "Sorry, man."

Rojas currently rented the house on Hope's Crossing Kennels land, but as part of the agreement, the rental payments were tracked and would be applied toward the cost if Rojas ever exercised the option to buy the house and the small plot of land it was standing on permanently.

"No use making a decision until I'm faced with the request." Rojas's tone had turned wry.

"I'll follow up with the info for you." Forte wanted to wrap up. Haydn was standing at one of the front windows in the sitting area, and the cat was on the windowsill. Both of them were staring at something outside. "I'm guessing we've got a late breakfast being delivered."

And if it was something else, he'd need his full attention to handle it.

*   *   *

Sophie took a quick shower, promising herself a long bath later when she saw the cute tray of teakwood holding a selection of carefully labeled bath salts. The bathroom had a separate shower and large soaking tub, big enough for two. Another thoughtful addition to the bathroom was a semi-permanent partition, making the toilet a bit more separate from the rest of the bathroom. It wasn't common, not even in modern hotels, but she did go on the occasional long weekend, and she loved hotels that included this in their floor plans.

Maybe it was a weird thing to notice, but any particular features that enhanced comfort were the things she remembered about staying at a particular place.

There were apple-scented candles in the bathroom, too, and she thought they'd be nice to light so she could turn the artificial lighting off when she took her bath.

All this she promised herself while she dried, then dressed in a fresh tunic-style tee and leggings. Forte had left both of their duffel bags in the bedroom she hadn't been using for her nap. The two bedrooms did share the full bathroom, which, in this case, worked out conveniently, but she wondered how other guests worked it out.

"I can hear you wandering around, so I'm guessing you can't find clothes or you're considering every detail of those rooms based on how you might set up a B-and-B." Brandon's voice echoed down the corridor, and she jumped.

"You know me so well." She decided to cut through the hallway back to the other bedroom instead of going by way of the bathroom again.

Brandon met her in the hallway, brushing a wet strand of hair from her shoulder and bending to press his lips against the place where her neck and shoulder met. Delicious shivers went through her at his touch.

"Do you need help getting your boot on?" he murmured.

"I don't need help, particularly, but I'd be faster joining you out in the living room if you did help." She smiled at him.

He sighed as he followed her into the room. "You're a capable woman, and I respect you for it. I also want to help whenever I can. Sometimes you don't pay attention to your own well-being and I intervene before you really do something bad to yourself. But times like today, when you're fine as long as you do things at your pace, I don't want to smother you or boss you around."

Ah. He'd absorbed what she'd said about giving orders earlier. She sat on the bed, looking up at him.

"I'm trying." He reached for her hand and lifted it, brushing her knuckles with his lips. "But could you meet me halfway and ask me for help to let me know when it's okay to take care of you? It'd give me a clear signal so I don't push you into having to push back."

His request made, he reached for her medical boot and brought it to her.

She smiled at him and lifted her right foot.

Her leg as a whole was looking a lot better. The angry red scrapes and cuts from hitting the asphalt and rolling to avoid the explosion were healing well. The skin around the cuts had faded to her normal skin tone. Luckily, they'd been able to avoid stitches for the deeper cuts and use butterfly-stitch bandages, which she'd been replacing daily right after her bath. The bruises were still showing up, though; rising up under her skin in awful blotches of black, blue, and purple with a crazy mustard yellow around the edges.

Swelling in her ankle was under control, but she could still tell the difference when she looked at it side by side with her good ankle.

Brandon studied the evidence of her brush with blowing up, his expression somber. Then he carefully pressed a kiss against every scrape and bruise, lingering over her ankle.

She parted her lips. Maybe the rest of the day could wait.

Then his gaze met hers and humor danced in his eyes. The desire still burned, but she couldn't help smiling in response, her mood lightening.

"We should get a sock on your foot to protect your skin from rubbing against the inside of the boot." Brandon worried too much. "But I guess this'll be good to get you out there for a late breakfast and we can ice your ankle while you're out there, then get a fresh sock on it before we put the boot back on."

She stuck her tongue out at him. "Okay, but we can ice the ankle with the boot on, too. I'd just as well have my toes bare to the air for a little bit if I'm not going to be on my feet for the next couple of hours."

He gave her a smile as he straightened to stand in front of her. Impulsively, she leaned forward and wrapped her arms around his thighs, rubbing her face into his abdomen.

One of his hands came to rest on the back of her head.

"Sophie." His voice had gone husky. "I promise I'll cuddle with you after you have a chance to eat, but if you keep doing that I'm going to forget I wanted to make sure you got breakfast."

She held on an extra-long moment and then released him, standing up and making him take a step back. Oh, he didn't have to, but he did for her.

"How are our four-legged friends?" she asked as she walked down the hallway. She was trying hard to walk with a normal stride now that it'd been a few days. Her doctor had said she could as long as there was no pain when she put weight on the ankle. She made it most of the way before little twinges told her it was too soon.

Brandon placed his hand on her lower back and urged her past the living room area and over to the sitting area with the settee. "They're fine. Not sure if they want to be friends yet, but war hasn't broken out, either. "

"That's g—oh!" She slowed and let Brandon lead her around the gorgeous setup on the low table. She sat and barely noticed as he coaxed her into lifting her right leg to rest on the length of the settee.

A selection of lovely dishes were spread across the table, each of them porcelain white with a delicate pattern of tiny blue roses around the edge. On one oval dish, spears of asparagus wrapped in bacon were stacked high. On another dish was a selection of tomatoes cut in half and broiled. A third specialty dish had hollows to cradle soft-boiled eggs partially shelled to display the rich, yellow yolk. A polished wood board was set to one side, offering a selection of at least five cheeses.

"I'm not a cheese kind of guy, but this looked like something you'd like to nibble on through the day, so I had them put it here for you." Brandon crouched down and balanced on his heels as Haydn walked by. The big dog was easily tall enough to lean over the low table and gobble up everything there. "Don't worry about Haydn; he'll leave the people food alone."

"It looks gorgeous, and I'm picky about my cheeses." She couldn't wait to pounce on them and start sampling.

He regarded the cheese with less affection. "What are all these, and is this one even edible?" He pointed to a white, crumbly cheese veined with blue.

She laughed. "Okay, so the selection on this cheese board hits every one of my top things to remember about putting together a tasty combination of flavors and textures. That's always a win for me."

"So what are Sophie's top things to remember about cheese?"

She giggled then blushed as he watched her, waiting. He actually wanted to know.

"Oh." He knew she loved food, but they'd never talked about food together. "Well, there's variety, for one thing. There's a nice sharp block of white cheddar; a nutty chunk of manchego; a creamy wedge of brie; a tiny fresh white wheel of goat cheese; a nice strong blue cheese, which you were pointing to; and a gooey wedge of something so soft it looks spreadable with a strong, funky scent. That's more choice than most cheese boards I've seen in restaurants. They usually only serve between three and five cheeses."

He wrinkled his nose. "You want funky cheese?"

She nodded with enthusiasm. "That kind is my absolute favorite to spread on a slice of thick, crusty bread. So good."

"And you're happy about this other stuff served with the cheese, too?" He gestured to a couple of tiny ramekins of preserves and dried fruits.

"I can't wait to taste them." She leaned closer to get a better look. "Dried apricots or cranberries are great to have with the brie or goat cheese. And there's any number of preserves you could pair with the nutty cheese. Maybe they make these preserves on site. A lot of B-and-B's do. This one even looks like it might be bacon jam."

"Seriously? They make jam with bacon in it?" He was definitely dubious.

"Bacon is a versatile ingredient." She was very serious about that statement. "It makes a lot of things better."

He snorted. "I'll try it later. For now, eat, please."

"Aren't you eating with me?" Her spirits took a dive as he stood, his knees creaking faintly with the motion.

He paused. "I'll have some if you want me to join you. Or you can fall into a book. I brought an e-reader with books already loaded from Lyn and Elisa on it. It's not connected to any kind of data plan, and we'll need to keep the Wi-Fi turned off. I've got to walk the property and make sure I've got as clear a line of sight as possible on the approaches to this place."

His consideration was overwhelming. This really was like a dream vacation. If someone wasn't trying to find and kill her. "Brandon?"

"Yeah?" His brows had drawn together as concern colored his tone.

She asked her next question in a very quiet, hopeful voice. "Could we pretend, just for a while, that the outside world doesn't exist? Could it just be us here, enjoying a remote getaway?"

He came to her side and leaned close. His lips met hers in a soft, lingering kiss full of promises. "You can pretend if you want, Sophie, and I'll keep your dream safe."

CHAPTER FOURTEEN

Forte woke at dawn out of habit. He didn't need an alarm clock anymore, but he reached for the current disposable phone and disabled the alarm he'd set for peace of mind. Might be a weird quirk of his, but it made it easier to fall asleep at night when he wasn't anxious about whether he'd wake up on time in the morning, or in the morning at all.

Sophie had rolled to the other side of the bed. She might be a snuggle monster on first falling asleep, but she definitely tossed and turned through the night. Apparently, she'd gotten too warm toward the early hours before dawn because she'd not only rolled to the other end of the gigantic bed but she also kicked off the majority of the covers. Only a single corner of the bedspread covered her hip, and the sight of her lying naked and mostly exposed like that was amazingly tempting.

He shook his head and pushed aside thoughts of a morning ambush for the time being. She needed her rest.

He got off the bed as quietly as he could, doing his best

not to disturb her, then moved around the bed to where Sophie lay and straightened the covers, tucking her back in so she wouldn't catch cold.

It was reasonably challenging to move around the cabin silently. The wood floors squeaked unpredictably. He might have been irritated normally, but this morning he found it a sort of challenge. Lighthearted, he crossed to the bathroom as quietly as possible. Once he'd taken care of his own business, he headed out to the hallway via the second bedroom and found Haydn waiting for him in the hallway.

Sophie's cat was nowhere to be seen for the moment.

Forte continued down the hallway, and Haydn fell in at his side. They stopped at the breakfast counter separating the kitchen from the sitting area. He grabbed his tablet, then Haydn's leash.

Sophie's cat hopped up on the breakfast counter and directed an imperious *meow* at him.

"After we go out for a walk, you both will get breakfast." He didn't know when he'd started talking to the cat, but it didn't feel awkward. He talked to the dogs he'd trained all the time.

Sophie's cat sat right there on the counter and proceeded to groom, extending one of her hind legs toward the ceiling and giving him the cat finger again.

All righty then.

He and Haydn headed outside, though Forte made sure the front door was firmly shut. The last thing he needed was for Sophie's cat to follow them and potentially take a trip into the woods.

These woods were dense and provided a home for plenty of wildlife. Raccoons were out there for sure. He thought he'd heard a fox or even two calling out in the night. Plus, it was a good sign there were bears in an area when the trash cans at the entrance to the clearing were all enclosed in latched cages.

Haydn didn't need the leash. Forte let him range out to the edge of the clearing on his own. Mostly, Forte kept the leash in hand to reassure anyone who might be out walking from one of the other cabins or someone from the main house.

Haydn stopped to sniff a tree, then turned and lifted his leg nice and high to mark it. Could be another dog. Could be a bear. Forte shrugged. "You do your thing. Probably can't hurt to have the scent of another large predator around this clearing to keep some of the deer from coming in and eating the landscaping."

The browse line in these woods was discernable, though not as bad as it could get up in the woods in Pennsylvania. He was happy to see there wasn't much underbrush in these woods, giving him a clearer view of what might be in the woods around them.

Haydn, for his part, had apparently decided to delineate the entire clearing as his territory and was patrolling the perimeter to establish it. This included a brief stop-and-piss on likely looking trees or stumps. Forte walked a full circuit with him the first time, then called him in and put the leash on him.

Haydn was ready and eager, standing with his weight evenly balanced on all four feet despite the prosthetic. All the recent activity had done him good, and he'd acclimated to the prosthetic faster than Forte had anticipated.

Forte strode over to the cabin's porch and pointed to indicate a spot under a bench where he wouldn't be immediately noticed. *"Hier."*

Haydn immediately placed himself where indicated.

Forte smiled. *"Bewaken."*

Leaving Haydn to guard the cabin, he walked up to the main house.

The household was just beginning to stir. They had full Wi-Fi there, but he bypassed the inviting wraparound porch and continued up yet another hill toward the tasting house.

They were at a cidery, actually, and he planned to bring Sophie up to taste ciders later in the day if she was up for it. For the time being, he parked on one of the picnic tables looking out over the area and fired up his tablet to connect to the public Wi-Fi they had there. From his vantage point, he could see all approaches coming into the cidery grounds.

Once the tablet was on the public Wi-Fi, he opened up the app for the virtual private network Cruz had set up. Safely anonymous on the Internet, he went to his e-mail and read through the messages there. It didn't take long.

Kennel business was mostly handled by Elisa now, and his family e-mailed him to check in occasionally, but more often, he was included on the family distribution list when someone wanted to let all of them know something at the same time. That was the way his family worked. Loving but not really bound tightly together.

One message sat in his inbox, out of place. The subject looked like spam, but the e-mail address was legit, so it hadn't been flagged by the spam filter.

Mr. Forte.

Please call this number for an exclusive offer just for you.

That was it, no logo or graphics. It was the e-mail address that caught his attention: Labs-Anders Corporation.

Forte opened up a new e-mail window and quickly typed out an update message for Ky including the client names Sophie had shared with him the prior afternoon. Then Forte added a request for Ky to look into a con-nection between the client names and Labs-Anders Corporation. It looked like Beckhorn had hit on the right organization. He also copied Rojas and Cruz on the e-mail so they'd be aware of the communication with Ky.

The e-mail address he was using to send the e-mail was different from his personal address. This was one of a set only he, Cruz, and Rojas used. Now Ky had it.

He wasn't actually surprised someone had found him. The personal e-mail address was available to the public and easy to find. It was what his family used, and the e-mail he provided when prompted to give one for interacting with the local community or businesses around the kennels.

But being contacted told him there was interest in him from an unusual source. The timing was too convenient for it to be unrelated to Sophie's situation.

"Hello. Labs-Anders Corporation. How can we help you?" The voice on the other line was female and bored. Or it sounded bored.

"This is Brandon Forte." It didn't hurt to give whoever this was his full name. Whoever had contacted him knew it if they'd tracked down his e-mail.

"I'm sorry, unless you have a specific reason for calling or know who you are trying to reach, I'm not sure I can help you." The woman's tone was flat and extremely unhelpful.

"I'm calling in response to an offer I received via e-mail." This could be a sign, countersign procedure, but the e-mail hadn't indicated any specific phrasing. Most likely, it was receiving the e-mail at all that would get him through the next security check.

There was silence on the phone for a moment, then the woman's cadence turned crisp. "Are you having car trouble? Spent time in the hospital recently? Or maybe experienced a recent break-in at your home? Our attorneys can help you get the money you might deserve."

Well, that was a triple coincidence.

"Yes, I've had some car trouble in the last couple of days, had to spend time in the hospital after that, and someone broke into the apartment I was in this week, too." The appropriate phrases were pretty obvious in this situation.

"All right, sir, I'll transfer you to someone who can help you right away."

Not the most formal sign, countersign procedure he'd ever experienced, but it was pretty organic as conversations went.

"Zerta." A male voice picked up the line. "Thank you for calling us, Mr. Forte."

Forte wasn't in the mood for word games. "This is starting to sound like a cheesy spy movie. What are you offering me?"

There was a pause, then a slow chuckle. The man on the other end of the call cleared his throat. "I apologize. I hope my laugh didn't add to the B-rated movie theme. To be concise, we'd like to offer you a position with our private organization. We're prepared to make the same offer to both of your partners. We feel each of you would be a valuable asset."

"Why do you think I would be interested in private contracts?" Forte had had the option, even been approached by one or two other private military organizations. He didn't have the same negative opinion of mercenaries as others might, but it hadn't been what he'd wanted for his future.

"You haven't lost your edge, Mr. Forte. Not even after five years of retirement from active duty. We need seasoned, experienced leaders of your caliber. Your knowledge of military working dogs would also allow us to broaden the range of services we can provide to our clients." The man on the other end of the line delivered his reasoning smoothly. He probably wasn't lying, either.

But Forte had the distinct desire to up his personal fitness regimen immediately and maybe get in some extra training on a few skill sets. Whatever he could manage on his own out here. Because this organization had financial means to send more than just one hitter after a target. They were going to be harder to discourage than a single stalker would be. No. This was going to have to be a thorough takedown.

Either way, it was time to end the call before it could be traced. Cruz had a redirect set up for the disposable numbers so it'd given Forte a few extra minutes and they probably knew he was on the continent. But he needed to drop off before they figured out the time zone.

"I'll think about it and call you back at this number."

The other man chuckled again. "Excellent. Please don't take too much time. We'll be waiting."

CHAPTER FIFTEEN

The chef responsible for the meals sent so far was equally good at presentation and flavor. Right in the middle of the afternoon, Brandon had intercepted the proprietor coming down the road from the main house to deliver a large picnic basket.

He'd been distracted today, though, and only laid out the food without asking her what she thought about it.

"Everything okay?"

Brandon paused and looked at her directly for the first time since lunch. There was that stranger in his gaze again, the man she didn't know from their school days. "For the immediate moment, yeah. I'm sorry I haven't been good company."

His words, his tone, the set of his jaw—none of them gave her a hint as to what was going on beneath the surface. This was the facet of him she was still learning. And she might never actually know what he was capable of or what he'd do.

He was still her Brandon, considerate and caring without being overt about it. But he was more, with a sharp edge and a deeper potential for...darker things. Now that she thought about it, he'd never trained in front of her. Rojas, and sometimes Cruz, trained in the open adult classes at Revolution MMA. Brandon only ever trained in private.

There was still plenty for her to learn about him, and she could spend a lifetime doing it, she realized. But only if he let her in.

She shook her head. "Is there anything I can do?"

He pulled the chair opposite the settee around the low table to sit next to her. Leaning forward, he rested his elbows on his knees and touched his forehead to hers. She closed her eyes a moment and savored his proximity, then she opened them and got a good look at his arms.

The position showcased his very nicely defined forearms. *Yum.*

As he straightened, she bit her lip to hide the tiny loss she felt as he moved away. Silly, probably, but this was a new level of...whatever it was and she was savoring every moment.

"You're doing exactly what I need right now." The corner of his mouth lifted in a lopsided grin. "It'd be a lot harder to keep you safe if you were being difficult about it."

She swept her hand out in a gesture to indicate the entire table covered in an impressive afternoon tea spread. "How can anyone be difficult when you feed them like this?"

He plucked a small tent card from the picnic basket. "There's a selection of teas in here, too. It says all this should be enjoyed with the tea of your choice."

"Our choice." She hoped he'd join her. "Don't tell me you're going to leave me to try to eat my way through this alone?"

He'd been going out on irregular security sweeps. When he did, she was left in the empty cabin with her imagination and anxiety, wondering what the chances were that he'd encounter the threats he was guarding against. At least when he was present, she could pretend they were on a romantic getaway.

He snagged a few brown paper bags from the basket, individually labeled with tea descriptions. "White plum, peppermint, orange blossom and tangerine, Lady Grey, Darjeeling, and Early Grey."

As she looked over the spread on the table, she spotted a small covered container. Leaning out she stretched her hand out to snag the container and peek inside. "And there are actual brown and white sugar cubes. Yes. Could we brew a pot of the Lady Grey, then, please?"

He tossed the rest of the packages back into the picnic basket. Turned the selected tea package in his hands. "Oh, cool. There's actual, sensible instructions on the back of this."

"You mean for the temperature of the water and how long to steep the tea?" She leaned as close as she could without tipping off the settee. This might be the first time he'd ever taken notice.

"Yeah. That's a thing?"

She nodded. "That is actually a thing. The electric hot water kettle is high tech, too. It has buttons for different water temperatures with added labels for corresponding teas, like whether you're heating water for white tea versus green tea or maybe oolong or black. So you should be able to fill the electric kettle and just hit a button, then go get the teapot to hang the tea bag into it."

"Copy." Brandon stood and grasped her shoulders gently, pressing her back onto the settee. He remained braced over her for a long minute, holding her gaze, then he kissed her. She was completely scrambled by the time he let her up for air, and he was already headed for the kitchen by the time her vision cleared. "Can you try one of the sandwiches and tell me what the heck they are?"

She was fairly certain the basket contained another card describing the food, if the chef had included a note about the tea. Still, he was prompting further conversation, and she was happy to talk about the food. Then again, he could be teasing her like this just to see what happened to her words when she got distracted.

If all his kisses were going to be that mind-blowing, she was okay with this particular game.

"There's a couple of different kinds of finger sandwiches here." She picked one up. "Ooh. This one is egg salad with thin slices of cucumber and microgreens."

"Why all the green stuff? Whatever happened to a plain egg sandwich?" He was handling the water and teakettle tasks fairly easily, even with Haydn underfoot in the kitchen with him.

Her cat hopped up onto the back of the settee and sat perched just behind Sophie. "This is a nice twist. It's on white bread with the crusts cut off."

"You don't usually cut the crusts off your sandwiches."

"No." She finished off the one sandwich in a few bites and reached for a second. "But these are all about the presentation. The whole point is for everything to look appealing and snackable. Tasty tidbits. Finger foods. This one is roast beef and watercress with what looks like a tomato jam, maybe?"

She bit into it to confirm. Because of course she needed to know if her guess was on target. She licked her fingers to catch every bit of the fantastic tomato jam. "Mmm. Yup."

He snickered. "Finger foods."

She widened her eyes at him in mock dismay. "Naughty!"

He only grinned at her and took a sandwich, inhaling it in one bite then slowly licking his fingers.

Instant nipple tightening. She cleared her throat. But she was saved from replying to his sally by the beeping of the hot water heater.

The water had heated in record time, and he was already pouring it into the teapot to steep the tea. "So what's the difference between Earl Grey and Lady Grey?"

She swallowed her bite of sandwich before answering. "I don't know specifically. I just know I feel like I want that more today. It's got a lighter taste to it, and I like the flavor when I add a lump of brown sugar."

"That's fair." He made sure her teacup and the container of sugar cubes were in easy reach. "How are the sandwiches?"

"So good." She handed him a finger sandwich. "This one looks like chicken and pesto with sundried tomato. I want to try the crumpets next."

He looked around on the table. "Since I recognize most everything else here, I'm guessing the crumpets are the pancake-looking things stacked next to the scones."

She nodded. "I haven't quite got the knack of making them yet. Mine don't ever show this many air pockets."

She proceeded to butter one, then added a dollop of strawberry preserves.

"Too sweet for me." He popped the chicken sandwich into his mouth whole, chewing thoughtfully.

"There's a place in Seattle near Pike's Place Market that serves crumpets and they're hearty breakfast sandwiches. There's a green eggs and ham with cheese crumpet where they mix pesto into beaten eggs and cook them to stack with the ham and cheese. It ends up being huge."

"When did you go to Seattle?"

"Hmm?" She glanced up and was caught by the intensity of his hazel eyes. "I don't think you'd come back yet from the military. I used to go traveling on long weekends every once in a while. Just to see places I'd been wanting to visit."

The lopsided grin was back. "Yeah? Where else did you go?"

Nowhere that hadn't made her wish he'd been with her.

"Oh, I don't know. I'd remember better if I had my phone so I could show you my favorite pictures from each place." She tried to remember when she'd started her adventures. "I think I started the long weekend trips right after my first internship. I had to save my pennies for each and every one. First on my list was Baltimore."

He reached for another sandwich. "Why Baltimore?"

She shrugged. "I wanted to see the Inner Harbor on my own, without anyone dragging me to go see anything in particular. I explored a couple of restaurants off the main tourist path, a few blocks away from the harbor area."

He nodded, a sparkle in his eyes.

It was sort of funny that they'd never talked about her trips in detail. She'd never brought them up because they were both usually so caught up in the present. What could be done to solidly establish the kennels, how to gain acceptance and support from the community, and more considerations to make *now* last as long as possible.

She nibbled at her crumpet and continued. "I mostly visited cities. Denver, San Diego, San Francisco, Seattle, Houston. I wanted a change of pace from the usual suburbia."

He reached for the teapot and poured tea into her cup. "Do you like cities better? Would you want to move to one?"

She added a lump of brown sugar to her tea and stirred with the amazingly cute teaspoon. "No. If I wanted to live in the city, I'd have gotten an apartment in Philly. The old city area is really nice. But I like living in the suburbs. It's quieter, with more room to breathe, but the fun of the city is only twenty or thirty minutes away. It's really easy to have whichever surrounding I'm in the mood for where I live right now."

"But what if you moved someplace else? Is there somewhere in the country you'd rather live? Some other country you'd want to try living in for a while?"

This was a faintly familiar conversation. She smiled. "We talked about places we wanted to go back in high school. I've been working through my list, visiting and having fun. I'm pretty satisfied with that."

He paused. "You could've gone anywhere. Why did you decide to stay in Pennsylvania? Why did you stay in town?"

She'd had enough of his dodging. "Why did you leave?"

He froze.

She set her teeth and waited him out. It wasn't fair for him to know what she'd been up to without him sharing the same.

"There were reasons," he said finally. "Multiple."

This was going to be like peeling back the layers of an onion. Fine. She could go one layer at a time as long as he didn't shut her down.

He sighed. "The simple answer is because I needed change."

She tipped her head to the side, watching the way he held himself still, completely controlled from his center of gravity out to his fingertips. "We were going to travel for a change in scenery."

He shook his head in a sharp, tight motion. "The kind of environment I was looking for wasn't any place I'd ever want you to see. I wanted a crucible."

Ah. She blew out her breath slowly and let go of the tension in her shoulders. His reason was something she could accept. Maybe try to understand a little at a time. This was so much better than just wanting to leave everything behind, including her.

She'd been selfish over these years, obsessing over what she might have done to make him go. It wasn't about her. "I was wrecked when you left. I won't lie. But I'm glad you went where you needed to go."

His jaw was still clenched, the way it was when he still had too much bottled up inside.

"I'll listen, if you want to tell me about where you were." She wasn't sure how else to invite him to talk to her without pushing. It shouldn't be about her wanting to know. Not for this.

"The places didn't matter." His gaze finally came back to her, and the impact of his hazel eyes stole her breath. "I thought about you every night."

"I thought about you, too," she whispered.

He smiled. "I plan to be the only thing you think about tonight."

She opened her mouth and inhaled, intending to respond, but ended up choking on crumpet crumbs. He reached across the table and held up her teacup. She took it from him and sipped carefully, glad it had cooled enough to drink without burning her tongue.

He chuckled. "So why did you choose that apartment complex?"

She prepared more tea for herself to give herself a chance to change gears, or calm down, whichever. She was off-balance, but she planned to follow the conversation where he led it this afternoon. Otherwise, he'd know he could distract her with sex whenever she asked a tough question.

"I dunno. I guess I didn't really think about it. It just made sense." She thought back to when she'd decided to move into her apartment. "I mean, living at home through undergrad let me save money. My parents would've freaked out if I moved far away for my first apartment. It took weeks to get them used to the idea of me living where I do now."

There'd been daily shouting matches over her decision to move out. Her mother would dissolve into tears and ask what she'd done wrong raising Sophie if Sophie wanted to leave so badly. And that was just to an apartment in the same town.

"It was very practical to stay close to home for the first few years, especially since I landed the job in Philly." She huffed out a laugh. It was a job she didn't have anymore. "My parents were so proud of the solid start to my respectable career, they eased up on their stance against my moving out and actually listened to me."

It'd been the first time she'd felt like an adult. She had no idea what her parents would say when they got back.

"I'd like to have a new job before they get back." She spoke about the near future quietly, because she wasn't in a position to plan for it. Someone wanted her dead, and she couldn't forget that for long, even when she tried. "I'm just not sure I actually want the same kind of job."

He shrugged noncommittally. Thankfully, there was no judgment in his expression. "Everyone can change careers once in a while. I did, for sure."

She picked out a custard tart covered in an apricot half. "You mean from the military to training dogs at your kennels?"

He nodded slowly. "That's the major example, yeah, but I progressed through a couple of different positions on active duty. It works differently in the military than it probably does in corporate America, but the opportunity to change course is available."

He'd never talked to her about his time on active duty from this perspective. There'd been a couple of quiet mornings when he'd first returned when he'd warned her he'd been through some awful experiences. Even those, he hadn't shared in much detail. But he hadn't talked about life in the military, the day-to-day.

"I guess what I'm trying to say is you could change course if you wanted to." He picked up a crumpet, took an experimental bite, then put it down on his plate.

She smiled. "Maybe we should try topping that with eggs and ham for you."

"Maybe." He took up another sandwich from the endless pile.

"The trouble is that I don't know what other career I'd want to do. I'm not sure what would make sense." She didn't have another career in mind beyond accounting. She had only a dream.

* * *

The afternoon with Sophie was nice, and she'd asked him to help her with physical therapy. It mostly involved helping her to a space open enough for her to do a bunch of core strengthening exercises without putting any weight on her ankle. She did a few Pilates exercises and several sets of "superman / banana" followed by what she referred to as "bow to boat." The boat portion of that exercise required her to roll onto her belly and reach back to grasp her ankle, though, and he hadn't liked her putting odd strain on her ankle in the medical boot. But she managed to elevate her heart rate and work up a fine sheen of sweat.

Since she was focused on working out, he busied himself with his own set of exercises. Otherwise, he would've tried to have his way with her right there on the living room carpet.

She might have had similar ideas, though, because she'd been sneaking sideways glances at him as he executed push-ups and burpees. She even helped him count out his burpees, laughing as he tried to keep up with her as she called out the numbers for standing, crouching, shooting his feet out to a push-up position, back to crouching, then jumping upward to land in the standing position again. He was glad he was in good shape because he'd enjoyed the enthusiasm she had for making him work to keep up with her, and it would've sucked if he couldn't keep up. He'd come away from the workout trembling, though, so he decided to take a shower.

When he came out of the shower, he was presented with a very nice view of Sophie's rear.

He came to a halt. "Whatcha doing?"

She rose up on her hands and knees on the bed and curved her back toward the ceiling. "Yoga."

"On the bed?" He moved forward quietly, hoping not to startle her but wanting to be closer.

She breathed in slowly and exhaled, arching her back and looking up toward the far corner of the room. "There's actually a few articles online describing how a couple of these simple stretches help you sleep better. I can't do the more challenging routines right now, but doing these simple stretches really feels good."

He tipped his head to examine her rear. "It really looks good, too."

She froze then straightened so she was kneeling on the bed, her upper body turned so she could glare at him. "Naughty."

"Oh, I'll give you naughty." He tossed the towel aside and lunged at her.

She giggled and let him topple her over on the bed, but squirmed as he tried to gently pin her. She'd taken several self-defense seminars at Revolution MMA, so she had some fundamentals for grappling. They tussled for a few minutes until he got inside her guard and took the opening for a kiss instead of pinning her.

Her legs locked around his waist and her hands ran over his biceps and deltoids to his shoulders.

He continued tasting her, feeding from her mouth, and enjoying the feel of her body under him. She nipped the corner of his mouth and he growled at her playfully. She pulled his head down for another long, lingering kiss.

Then his disposable phone beeped a notification.

Damn it.

He came up for air. Her legs tightened around his waist.

"Tempting, snuggle monster, very tempting." He tapped her hip twice. He had never imagined he'd be tapping out just when things were getting hot. "The phone is probably important."

She sighed and let him loose. She gave him a momentary pout then wrinkled her nose and smiled. She was so cute sometimes, his heart stopped.

This better be important.

He grabbed the phone and took a look at the text, or texts, in this case. "It's from our new friend, Raul Sa. Looks like his teammate, Arin, made it to Europe just fine."

He didn't expand on the fact that Sa's teammate had a replica of Sophie's passport with her photo transferred onto it. Sophie wouldn't have wanted someone to cross the legal line because of her.

But he would, and he worked with people who had.

"Arin will be headed back soon." Under her own identity.

Sophie rolled onto her side and propped herself on her elbow. "So, I didn't like the decoy plan when you told me about it during the drive down here. But I'm glad she made it there okay. Was there any trouble?"

He shrugged. "Possibly. Nothing she couldn't handle if Sa didn't mention it in the text. Rojas will get a full debrief, and I can follow up with him if we need it."

Sophie sighed. "I didn't like the idea of someone going out there to draw the threat away. What if she'd been hurt?"

Forte reached out to caress her cheek. She had a much better heart than he did. "This kind of work is what she does for a living, and from what I can tell with limited information, she does it well. She chose this line of work, all the associated risks included."

Sophie leaned into his caress. "I can respect that. I just wish it didn't have to be risks taken on my behalf specifically. It sounds much more heroic when it's for our country or for a good cause."

He adjusted his hand to lift her chin so her gaze met his. "You are a part of this world and what any soldier is out there to protect. And you are worth any risk to me."

She bit her lip. "I'm afraid, Brandon. It's been too easy, too beautiful pretending this is a vacation or a getaway with you. I shouldn't want this while someone else is out there risking her life being me."

"She isn't you." He kissed her to prove it, pulling her close. Then he drew back just enough to see her face. "It's okay to be afraid. We're not completely safe. What we're doing is buying time. And it's okay to make the most of that time because there's no guarantee we'll have more later."

CHAPTER SIXTEEN

As early as she liked to get up in the morning, Brandon still beat her to it with his habit of waking before dawn. She'd sort of come to consciousness when he'd left the warmth of the bed they'd been sharing, giving him a sleepy giggle when he'd run his knuckles over her rib cage. He might've teased her into turning to him for a long kiss, too. Or that might've been a dream. It was very nice, regardless.

He'd been right last night. She'd decided to savor the time and enjoy, fully aware it might end as easily as any other dream when it came time to wake up.

Or not wake up, ever again.

Shaking off sleep, she sat up and swung her feet over the edge of the bed.

"I'll live." Saying it out loud was more of a decision than a hope. Even if all this ended badly, she'd take the time he'd bought for her and make it wonderful. No regrets.

Washing her face chased away the last fog of sleep and gloom. She decided to pull on one of the tactically altered tunic T-shirts for the day. Elisa had a knack for simple, quick sewing alterations, and the effect was fun. The formerly loose T-shirt now clung to her form, accentuating her slender curves.

The act of putting on clothes that made her look the way she liked did wonders for her confidence. She walked down the hallway, looking for other signs of life in the cabin.

Haydn was a shadow at the end of the hallway.

"Hey, Haydn, where is Brandon?"

The big dog gave her a doggie grin, his tongue lolling out as he panted at her.

"It is a mystery." She stopped in front of him, placing her hands on her hips. It wasn't as if Haydn was going to talk to her, but he also wasn't going to particularly do anything in response to her chatter, either. She'd learned from Brandon a while ago that his working dogs responded best to clear, concise commands. But she liked to talk to the dogs, and he'd never said it was bad. "I was about to do some morning yoga out in the living room. Are you joining me?"

She walked past Haydn to the living room and he followed her. Her cat was curled up on the back of the couch but roused and let out a *meow* as Sophie entered.

Her new cat really needed a name. Maybe Sophie would come up with one as she went through her yoga routine. Part of the reason she enjoyed it was the way thoughts that'd eluded her while she was thinking too hard came to her in the middle of a workout once she'd relaxed.

A cat's name seemed like a reasonable thought to search for, as opposed to the bigger answer of what the hell to do with the rest of her life.

She decided to start in the middle of the open space in the living room. This would be the first time she was trying a session while putting weight on her injured ankle.

Her cat decided to come down to the floor to walk in a circle around Sophie with a quiet *meow*. Sophie stood tall with her feet together, making sure to keep her shoulders relaxed and her weight evenly distributed over her feet. She'd be careful to pay attention to her right ankle and stop the minute any pain started there. She kept her arms loose at her sides. Her cat sat directly in front of her and watched as she took a deep breath, raising her hands overhead, palms facing each other with her arms straight. She reached up toward the ceiling until she felt the stretch all the way to her fingertips. After a good long moment she lowered her arms to her sides.

Just that started her blood flowing and she focused on steady, even breathing as she repeated the move.

Her cat moved to her side and *meow*ed again. Haydn stood on the other side, watching her with his head tipped to one side in a quizzical pose.

She placed her hands flat on the floor and stepped back first with her good foot, then her booted. Once she was sure of her balance, she pressed her palms into the floor. Her body leaned into an inverted V, her hips lifted toward the ceiling, and she was careful to press her shoulders away from her ears.

After studying her, her new cat executed a stretch of her own, mimicking the downward dog pose. Sophie giggled lightly under her breath. Best not to tell the feline the name of the actual yoga pose. Then, on her other side, Haydn whined and stood for a moment, then bent into a similar stretch.

Now all three of them were in downward dog.

"Seriously?" Brandon's voice made Sophie jump.

She stood too quickly, and the blood rushed out of her head. "Whoa."

Brandon was suddenly there in front of her, hands gently gripping her upper arms and steadying her. "Too fast. Aren't you supposed to stand up out of those positions slowly?"

"Everything about yoga is in its own time." But her mind wasn't on what he'd asked her or even what she'd answered. Instead, she was picturing mathematical representations. "I figured out a name for her."

"Yeah?" Brandon nudged her toward the couches.

Too excited to resist, she grinned at him as he sat her down and had her lift her right leg to rest on the length of the couch. "Yes! Tesseract! I'll call her Tessa for short."

The cat in question hopped onto the couch and walked up onto her chest, butting Sophie's chin with her head in an imperious demand for petting.

"I'm almost afraid to ask." Brandon sat on the couch next to her. "You like math and all, but how did you come up with that one?"

"Well, I was starting my yoga routine, taking it nice and easy." Sophie wanted to express her thought process before she forgot how she'd come to her epiphany.

"So I was a single point of origin. Then Tessa followed my lead. She became a second point with a line of action between us. Two-dimensional. Then Haydn joined us and made us three-dimensional. Then you came along and added a fourth dimension to us."

Brandon stared at her a long time. "But when Haydn joined you, you became a triangle, not a cube."

"Okay, so the mathematical logic gets fuzzy there, but my abstract thought process saw the point turn into a line between two points, then the line become two parallel lines connected to become a square, and the square become two squares connected at the corners to become a cube, and then you surprised me and the cube became two cubes connected at the corners to become a hypercube." She drew in a deep breath. "It totally made sense at the time."

Brandon chuckled. "Okay, your brain did geometry. For

fun. Because a dog and a cat joined you. I'll admit I've never seen that before, by the way."

She leaned into him, exceedingly happy with herself. "No?"

"It's good to see Haydn put weight on the prosthetic and use it to his advantage. A stretch like the one he was doing with you wouldn't have been as doable without his prosthetic on."

"Mmm." She looked over at Haydn, who was now lying on his belly in the middle of the carpet. "Maybe you should incorporate yoga into his physical therapy."

Brandon stiffened against her. "I don't think so."

She sat up and turned to face him. "Why not?"

"You're talking about a dog doing yoga." Brandon shook his head.

"There are articles out there on the benefit of yoga and massages for dogs." She was sure she'd seen some online in the past few months.

Brandon raised both eyebrows, probably because she'd made the statement so vehemently.

She narrowed her eyes at him as he remained silent, though. "I'll cite my sources as soon as I can get online again."

And just like that, she remembered she couldn't go online because someone was out there trying to find her so he could kill her.

* * *

Forte watched the joy bleed out of Sophie's expression. Her smile faded, and her gaze dropped away from his. There were other minute changes. Her eyes dilated slightly as her thoughts turned inward and the sweet, natural blush on her cheeks when she was tweaked into being angry with him faded. Her shoulders drooped and she absently rubbed her upper arms from the chill of thoughts rather than the temperature of the room.

"Hey—"

His current disposable phone rang. Cursing, he held the phone to his ear and used his free arm to gather Sophie in against his side. She came to him unresisting and curled up against his body.

"Forte," he growled into the phone, but, hell, anyone calling this phone could take it.

"Ky here." Ky's voice held a note of wary reserve.

"Yeah." Forte wasn't in the mood to go for camaraderie at the moment.

"I've got an update on our friend's former employer." Ky matched his tone. Apparently, he'd had a bad day. "We've had attorneys buzzing around since we began a direct investigation. They're trying everything and anything to make things difficult, and it's a huge pain in the ass."

Sophie's safety was worth it.

"That's a lot of energy and money to throw around if they have nothing to hide." Forte was actually cheering up thinking about it. It was probably a sign of how bad a person he actually was because he was glad Ky was buried under attorney bullshit. It meant Sophie's employers were guilty of something.

"There are quite a few clients who like to provide their records and expenses in amazingly awful condition. It's a mess to dig through. And what do you know, but the worst files have neat little notes in the margins indicating where the numbers need to be reconciled. They're accompanied by a certain friend's initials." Ky sighed. "She was too detail-oriented. It had to have taken her multiple nights of long hours to plow through all this. There are other files she must not have seen, though, or she would've seen the trend across the different shell companies and client names. We're seeing a bigger picture than she had access to, now that we're investigating."

But Sophie wasn't daunted by long hours or hard work. She dove into it, and once she got hooked on a particular task, she wouldn't stop until it was complete to her satisfaction.

"Our friend has a passion for math." Forte gave Sophie a gentle squeeze, then rubbed his hand up and down her upper arm. She responded by leaning her head into the hollow of his shoulder. "She comes up with weird applications for it."

"Accounting is definitely math, and you definitely have to be a particular kind of personality to want to do it day in and day out." Ky's voice took on a wry tone. "It's killing me just going through all these files. Just about half the files of interest are ones where she found issues and made notes to talk to the client to reconcile. It adds up. If she'd come up out of the nitty-gritty details and added it across the multiple files, or had access to the other documentation, it accumulates into significant amounts of money."

Ah. "Let me guess. All the issues look like typos or errors in notation."

Ky grunted. "There's a lot of missing zeroes in some places and added zeroes in others. A couple of places where digits are switched."

Sophie's employer, or possibly the accounting firm as an entity, was hiding the ebb and flow of a lot of money. Sophie might not have encountered the real evidence of it, but she'd gotten too close with her detail-oriented knack for wanting to make sure everything reconciled to the last cent.

"Does her employer have a hobby of putting together car bombs in his garage?" Forte was half joking. It couldn't be that easy.

"No evidence pointing to such a hobby." Of course, Ky would've gone to the man's home to check. "I was honestly thinking it'd be overzealous trying to have her eliminated. It would've been fine to just fire her."

"But there was a bomb in her car before she was fired." There were pieces scattered all over the place. Forte wanted to be able to put them together to make a whole picture, but he wasn't seeing it yet.

He already had an idea of where to look, though.

"And it was her employer who told her to take the rest of the day." Now the anger was starting to come through in Ky's words. "He's involved. This man is neck-deep in it, and he's too panicked to lie well. I'll get to the meat of this."

"Any of those shell companies or clients connected to Labs-Anders Corporation?" Forte hadn't shared earlier because Ky needed more to go on than a hunch.

"Not on first look." Ky was silent for a moment. "But I'll take a harder look."

Good enough. Forte was betting Labs-Anders Corporation did more than recruit in the Philadelphia area. And it was no coincidence that Cruz had encountered them actively recruiting not too long ago. It made sense for them to have other business interests in the city.

"Anything we can do?" Forte was glad Ky was continuing. Others might stop at the surface reasons and decide they had enough of the truth to call it a day. Not Ky.

"Keep our friend hidden." Ky was sober, sincere. "There's no way the former employer had the knowledge or skills to be directly responsible for either the car bomb or breaking into her apartment."

Forte did his best to keep his own tone light. "Is there evidence your man hired someone else to go after our friend? Is there any connection?"

Ky would look into Labs-Anders Corporation and understand why Forte was asking. And then the police officer would tie in the evidence he had, hopefully.

"I've got some e-mail exchanges, but it's like one side of a conversation. The other party was good about trimming e-mail threads and hiding their tracks on their ends." Ky sighed. "So this former employer is responsible for searching for a fix to his problem, but it looks like he contacted a vendor to design and execute the solution."

"A vendor." Forte heard the word "mercenary" even though it went unspoken. If Ky had intended to indicate hired muscle, he'd have just said so. But a vendor tended to respond to requests for proposal and work via contracted agreement.

For a few moments, Forte considered Raul Sa's mercenary squad. The man had been very eager to help. But, no, mercenary teams tended to develop defining characteristics. Beckhorn would've sent Forte, Cruz, and Rojas a red flag instead of a recommendation if Sa's mercenary squad was the type to take on shady jobs like eliminating a civilian like Sophie.

"Please let me know if you gather enough to identify the vendor." Forte made the request pleasant, but he was already looking into Labs-Anders Corporation. The thing about his kinds of connections was that years could go by, but good friends never forgot. He'd be able to reconnect. And if he didn't find what he was looking for, Cruz and Rojas had their networks, too.

The importance of Ky's investigation was to cover the legal side of things.

"I'll keep you up to date." Ky paused. "Will you do the same, in a timely manner?"

Forte hesitated to answer. He wouldn't lie to Ky, and he

would've definitely shared any information he found eventually. But Ky's definition of timely and his were almost assuredly not in alignment in this situation. "I hear Labs-Anders Corporation is a vendor that doesn't like dogs. I'd have to think hard about working with them."

A few months ago, Cruz had run across a military contract organization in the process of forming. The highest-ranking individuals were building their mercenary group carefully and taking steps to ensure they had potential international contracts in place when they eventually did establish the organization officially. At least one SEAL team, probably more, had found themselves in a questionable circumstance and pressured into committing to more than just their service in the military. At times like those, right and wrong weren't easy to identify. They were hazy, gray areas. A man did his best to make a decision he could live with, even if that decision wasn't ethically ideal.

Forte had been caught in several moments like that, when he'd had to make choices where there was no simple right or wrong. He could live with the decisions he'd made, but they definitively ensured he was going to hell.

If he'd chosen to go private after he'd retired from active duty, he'd have gone further down the rabbit hole. Decisions would've gotten easier because the darker it got, the less a person looked for the light of doing the right thing. It was easier to just complete the mission and let someone else decide if it was right or wrong.

He hadn't wanted to take the easy route.

But that didn't mean there weren't a lot of other men out there who had chosen that path.

"Cruz should probably check and see if that vendor is involved in this particular project," Forte said finally.

CHAPTER SEVENTEEN

Let's go for a walk."

Sophie sat up as Brandon eased out from under her on the couch. They'd sat in silence for a few minutes after he'd ended the call with Ky. "Are you going to contact Alex and David?"

Brandon rose to his feet and held out a hand to her. "Yup. But we can do that as we walk. Then I'm going to need to leave you for a short while to ditch this phone."

He had an almost expressionless look on his face. Only she noted the way his lips pressed together slightly and his eyes were narrowed just a bit more than his normal expression. He was thinking, hard.

"Things are getting more complicated, aren't they?" She took his hand and let him pull her up to stand next to him.

"How's the ankle?"

Oh, he could sidestep the conversation some, but she wouldn't let him get away with it for long.

"Better. It didn't hurt at all in the few minutes of stretching I just did, and I've got no problems standing." She headed over to the door where her sneakers were waiting and slid her left foot into one. "Why?"

"Because we'll be walking a short distance, and I want to be sure you're up for it." Brandon joined her.

She glanced at Haydn and his prosthetic left paw. "Where he can go, I can go."

Brandon chuckled. "Probably not quite yet, but we can use that as a rule of thumb if you want."

She didn't respond as they headed outside.

It was a beautiful morning, actually. The sun was beginning to rise up over the trees and filter through the leaves. Brandon led her around to the back of the cabin and directly into the woods.

"This isn't a stroll for the fun of it, is it?" She picked her way across the wooded ground, wincing as branches cracked under her steps. Haydn was managing better than she was, keeping pace easily with Brandon.

"Well, it's a nice walk. And it's always good to have options in case things come up." Brandon's attention was on the woods around them, his gaze scanning the area as they made their way slowly along. "So I'd like you to remember where we're going so you can find your way back again."

Ah. She tried to look up more often and take note of unusual trees or shrubs as cues to mentally mark their path. "This seems easy to navigate."

Brandon nodded. "If something comes up and I tell you to run, this is the way I'd like you to take if you can."

"I'd be making a ton of noise." Didn't seem like the best way to bolt if she was running away from someone.

"You'd be making a lot of noise no matter where you went." Brandon paused and held out his hand to her to help her over a log. "The idea here is for us both to know which way you're going and be familiar with what's going to be around you. It'll give me a better chance to take out whatever is pursuing you if I know your route."

Okay, that made more sense than a simple escape plan.

"You do run faster than I do." And Haydn did, too.

In fact, both Haydn and Brandon were moving through the woods more quietly than she was managing. With or without the awkward medical boot encasing her right ankle and foot, she was managing to step on every dry twig in this entire forest.

"I wish I could be more capable." She hated being helpless. So far in this, she'd treated it like a mini vacation. It'd been easy to pretend Brandon was a super thoughtful boyfriend spoiling her with this retreat tucked out of the way. In reality, he was working to keep her alive. "You've taken care of everything, and I've done nothing useful at all."

They crossed a small creek bed, dried up but still there. As they reached the top of the slight rise, Brandon turned to face her. "You've been cooperative. You listen. You ask intelligent questions. That's more than most people could manage. This isn't exactly something they prepare people for in college."

She huffed out a laugh and closed her eyes. Tiredness washed over her in a wave. "I'm an accountant. There can't be many other things in this world more normal and more boring. I think I got more preparation for this situation back when I was in the Girl Scouts than I did in college."

Brandon nodded. "No one expects to be in this kind of situation. It's amazing you're not still in denial. But you didn't waste precious time that way. You accepted what was happening and you did what I asked so I could keep you safe. You're still doing it."

And he would save her, over and over again. She believed that with every cell in her body.

"You wouldn't lie to me." She looked up into his eyes, a striking combination of gold and green in the changing light. "You said we had to do this, so we are."

He reached out, gathered her into his arms. When he spoke, his voice was so intense it cracked. "Your faith in me is unbelievable."

"I don't know why someone is trying to kill me," she whispered into his chest. "I don't know what I saw in those client files, but that has to be it, right? The reason I got fired, too."

Ky thought so. She'd heard the conversation, and if Brandon thought a...vendor...was after her, then her employer had hired professionals to kill her. If it hadn't been for Brandon and Haydn, she'd have died in her car and no one would've known it'd been anything but a freak accident. People would've shaken their heads and missed her, maybe, but they wouldn't have imagined it could've been anything but coincidental.

Brandon continued to hold her close. "We thought it could've been because you knew me, Rojas, and Cruz. We haven't exactly been making friends over the last year, and someone could've been targeting you to get at us. There's people out there watching us."

She drew her head back so she could look up into his face. "If you blame each other, you have to blame Elisa and Lyn, too. And don't you dare feel bad or sorry because I care about all of you. I wouldn't give up a single one of your friendships for anything."

He bent his head and pressed his lips against hers.

She clung to him, opened, so he could send them drowning in this newfound thing between them.

A few moments later she was breathless, and his voice wasn't exactly steady, either. "It makes it simpler to know it was your boss who hired somebody. Now that we know who to look at, we can find the connection to whoever is coming after you. It's a matter of timing now. Either we find them first and you'll be fine, or they'll find us and I'll need to take them out here."

He made it sound straightforward, but she turned over the possibilities in her head. "What if you don't find who is coming after me, though? What if they break off and don't come after us here? We can't stay here forever."

She was enjoying it. She was. But she wouldn't hide much longer. There were practical things to think about, like how much this was costing.

"I need to get back to the real world, get a new job." She fretted about the cost now that she was thinking about it. "I'll want to pay you back and then there's fixing my apartment back up."

And when they returned, would this thing between them still be real?

"Sophie. I want you to listen and not answer right away. Just think about what I'm about to ask you." Brandon released her and gently grasped her upper arms instead. "This might not end. You might have to start over. Would you consider the pros and cons of disappearing, letting the world think you are dead?"

The concept shocked her.

"You mean you might not catch the person trying to kill me." She forced the thought out.

"Or you might have to testify against your employer and go into protective custody." Brandon's tone was gentle. "There are a lot of reasons to be legally dead. It's a lot better than letting someone actually kill you."

No! She didn't want to disappear. "My family."

"Would be hurt. They couldn't know."

"My friends." Hot tears burned as they fell down her cheeks.

"Not even Elisa or Lyn or Boom could know." His tone was grim. "They'd be the first anyone would look at to try to find you."

"What's the point of living if everything you care about is gone?" She didn't want to be practical or reasonable about this. Her heart was breaking into pieces and it wasn't fair.

What was worse, she hated herself for indulging in being counterproductive.

Elisa had left everything behind, but that was because she'd hated the life she'd had and wanted to build herself a new one.

Sophie loved her life.

This was a completely different scenario. And she hadn't made the choice to give up her life; she'd been chased out of it. Why? Because she was good at her job? Because she was friends with wonderful people?

"I'd go with you, Sophie. You wouldn't be alone," Brandon promised her.

She shook her head blindly. "The kennels. The dogs."

He tugged her close, his strong arms wrapping around her. "I'd start over again with you."

How could her heart expand so much to hear those words and break at the same time?

She melted into him, pressing her face into the hard planes of his chest and leaning into his strength. Extending her arms around his waist, she held him to her every bit as much as he crushed her to him.

"Sophie." He whispered her name into her hair, and the darkness in his voice sent delicious shivers over her skin.

She tilted her face upward, and his mouth covered hers. His kiss was hungry, demanding. But she had some demands of her own to make, and she nipped at the corner of his mouth until he paused.

"Haydn's still here." First order of business. No watchers. Even in the woods.

Brandon's eyes were stormy, but he gave her a squeeze and let her go. "Haydn, *hier*."

The two of them crossed the creek bed and disappeared. Brandon returned alone a minute later. "He'll stand guard at a distance. No one will sneak up on us."

She laughed, half full of nerves and half eager. "You said that the first time, out in the woods behind our houses."

His gaze was steady on hers. "Yeah, and no one did."

The first time. Their first.

Her first.

It'd been the week of graduation, only a few days before they'd finished high school.

He was so many firsts for her, she didn't want to think anymore. She closed the distance between them and gripped the hem of his shirt. "Off."

It was her second demand. Because this time, she wanted to take the lead.

Brandon complied, wordless, with the sexiest hint of a smile playing over those incredibly kissable lips of his. He didn't just drop his shirt, though; he knelt and spread it out on the forest floor at the foot of the big tree next to her.

Still kneeling, he ran his hands up the sides of her legs. "Do you want the boot off?"

"Yes." Staring down at him, everything inside her burned hotter. She placed her hands on his shoulders as he helped her out of her medical boot, then her other normal shoe.

He gripped her thighs then, looking up at her. "Do you

want to walk back with no pants, or do we take these off carefully?"

Another choice. The first option tempted her far more than she'd anticipated. But...

"Pants. I want pants when we walk back." That was about the end of her capacity for rational thought at the moment.

He slid her pants down her legs, pressing a trail of searing kisses along her bare skin as he revealed it. Once she stepped out of them, she decided to push again. "Yours, too."

"Yes." He gave her the simple word and rose smoothly. His gaze never left hers as he unbuttoned his pants, pushed them down, and stepped out of them. When he straightened, standing there naked, she couldn't help staring at his very tempting erection.

She reached out and wrapped her hands around the length of him. He groaned as she caressed his shaft, cupped his balls. Their first time, she hadn't had the courage to do this. And now, she wanted to take every advantage. She took her time to enjoy the texture of his skin and played with the tip of his penis, trying to find the most sensitive spot.

Brandon groaned. "Do you still want your shirt on?"

She let go of his erection for a moment to run her hands over his abs and chest. "No."

She wanted skin to skin.

He helped her out of her shirt. Her bra followed a second later and she pressed her bare breasts against his torso, enjoying the tease of the sparse hair across his chest on her nipples.

His hands wandered over her upper arms, her shoulders, her back. He pressed his lips into her hair but let her continue to do as she pleased. And she wanted to taste him.

She started with soft kisses across his chest. She flicked one of his nipples with her tongue, making him chuckle.

Smiling, she made her way down his front, spending time kissing every inch along the V down to his groin.

She nuzzled his penis, enjoying the way it teased him into burying his hands into her hair, then she took as much of him into her mouth as she could, all at once.

"Sophie!" Her name fell from his lips in a gasp.

She steadied herself with one hand on his thigh and worked his shaft with her tongue, enjoying the ultra smoothness of his skin.

"Let me taste you, too, before I lose it." Brandon's voice was coarse with need. "This time, you're going to come first."

He wasn't including their recent encounter. He was thinking back to their first time as much as she was.

"Every time with you has been good." She backed away with one parting lick to the tip of his cock. Sitting back on the shirt he'd laid out, she watched in anticipation as he knelt before her.

He licked his lips as he gently pressed her knees apart and looked her directly in the eyes as he slid his hands under her behind. "There's no one around. You can enjoy all you want. As loud as you want."

She started to respond, but he ducked his head between her legs and ran his tongue the length of her.

She leaned back, braced on her elbows, and closed her eyes.

The man had learned to do so many things with his tongue. He started in long strokes, drawing out her pleasure until she whimpered. Then he found her clitoris and pressed it over and over with the tip of his tongue before returning to lick her again. He explored every fold of her most intimate places. And then he darted his wicked tongue inside her.

She bucked in his hands, helpless. He cushioned her behind, then shifted his grip to hold her hips. And then he started licking her again, interchanging long strokes with short ones directly over her clitoris. She squirmed, but his hands held her captive, and his hold only turned her on even more.

His lips closed over her clitoris then, and he sucked. A shout ripped out of her as the pleasure of it shot through her body. He murmured an approval and swirled his tongue around before doing it to her again.

The sensations built, wave after wave, and she raised her hips to meet him as he continued to feast on her.

"Please." She was completely on her back now and reached to bury her own fingers in his short hair. "Please, I want you inside me."

He paused, gazing up at her over the length of her body. The intensity of the hunger in his eyes shot her sensitivity higher than she'd ever experienced. A breeze passed over them, and she felt it over her skin, her nipples, everywhere.

"Brandon." She made his name a plea.

He straightened and then kneeled over her, pausing to lick first one nipple then the other as he watched her watch him. "Do you want me, Sophie?"

"Yes." She was almost sobbing with the need for him. "Yes!"

Bracing himself on one elbow, he reached between them with one hand. Grasping his erection, he dragged the tip of his penis along the length of her.

She threw back her head and groaned.

The tip of his penis swirled around her clitoris once, twice, and she lifted her hips, trying to guide him into her. He nudged at her entrance and held them both just at the edge.

"Do you want to scream?" Brandon's whisper caressed her ear.

She didn't have any more words. She only nodded.

He slid inside her so fast, filled her so quickly, she screamed.

He pulled back, almost out. "Good?"

In answer, she grabbed his hips with both hands, pulling him to her. He plunged back inside her to the hilt and she called out again. He set the pace then, hard and fast and so good. Every stroke drew a sound from her and she had no idea what it was. She didn't care, either.

"Sophie." Brandon's voice was completely out of control.

So was she. Her body tightened around him as he filled her over and over again. "Brandon!"

He adjusted his hips, plunged deep inside her, sending even more sensation through her. "Louder, Sophie. Louder."

"Brandon!" she called out, and it sent her over the edge, the orgasm crashing through her as she bucked wildly.

He drove into her twice more, and with an inarticulate shout, he came, too.

They lay together, shuddering, limbs entangled.

After a moment, he murmured against her ear, "Wherever you go, I'll go with you."

She buried her face into his neck and tried not to doubt. He'd left right after their graduation, after their first time together, after he'd said almost the same thing. Things were changing between them but were frighteningly the same.

She wrapped her arms around him and shoved her doubts as far back in her mind as she could. She wouldn't be afraid of change. This time, she'd give them a chance; she'd try, and if it got rough, they'd take it at a different angle. But she wasn't going to give up on this dream.

Yes, it could get worse, but what if it turned out better?

Here, with him, was better. She was sure of it.

CHAPTER EIGHTEEN

Forte stood on a high hill overlooking the road and the woods around the cidery. His vantage point gave him an unimpeded view of the entire area surrounding his Sophie. The building he'd left her in sat on a hill of its own, too. Even better to be sure no one unusual was approaching her while he was taking care of logistics.

A nondescript four-door sedan pulled up and Sa climbed out. The man lifted his chin in greeting to Forte before turning to open the back door of the car. A dark black-and-tan German Shepherd Dog hopped out, his attention on Sa as the man took his leash and led him over to where Forte was standing with Haydn.

"How's Taz working out for you?" Forte asked, stepping forward and giving the dog a good scratch around the ears.

The big dog leaned into the petting, his tongue lolling out to one side.

Haydn, for his part, stood apart and mostly ignored the other dog. They weren't strangers—having trained on the same property—but Haydn seemed to be going for the mature, no-nonsense attitude at the moment. Or he was jealous.

"I was glad to get your call." Sa shook hands with Forte once Forte had finished greeting Taz. "We just got back from Hope's Crossing and were wondering how you were holding up."

"It's been quiet." Forte looked back out over the cidery. "I don't like it."

It was going too well. Moments like these, in Forte's experience, were intentionally created to lull him or his teammates into a false sense of security. Get too comfortable and awful things happened.

Sa grunted. "My colleague is almost back from her flight to Europe. There were signs of her being followed on the way out of the country, but nothing on the return trip so far. Either she lost them, and she wasn't trying too hard to do it, or they figured out she was a decoy."

So for at least a portion of the time, Sophie's pursuers had been successfully distracted.

Forte nodded. "Either way, it's only a matter of time."

Cruz was good when it came to laying down false trails in computer systems. He'd helped blur the record trail for renting the car. But if the person looking for Sophie was as good as Cruz, Rojas, or Forte, or if they had more resources at their disposal, they were going to home in on this location eventually no matter how careful they all were. If Murphy's Law was involved, it'd be sooner rather than later.

"How can we be of help?" Sa wasn't the type to waste time. Forte appreciated his direct approach.

"We'll invoke the secondary clause in the contract. I'll want twenty-four-hour support." Forte wasn't going to run yet. Sophie hadn't made her decision and he wanted to give her as much time as possible.

Besides, even though he'd offered to go with her, he hadn't planned it. It'd been an impulse. He wouldn't go back on his word to her, but he did need time to set his affairs in order. Hope's Crossing Kennels and anything else in his estate would need to be taken care of so Cruz and Rojas could either keep running the place or go on their own way. Making the change now would be too obvious to someone who knew what to look for, so Forte would have to think carefully about how to make sure his leaving wouldn't screw over good friends.

"You got it." Sa spoke with easy assurance. "We'll be in range to respond within five minutes or less."

Forte nodded. Any closer and it'd be too obvious where he and Sophie were hiding. Having support at some sort of distance still left the chance open to their pursuers passing them by. If shit started, though, Forte could hold off attackers until Sa and his team could arrive.

"We're still at an information deficit." Forte sighed. "We know her employer was laundering money for several clients. She had too much initiative and was too detail oriented, got into files her employer didn't want her to see. There's enough evidence to convict him. But we don't have enough evidence to put away the actual individual responsible for the bomb or the break-in at her apartment. Could be the same person or it could be different people. But we have an idea of what organization they work for."

"Seems redundant to invest in more than one resource to eliminate a single civilian target." Sa sounded hesitant to offer the observation. Then again, they hadn't worked together in the past. They were feeling each other out.

"Maybe. One of our close friends had a series of incidents in the last several months. There was a single private investigator hired to track her and a backup team watching him in case he managed to flush her out but didn't get ahold of her." Forte didn't like the way the situations were escalating over the course of the year. With first Lyn, then Elisa, the situations and people responsible had been unrelated for the most part. "We made sure all the parties involved were unsuccessful in acquiring their target."

Sa chuckled. "No offense intended, but you all are victims of your own success. You were already making names for yourselves based on the qualities of the dogs you trained. You might be retired from active duty, but it's obvious each and every one of you is fit for duty with the experience to make you incredibly valuable assets. My squad wants you as allies, but others?"

"Maybe not so much." Forte was inclined to agree.

There was a demand for quality private services, for mercenaries. As long as there'd been acts of war, there'd been a market to hire those with the right skill sets and experience. And it was a valid career choice after service in the armed forces, or even without experience in the military at all. Like any other industry, there were always up-and-coming companies being created and establishing themselves. The best any one person could do was decide what organizations were the right fit for them.

Different companies with varying levels of ethics and corporate goals meant some would be a cultural match, and some wouldn't

"We've had a brush with at least one group. The outcome didn't leave anyone walking away with warm and fuzzy feelings," Forte admitted.

Sa grunted. "That's going to happen. Sometimes you respect each other in the morning and sometimes you don't. You think they came after your lady to make a point?"

Yes. "More likely someone offered them money and they

were happy to accept a contract on a civilian connected to
me and my colleagues."

"Gotta love the assholes out there who jump at the
chance to be paid for something they probably thought
about doing for free." Sa bent and picked up a stone, tossing it up in the air and catching it. "Can't say I haven't
considered something similar, but involving a civilian isn't
right. Going after a target like your lady? She didn't have
a chance on her own."

"She's a smart woman." Forte was sure Sophie would
make good decisions in an emergency situation. "Level-
headed."

Sa nodded. "Not arguing. But a bomb in the car. Without
your dog there, would you have known it was there?"

No. Haydn had been with Forte by coincidence. Forte
could've had a different dog with him for the outing, one
with alternative training like narcotics or corpse detection
or human search. And he'd run into Sophie unexpectedly,
too.

"Exactly." Sa took his silence and filled it. "You all
haven't shared much, but I can piece together the hints. They
didn't intend to give her even a chance to walk away from
the encounter. They'd intended to do the job. It was a freak
accident she came away from it alive."

Forte wasn't going to argue. He'd gone through the same
logic, but there was a sense of validation in hearing it come
from someone else. Plus, gave him the chance to take a step
back and view the entire situation with some perspective.

"The break-in, from what I gather, was intended to look
like a robbery, but she would've been just as dead." Sa's tone
was grim. "They wrecked her stuff to hurt the people who'd
be there to gather up her belongings, to let the people in her
life know it'd been done out of spite. The second time wasn't

just about the job and eliminating the target; it was about sending a message to you."

The thought process made sense. "They won't leave room for accidental survival the third time. They'll want to make sure."

"Yeah. They're going to send in a backup for their backup. It'll be overkill to make sure nothing goes wrong this time." Sa dropped the stone and dusted his hands off on his jeans. "You've taken steps, but I think my team had better be prepared for things to get messy."

"There's not a lot of time to dig up and figure out the connections from her employer to the person he hired to the group they work for." Forte was finally admitting the issue that'd been digging at him since he'd brought Sophie there to hide. "If the police don't come through, she'll be on the run for the rest of her life."

"And it won't be a long time if an entire organization needs to track her down just to prove they don't leave a contract unfinished." Sa sounded grim.

"We need to face them head on and make this a professional meeting of minds." It wasn't about her former employer anymore. Bastard was going to be convicted for his money laundering and anything else the investigation turned up. Now it was about the mercenary group who'd put their reputation into being able to complete the job.

Put them out of business and Sophie could choose how she wanted to live her life.

"This ought to be interesting." Sa turned to him and offered his hand. "You and your friends are good people. It's a pleasure to be working with you on this."

Forte shook the other man's hand.

* * *

"Hi!" Sophie smiled at Brandon. "You asked me to wait here and try some hard cider. It has *alcohol* in it. You were gone a long time."

Brandon stood in the doorway of the cidery, his expression carefully neutral.

She frowned and squinted. "There's a smile there for me. Somewhere. There's always a smile there somewhere."

"If you say so, dear." The proprietress came and took away her latest glass and replaced it with a tall, sealed bottle. "Here's your favorite to take away with you this evening. Your gentleman friend doesn't look to be in the mood to sit and stay. Though he's welcome to, if you'd like, him and his dog."

Haydn was with Brandon, a shadow in the door frame. Even his prosthetic had a matte finish so Sophie hadn't realized he was there at first. But then Haydn dropped his jaw and let his tongue loll out in a friendly pant.

Sophie beamed at the wonderful woman. "Thank you, for everything."

Kind eyes, gentle smile. "Of course."

Brandon was suddenly standing there, next to the table.

The proprietress looked at him. "You are a quiet one, aren't you? No worries. Your young lady mostly sat here and wrote ideas in her day planner. She was very nice to listen to me natter on, but she's been doing quite a lot of thinking this afternoon. I was hoping she'd share a sweet story with me, maybe about how the two of you met or what brought you here, but mostly she's just been thinking real hard."

Brandon nodded.

Sophie sat still, staring at her day planner and the colored pens scattered across the table. She'd been happy to see him, really she had, but she had questions and thoughts to share with him. For the past hour, as the woman chatted with her, she'd used the different colors to write out her questions rather than talking about how she felt about them out loud.

Looking up into Brandon's hazel-green gaze she thought she might dive in and drown. "I used erasable ink. My questions will go away if you don't want them."

"It's okay." He gave her those words and waited.

He could mean a lot of things. Mostly, he usually gave those to her at face value, which meant everything was okay for the time being. He wasn't worried and they didn't have to run anywhere and he didn't need her to erase her questions.

Later, though, he might not like her questions. He hadn't said it *would* be okay, after all.

Sober, maybe, she gathered up her pens and tidied up the table. "My favorite cider was the original Honey Hard Cider. It's sweet but not too sweet, and it has a hint of ginger at the end of it. It'd go really well with my recipe for red currant scones. I thought maybe you'd like to have some, too."

"Could be interesting." He took the bottle in hand.

Which was good because she might not be the best person to carry a glass bottle right about now. Instead, she clutched her day planner and her pack of pens to her chest as she stood. His hand pressed gently against the small of her back, steadying her. He didn't rush her out to the car. Instead, his presence was a solid reassurance. If she stumbled, he'd be there to catch her before she fell.

She got into the car without a word and waited for him to close the door, get Haydn safely in the back, then climb into the driver's side. "I guess it felt like you were gone longer than you were."

Brandon started the SUV. "I was gone about two hours, total."

She nodded. "It felt like all afternoon."

"I'm sorry." His voice was soft.

She shook her head. "I'm not mad. Not at all. It's just, I missed you. Which is the wrong thing to say."

"Why?" He directed the SUV down the gravel road and out onto the service road leading away from the cidery. "Would you like to drive for a while, see some of the area before we head back to the cabin?"

"Yes, please." She watched the rolling farms alternate with bare woods. There was a stark beauty to it all, and she imagined it would all be a verdant, lush sort of green in summer.

"So why is missing me the wrong thing to say?" Brandon's prompt held a sort of cautious tone to it.

She shrugged. "I had time to try all seven ciders. I had questions I wrote into my day planner so I wouldn't forget to ask you when it seemed like a good time. But you've devoted days to being with me every moment. Even when you're not right next to me, I've woken up and known if I called for you, you'd be within earshot. It's silly for me to say I missed you after just two hours. Clingy. You never liked clingy."

Which was something he'd told her back in high school when girls would hang on to him. He didn't like the way girls followed him around or tried to talk him into asking them out on dates. She'd paid attention because she hadn't ever wanted to be the kind of girl he avoided. She hadn't thought she could bear it if he started to brush her away the way he did those other girls.

"I wouldn't." His statement startled her.

Had she said some of that out loud? Maybe. She talked to herself sometimes.

"Which is why it's good to have dogs around so you can at least pretend you're talking to someone." He chuckled.

"Lyn does it all the time and so does Elisa. I figure your cat will do for you, too."

"But Tesseract isn't here." She crossed her arms across her chest. This was weird.

"She's back at the cabin and we'll be headed back shortly." Brandon didn't seem worried. "I just wanted to give you a change of scenery before we head back."

"I appreciate it." She was losing her buzz, though, and with it the courage she'd been trying to build while waiting for him. "I did have questions for you, though."

"Go ahead." He sat there, relaxed, his gaze focused on the road ahead of them. His hands rested easy on the steering wheel.

She took a deep breath and opened her day planner. The first question was in blue. "Do you really think I might have to disappear?"

His lips pressed together, and he nodded. "It's very possible. If we can't resolve this with whoever has been coming after you, they won't stop until they succeed in killing you. If they think you're dead, you'll be safer."

She'd been thinking about it ever since he'd suggested it. "People make this choice all the time when they go into witness protection, right?"

"Some of them might not consider it a choice." His tone had turned wry.

Well, that was fair. In a life-or-death scenario, the normal thought process probably would consider it the only option.

Her next question was in green ink. She'd surrounded it with lots of question marks because the thought had triggered a whole bunch of baby questions.

"Did you mean it when you said you'd stay with me?" She hunched her shoulders. She wanted to know if he meant it, but if he hadn't, it'd be like a smack to the face. Then again, he could get mad at her for doubting him.

"Yes." He didn't add to the simple response. Instead, he reached over with one hand and held it out to her, palm facing upward.

She stared for a long moment, then placed her own hand in his.

"Why?" she whispered.

"Because." He glanced over at her before returning his attention to the road. "Why are you afraid I don't mean it?"

She drew in a slow breath and let it out. This was her last question. She'd written it in big, red block letters. It'd seemed like a stupid question to ask when he'd suddenly returned from the military. And then in the years while he was establishing the kennels, she hadn't wanted to ask because she'd been so happy to be a part of his life again. He'd let her in, accepted her, let her become a part of the day-to-day routine of the place he'd created and the life he'd built for himself.

Asking the question had been a dangerous thing.

"Don't you believe me, Sophie?" His hand gently squeezed hers. "Can you tell me why you're afraid I won't stay with you?"

There was an urgency in his voice now. He was getting worried.

She withdrew her hand from his. It was time to ask. And then, when she heard him give her the answer, the two of them were going to have to figure out where they would go from there.

"Why did you leave me the first time?"

CHAPTER NINETEEN

Not "why did you leave" this time. She'd specifically asked why he'd left *her*.

He didn't know how to answer her.

Shit.

He knew the answer. He'd even thought about telling her. But this was his Sophie, and she'd never needed him to talk about it before this. It'd been enough to see her smile, to know she'd welcomed him back.

His life had started again the minute he'd seen she was glad to see him again.

"I need to know, Brandon." Her voice was strained. She'd started to hug herself as she waited for him to answer.

"Why?" His own voice was cracking. How was he supposed to answer her if he couldn't make words?

She laughed, but it came out half sob. "I didn't need to know at first. I had a life. I'd accomplished a lot of things for myself. I was living out on my own and had a good head start on my career. I had enough established for myself that when you came back, there was this life I had and you could be part of it again. But all of it is gone now, and I've got literally nothing but the clothes we brought with us and the cat you helped me adopt. With so little left, I've got a whole lot more to lose if you decide to disappear out of my life again."

And she needed a reason to believe him. Damn it.

"I didn't plan to leave." It sounded like he was making excuses, and he didn't want to. He could take accountability for what he'd done. "I thought it was the best thing to do."

"I don't understand." She wanted to, though. The yearning was there in her tone and her eyes when he glanced over to look into her face.

"After you asked me to take you to prom, I knew what your father's rules were."

"P-prom?" She was bewildered, and he didn't blame her.

"That was when I decided." He struggled to figure out how best to explain it to her. This was the beginning, but it hadn't been her father's fault. It'd just been the trigger for everything. "Because I didn't want you to have to fight your father to go to prom, so I went to him, and I asked him for permission to take you. Those were his rules, and even if you asked me, the least I could do was ask him."

Sophie had been a headstrong teenager. She'd defined the term. But she'd also been a caring and considerate daughter, had grown into the same kind of woman. So she'd lived by her family's rules and traditions and carefully chosen when she would do her own thing.

He hadn't wanted to be the reason she'd go against her father.

"Your father didn't want you to be with me, and he was so right." The last, he added hurriedly because it hadn't been her father's fault. Not any of it. "I wasn't good enough for you in any way. I was a pain in the ass and had this attitude of entitlement. The world owed me everything."

"No." So much conviction in her voice. "You've always been the best kind of person."

"You gave me the benefit of the doubt." He had to correct her. "Being around you brought out great things in me. I was a nicer person because you believed I would be. I did better in school because you thought I was smart. I worked hard on things because you asked me for my help. Left to my own devices, I was a lazy brat."

And her father had seen it all. Her father had told him she deserved better.

"You weren't." She still believed in the person he'd been even if he'd grown into somebody else.

"I was. There's no sense in pretending different." He was driving them in a big loop. No sign of anyone following them. Traffic was sparse on these back roads in the middle of the week, this late in the afternoon when it was still just a little too early for people to be heading home from work. "Your father wanted better for you, and he was right. You did deserve a whole lot better. But you wouldn't look to anyone else while I was still around."

And he hadn't known how to change yet. He'd only been angry and frustrated. He hadn't known he'd be capable of becoming anyone worthwhile.

"None of the nice Korean boys turned out to be worth anyone's time." Her words were bitter. "They could say all the right things and smile nice to my parents, but they were all fake. Half of them still live at home off their parents' paychecks, expecting their mothers to wait on them hand and foot until some girl is stupid enough to make a home for them."

"Your father didn't want that for you." Okay, maybe Forte was growling at the thought. But he figured it was justified.

Out of the corner of his eye, he saw her shake her head. "No. Once he figured it out, saw them come out of college and not do anything with themselves, he didn't like any of them. It doesn't stop him and my mother from looking for someone, though. Every year, every birthday, they get nervous about my getting older."

They'd wanted so much for her. They'd worked hard to give her opportunities. Forte had understood at least that much.

"They wanted you to be happy." He thought she'd understood.

"Yeah." She sighed. "But you can't make someone happy with what you think they should want. It's not the way the heart works."

True. And his ached hearing her. He wanted, hoped, to be the thing that could make her happy.

"Maybe not, but I wasn't the right person for you back then, either." She'd understand. She always did. "So I went where I could do things you'd be proud of. I went into service and tried to figure out what things I was good at. I learned. I did a lot of things."

"And then what?" Her voice had a surprising edge to it. One he'd never heard directed at him. "Then you came back a new man? It's not like you came in and swept me off my feet. You came back into my life and stepped right back into the spot you left. Friends. Nothing was different."

"You deserve better. I still believe that." Because he hadn't become a better man. Different, yes. Scarred. Damaged. "I'm not a good person."

He'd killed people. Not all of them had deserved to die. Only some of them had been trying to kill him first. He'd given up on doing the right thing and he was going to hell.

"So you came back just to be my friend?" There was so much hurt in her voice. "Or were you waiting for me to yell at you until you gave in? Like I did the other night."

"No." It hadn't been his intention. "I didn't mean for that—"

"Don't you dare say sleeping with me was an accident."

He swallowed hard. "It wasn't."

"And however much stress I've been under, I've been in full possession of my cognitive abilities. You in no way took advantage of me." She was sitting up straight in her seat. "I knew exactly what I wanted."

"You always have." He smiled. It was something he'd held on to through the years. Her conviction was amazing. "To be honest, I came back and I wasn't even sure you'd be willing to be friends again."

"Why not?" she snapped, still riding the momentum of her temper.

"Because I left. I knew you'd be mad."

"You left without a word. Without saying good-bye."

"Yeah."

She was silent.

"So I came back and I figured you'd either hate me or be my friend again. It was worth the risk to find out." He'd just about had a heart attack when she'd shown up on his property. He hadn't been sure if she'd come to yell at him and leave or if she'd been intending to cry and throw something in his face. She'd done none of those things. Instead, she'd asked him to introduce her to his first dogs.

"You needed to build a life again in the civilian world." Her statement was quiet, full of compassion.

He nodded. They were almost back at the cabin. All was quiet. "To a certain extent, yes."

"It still doesn't help."

His heart stopped. "Why?"

She knew now, or at least he thought he'd explained it. "Your dad didn't mean to chase me away. He just didn't think I was the right person for you, and he was right. I wasn't. Not at the time."

"That's just it." She popped her seat belt as he brought the SUV to a stop. "You still agree with him. You don't even know what he thinks of you now and you still agree with what he told you years ago. And if you do, then you're just going to do the exact same thing to me again. You're going to make a decision all on your own and not give me any choice in the situation. You're going to be with me for as long as you think it's the right thing to do and then one day I'm going to turn around and you'll be gone. Again. Or dead. Either way, it's the same."

Her voice had gone flat. "I broke the day you left me the first time. Everyone just watched who they thought was Sophie grow up and do all the things they expected her to. I didn't live, not one single day between then and when you came back. And now, I know you could decide to disappear again at any moment. Only this time, I won't have any sort of practical guide for how my life should be able to go on without you."

* * *

"That's not true."

She didn't want to listen to him anymore. Mostly because what she'd said was true. Oh, she'd proven what other people had believed of her. She'd been smart enough, worked hard enough, been independent enough to go out and exist on her own. They'd all been so proud of what she'd accomplished.

But there was a difference between existing and living.

"I've been practical and realistic." She let her head fall back against the head rest of the SUV. The exhaustion weighing her down was more than the stress of the past few days or the elation of finally having gotten through the barrier Brandon had erected between them. It was finally having nothing left to hide behind when it came to taking a long, honest look at herself. "What I want isn't something I've ever admitted, even to myself, until I decided to seduce you into admitting you wanted me as much as I wanted you. Doesn't that make me a bad person?"

"No." He could deny it all he wanted, but his voice had gone gruff.

"I thought I could forgive you." Hot tears started down her cheeks. She didn't bother to try to hide them or wipe them away. Let him see. "I can't. Or maybe I won't. You didn't give me a choice when you left. You just did what everyone else did, what all of you thought was the right thing for me. And you, of all people, I trusted to believe in me. Now, I don't even know what you think of me, but whatever it is, I don't have much faith that you actually know me better than anyone else."

He could say whatever he wanted. Hang around. Even blow her mind with amazing sex again. Not a thing he could do would make her believe him at this point. And she only had herself to blame. She'd been the one to finally ask him why he'd left all those years ago.

And it really had been enough to make her stop believing in the both of them.

"Sophie!"

Brandon's hand shot out as he yelled her name. He grabbed her shoulder and yanked her toward him. There was a strange sound like a dart hitting a board, then he was shoving her farther down toward the floor of the front seat. "Stay down."

The SUV started to reverse, but there were more popping sounds and the whole vehicle lurched to one side.

Someone was shooting at them. *Maybe?* None of it sounded the way she thought it would. Too many movies. All she recognized was the sound of glass breaking, but the windshield hadn't shattered.

Brandon cursed. "We're not going to make it to the service road like this. Both headlights are out. I'm going to break an axle in the dark."

He yanked the steering wheel, and the whole car swerved and collided with something. Maybe the corner of the cabin? She kept her head down, protecting herself as best she could with her arms, and sobbed.

"Ten seconds, Sophie, then I need you to open your door and roll out. You'll be near the woods. Run like I showed you. Can you do that? Sophie?"

His words cut through her panic, cold and hard.

"Yes." She forced the word out of her throat.

"Keep going, no matter what you hear." His instructions were delivered in concise cadence. There wasn't a hint of the earlier tension or emotion.

This was Brandon when someone was trying to kill him. Actually, someone was here to kill her. He was just in the way.

"I could step out. Let them—"

"No." Still calm. The authority in his voice brooked no argument. "Not because it's not your choice. Because it won't work out the way you want it to. They'd still kill me. Do you want to die and just have me killed because I saw it happen?"

"No." She choked on the word.

She didn't want him dead. Especially not because of her.

"Then don't make that choice." He was so reasonable. "You're down to three seconds."

Oh no. Fear stabbed her in the chest, and her stomach twisted as she turned toward the passenger-side door. The SUV swerved again.

She couldn't do this.

But she had to. He wouldn't tell her to if it wasn't what had to be done. He needed her to do this.

"Go. Now."

She yanked the door handle and shoved the door open. Rolling to the ground, she scrambled to get her feet under her. Her medical boot had almost no traction on the dry leaves at the edge of the forest. The woods were right in front of her, and she dove into them, sobbing as she crashed through the undergrowth.

Twigs and branches scratched her arms, snagged her clothing. She pushed through and hoped she wouldn't trip and impale herself on any broken tree stumps. There'd been a few thickets, canes of wild blackberries. She'd been delighted to see them before, but now the thought of blundering into them made her reach her hands out in front of her as she rushed forward.

They'd walked through here during the day. But the winter days were short. Sunset came early. The sun had gone down already, and darkness fell fast in the woods. She tried to find the visual markers she'd noted earlier in the day—the tree struck by lightning years ago that'd kept growing, the huge moss-covered rock. They'd become shadows against the night, and she reached out to touch them, lean on them, as she ran to each one.

There were shouts behind her. And growling. She heard gunfire, this time the way she'd imagined it would sound, loud and sharp in the night. Bark cracked next to her head, and splintered wood hit her cheek.

Panic blanked her mind. She ran again.

Her ankle started to throb. Within a few steps, sharp pain stabbed up through her right leg. The medical boot was heavy and had started to twist on her foot with the running over the uneven ground. She stumbled across the dry streambed and scrambled, trying to get up the bank. Any moment, she expected to feel sharp pain in her back. Or maybe she wouldn't feel anything at all when whoever it was finally managed to shoot her.

All she knew for sure was that she had almost gotten up to the higher ground Brandon had shown her, and she didn't know where to go from there.

Her throat was raw and the air burned in her lungs as she rolled over the edge of the bank. There was a loud, crashing noise, and brilliant light flashed back in the direction from which she'd come. Far through the trees, she thought she could see gold and orange.

The cabin was on fire.

CHAPTER TWENTY

Forte lay low under the cover of the underbrush as their attackers continued to circle the cabin, searching the flames for signs of him or Sophie inside or around the building. Haydn remained next to him, steady and watchful. The big dog was alert, tense, ready for action.

Shit. Fuck. Damn.

They had to find him and Sophie sometime. He'd already figured it'd only be a matter of time. But they'd managed the worst possible moment. He needed to get Sophie through this alive and then, maybe, he'd manage to repair the trust he'd broken.

Despite the current threat, Forte kept an eye out for Tesseract. There'd been several windows broken when he'd detonated his small charges around the outer walls of the cabin, and the cat had had time to escape before Forte had set off the charge in the fireplace. He'd hated to destroy the cabin, but Sophie's belongings were replaceable. Her cat wasn't.

There hadn't been time to make sure the cat cleared the building, though; not when giving Sophie time to get clear had been the priority. It was another reason for Sophie to hate him for the rest of their lives.

He'd worry about it once he made sure she had a life to live.

Two of their attackers broke off the search around the cabin and headed into the trees in the general direction Sophie had taken. Hard to say if those two had found her trail yet based on where they entered the forest. He needed to leave his position and get ahead of them before they found her.

It'd leave them vulnerable to the remaining men, but Forte was on his own for a minimum of five more minutes. Sa and his team would be providing backup, if he and Sophie could survive that long.

Forte eased backward on his belly, watching the two figures backlit against the flames consuming the cabin. Both of them had their backs to him. One was turned away from the flames, searching the area around the now abandoned rented SUV. The other had a compact radio in his hand.

Possibly in contact with another fire team. Or, more likely, communicating with the two men who'd gone into the trees in pursuit of Sophie.

He inched back, withdrawing from his vantage point down into the shallow ditch created by the dry creek bed. Haydn followed, the dog's black fur rendering him almost invisible in the dusk. Forte stood slowly and then remained still for a moment near the base of a tree that kept his profile from silhouetting in the fading light.

Blinking deliberately several times to help his eyes adjust to the darkness a touch faster, he quieted his breathing and strained his hearing. A patch of his eyesight was burned out from staring at the bright flames. It took precious moments for his vision to resolve. Once he could see through the failing light, he advanced on a parallel course from the path he'd seen the other men take.

He'd scouted the area thoroughly since they'd arrived. Their attackers were intent on finding Sophie. He had the advantage of knowing the terrain and being focused on eliminating them. As long as Sophie had gone where he'd told her to, there was a chance he'd be able to take them out before they reached her position.

Despite the urgency, he moved on light feet, careful to make as little noise as possible. Slow was smooth, smooth was fast, and in a forest like this smooth was quietest.

Haydn moved along at his side, the prosthetic leg rendering the dog somewhat less than silent, but not enough of a disturbance to outweigh his value as a partner. Forte needed the help.

Confusing shadows danced in the forest dusk. Fading natural light was tricky enough to navigate by, but the licking flames of the burning cabin added an entirely new level of complexity to seeing through the dark spaces in the deep woods. Small, unruly gusts of wind kicked up as the fire grew, making the flames behind him swirl. Which made the shadows dance.

Hadyn bumped his leg, and Forte froze with his knees bent, listening. Hadyn moved away from his side by a half step, waiting. Forte shuffled to him and reached out an arm. He'd nearly face-planted into a huge old green-ash tree. Smiling, he palmed the top of Haydn's head in thanks.

Refocusing, Forte began to move more quickly. If that was the same tree he recalled from his other walks, they were already halfway to where Sophie should be waiting. He would have to sacrifice some elements of stealth. He'd be damned if he'd allow those men to reach her first.

Never.

Haydn moved with him toward the rain-eroded path at the bottom of the hill. The flatter ground, with less undergrowth to avoid, allowed them to break into a trot. His night vision sharpened with the distance from the fire, and he broke into a flat-out run.

Hadyn ranged out in front of him by several yards but slowed and glanced over his good shoulder. A part of the dog's training was to check to ensure his handler remained close. Especially in these conditions, it'd be hard to keep line of sight on Haydn because his coloring allowed him to disappear into the night.

But Forte wasn't moving fast enough. His gut twisted as he worried about Sophie. No. One of them was going to need to get to her at speed.

He made a decisive, simple hand gesture. *"Zoek. Zoek* Sophie, Haydn."

Haydn had been standing awkwardly to keep his prosthetic limb from sinking in the mud. But the command sent the dog into a blur of motion, and he shot down the creek bed.

Watching, Forte allowed himself a hint of hope. Three legs and a whole lot of heart were headed Sophie's way. Haydn would be able to catch her scent and home in on her faster than Forte's memory and limited two-legged stride could. And the dog had a better stealth advantage.

Several hundred yards ahead, Haydn changed course, veering sharply to charge up the steeper bank. Forte crouched low as he advanced, scanning the higher ground for the danger. He took the bank at an angle, slowing down as rocks and loose chunks of partially dried dirt broke away from the incline under his weight.

There was a hard thud as a body hit the ground with a surprised curse.

Forte ran up the rest of the bank, his thighs burning with the effort. He had his firearm ready, safety off, as he came over the edge. A man lay belly down in the dead leaves, both hands shielding the back of his head as Haydn stood over him. The German Shepherd Dog had a jawful of the man's shirt and protective vest.

"*Los*." Forte approached warily, searching the ground for weaponry. The man had been armed.

Haydn released his prey and stood back, ready to pounce on the man again if he tried to get up.

"Don't move." Forte issued the warning, flat and cold. He didn't bother with a follow-up threat. This was a mercenary, not a civilian. The man had covered his head but otherwise hadn't tried to fight Haydn. He'd known the damage the dog could've done.

Working dogs could bite to rip and tear. They could break bones. Overseas, in intense combat situations, they were trained to deliver even more decisive damage. It was a hard truth and necessity. Here, on US soil, Forte would use minimum force required to subdue his adversary, but he would not give the man the chance to take advantage of the mercy.

The man stayed where he was as Forte circled him, spending precious seconds ensuring a weapon wasn't within reach. Whatever weapon the man had been carrying had been knocked away when Haydn had taken him down. Bending close, Forte tapped the man's skull with the butt of his gun.

Okay, maybe it'd been a touch more force than the minimum required. Either way, the man went limp, unconscious.

Forte directed his attention to his partner. "Haydn. *Zoek* Sophie."

The dog turned and left him.

Temporarily holstering his weapon in the hidden harness

under his T-shirt, Forte pulled a few zip ties from his pants
pocket. Zip ties were as handy as duct tape in a lot of situations and he always had a few randomly in his pockets.
Made it a pain in the ass when it came time to do laundry, but
now he was glad to have them. Sophie had tried to tease him
about them, but then she was always finding random pony-
tail holders in her pockets.

Forte kneeled on the man's back and secured the bastard's hands. This one was neutralized.

He searched the man anyway, patting him down and removing anything the guy might use to free himself once he
woke up. A small secondary gun in an ankle holster and a
long, wicked knife strapped to his lower leg became loot.
Satisfied, Forte dragged the inert man a few yards to the side
and dumped him in an indentation in the ground under a low
growing shrub. If the two by the cabin came this way, they
wouldn't see their comrade immediately. Forte was going to
have to hope the man's primary weapon stayed lost in the
piles of leaves.

One threat out of the way. One ahead. Forte drew his
gun again. Arms straight, elbows slightly bent, he kept his
weapon pointed at the ground as he continued in the direction Haydn had gone.

* * *

Silence would've been frightening, but the darkness in the
woods was the opposite of quiet. Leaves rustled all around
her. Trees groaned as the wind passed through the upper
branches, and twigs snapped out along the forest floor.

If there'd been a hooting owl or a fox calling out in
the night, she could have breathed easier. But the signs of
wildlife were absent, too. Night had fallen, and there were

none of the haunting sounds of nature to reassure her. The animals were in hiding, the way they were when humans hunted in their world.

Here she was, sitting vulnerable, waiting for Brandon exactly where he'd told her to be. She'd curled up in the darker shadow of a huge tree trunk, hoping she'd be less conspicuous. But she was exposed to the night breeze and the growing chill as the night settled around her. At first, she had debated internally, and then she'd removed the reflective cat's-eye pieces he'd marked the tree with earlier in the day. He'd intended for them to serve as a marker for their "fallback DFP," and they had helped her find the exact place where he'd wanted her to wait. Though the small reflective pieces were hard to see, she'd rather not give anyone other than Brandon a reason to come investigate her tree.

A few minutes—five, or maybe even ten—went by. She didn't wear a watch and she didn't have her smartphone with her. She'd have laughed if she dared, sitting alone as she was. Days without her phone and this was the first time she truly missed it, because she desperately wanted to note the passage of time, as if it would be of help to her. Calling for help would've made more sense. But no, the logical portion of her mind wasn't in control at the moment.

She'd have given anything to know how long she'd been waiting. Or even to know for sure that she'd heard an animal noise earlier. Hopefully a dog? Hopefully not gunshots.

More twigs cracked, closer this time. And then silence did fall.

Her heart stopped for a long, agonizing moment as a silhouette became discernible against the backdrop of the dark trees. The figure approached, placing each step carefully as it climbed the bank.

Then her heart rate kicked up into overtime.

It wasn't Brandon.

She shrank into the tree trunk, trying to make herself as small as possible. Maybe they'd pass by.

But the footsteps stopped near her. She made herself look up to see the figure standing over her, raising its arms to point a gun at her.

Move.

She tried, started to rise to her feet, but pain streaked up her ankle into her knee, and she fell backward onto her butt. Scrambling backward, she tried to utter a plea, a request. Something.

She wanted to live.

Wind rushed through the trees and the trees groaned. The mud under her seeped damp cold through her pants. More leaves rustled.

A dark shape hurtled up the bank and into the man in front of her.

Her would-be killer uttered a shout of surprise, then there was a solid thud as he fell to the ground. Fabric ripped and the man cried out again, this time in pain. She struggled to her feet, managing to stand by clutching the tree trunk for support.

Peering through the dim night, she made out a black silhouette crouching over the man. It had hold of the man's arm and was shaking its head back and forth. A wolf? No, it was a dog.

Haydn.

Sophie did sob then. Brandon couldn't be far behind, not if Haydn was here. She was saved.

The fallen man swung his free hand at the dog's head again and again, but the dog's side-to-side head motions kept most of the blows from landing. Most. The butt of his waving gun connected audibly with the dog's jaw, skull, and false leg, but Haydn refused to let go.

There was a sickening crack and the man's curses turned into a scream of agony. Sophie could see the man fumbling with something on the ground. Hadyn was forced to shift his weight toward the man, who now seemed to flail with every fiber in his body. The dark, glinting shape reappeared in the man's hand. With a grunt of manic delight he pressed the muzzle of the gun against Haydn.

"No!" She tried to run forward.

The gunshot split the night, and Haydn yelped in pain.

Cursing fluently, the man shoved the dog's body aside and got to his feet.

Sophie didn't think. She should've run the other way. Instead, she ran toward them and fell forward to her knees, wrapping her arms around Haydn's broad form. The big dog grunted as she hugged him close. His chest rose and fell against her, and she dropped her forehead to his shoulder, letting her tears fall. She spread her fingers through his fur, searching for the wound. Her fingertips came into contact with hot blood and she hurried to apply pressure, slow the bleeding any way she could. She was keening, letting out a small desperate sound as the flow of her tears mixed with the flow of the dog's blood.

"The fucking dog is the least of your worries." The stranger's voice was harsh, guttural.

She refused to look up at him this time. She'd freeze again if she saw the gun pointed at her face, and Haydn needed her now. She couldn't outrun the man, but she could help the dog at least. For as long as she was still alive.

She was afraid. So incredibly terrified. And she didn't want to die. But she wouldn't go out as a coward. "Go to hell."

The man paused and laughed at her, the sound mocking.

"What a smart-ass little bitch. Do you know how much trouble you've been?"

"Thank you." She struggled to keep her tone even, maybe somewhat confident, if a bit stuffed up and nasally from the still-flowing tears.

At least she could try.

"What?" A hand shot out and grabbed a handful of her hair before she could flinch. He twisted a handful, forcing her to turn her face up toward him. "For what?"

Keep talking. Even if it made the bastard happier, every minute he spent full of himself was another to give Brandon time to get to her. *Don't fight. Not yet.* This man was a professional mercenary according to Brandon, better than the best of her self-defense classes. She'd need an incredibly lucky moment to get away from him. Think. Look for a way out. And keep him talking.

"Smart-ass." She tried not to gasp as her scalp burned. "Trouble. I kind of like those nicknames."

He shook her, and stars blew up behind her eyes. "Do you even realize the situation you're in? You're already dead. You're a corpse. All I need to do is put a bullet in you. And what's better, I'll get paid to do it. Do you know that, bitch? Do you want to know how much it's worth to erase your sorry existence from this world?"

"I'll pass. Thanks." She'd had to croak on the last word. Her throat and mouth had dried out with her fear.

"No?" He shrugged, the motion tugging on her hair more. "Then I should just shoot you and put you out of your misery. I'm betting no one in this world is going to miss you as much as your sweet heart hopes they will. That's the problem with you girl-next-door types. All romantic ideas. Face a real life-threatening situation and it's never as amazing as the movies make it. Have you pissed your pants yet?"

No, but the thought had crossed her mind. "Went before I got in the car. It'll be a while before I've got enough in my bladder. Do you want to wait?"

He cursed and gave her head a shove, then dragged her back to an upright position. She scrunched her eyes closed against the searing pain in her scalp.

He sighed. "I should just shoot you."

But he hadn't yet. He was waiting. Hope flared inside her chest and she reached with her hands, searching along Haydn's side.

"Let her go." The quiet command carried in the cool night air.

Brandon's words could carry through a crowded room. He never had to shout. His deep voice just cut under and through it all, and everyone in range felt it resonate in their chests.

Her captor laughed. "It took you long enough to get here."

CHAPTER TWENTY-ONE

Yeah?" Forte took in the situation in a glance, but for his adversary's benefit, he made a show of looking over the tableau the asshole had set up from the ground up.

Haydn lay on the ground, probably bleeding out.

Sophie had her arms around his dog, leaning over him as protectively as she was able.

Asshole stood over Sophie, and while he had a grip on her hair, he obviously wasn't serious about keeping her under control. Either the idiot didn't think she'd be a problem or the real intent wasn't about controlling her.

Her hands were buried in Haydn's fur, and there was blood on her.

Forte hoped it wasn't hers. But fear didn't ice his veins. No. Anger burned him up from the inside out. The cold night air helped remind him of his surroundings. He listened for possible threats approaching from behind and also for signs of backup. He watched not only his immediate opponent but also his allies, however helpless the other man might think they were.

And because Forte had listened to Sophie manage the man, chances were fairly reasonable in favor of the man being an idiot.

"I wanted to meet you." Asshole definitely had dirty laundry to unload. "Your name, Brandon Forte, has come up a lot recently. Right up there with David Cruz and Alexander Rojas. The three of you have reputations, you know. You're supposed to be the badass super professionals every mercenary team wants. You and your dogs. Fucking exceptional or some shit."

Forte raised his eyebrows and shrugged. Not easy to look unconcerned when you had a weapon in your hands, but it could come in handy if you could master the art of it.

To be honest, he hadn't thought of the possibility of them developing reputations in the circles of influence maintained by mercenary organizations. He figured they'd made a few enemies, yeah. But building reputations had a different connotation to it.

And he should've had better insight into it because even Raul Sa had mentioned it. If one established organization acknowledged them, others would, too.

Forte had assumed he and Cruz and Rojas hadn't needed to know more about the private sector than what it took to assure themselves their dogs were going to ethical companies. They'd been more focused on the welfare of the dogs and what purposes the working dogs would be used for rather than the influence the organization had in the industry as a whole.

If he survived the night, he was going to have to take steps to be more aware. For himself and his partners. "It's good to know we're well thought of in the industry."

The other man scowled, his mouth twisting into a bitter

grimace. "You fucks screwed up the prospects of a close friend of mine. Brothers in arms. He's worth ten of you fuckers. We served together, planned to go into private contract together. He's in jail now. Because of you fuckers."

Aw, c'mon. Forte cursed as much as the next man. And he was a firm believer there was a time and a place where a solid curse expressed a sentiment more clearly than any twenty-dollar vocabulary word could. But damn, a lack of variety when a person indulged in cursing was just lazy.

"Ah, well…fuck. Sorry you feel that way." He wouldn't apologize for the actions Cruz had taken to protect Lyn almost a year ago.

Cruz had incapacitated several kidnappers when he'd pulled Lyn out of a warehouse in downtown Philadelphia. More than one man had ended up behind bars as a result, but only one of them had been a former military veteran. Actually, that wasn't true, either. Forte had an idea of who this guy was referring to.

Cruz had gone head to head with an ex-Navy SEAL, dishonorably discharged. There were bad examples of humanity in every branch of every military in the world, and this guy had been one of the irredeemable. He'd been willing to stoop to stalking, kidnapping, and potentially killing Lyn just to get ahold of Atlas.

There were good men and women both actively serving in the armed forces and retired from them. But like any other aspect of the universe, there were twisted, bad individuals in the mix, too.

Seemed like it was his turn to come face-to-face with his share of them. Again.

A soldier could survive to walk off a battlefield, even go home. But life had a way of making every day a different kind of fight.

"You know the company I work for was impressed?" The man spit to one side, on Sophie's medical boot. "You all kept it quiet. Neat. Minimal issues with the local law enforcement. Excellent public relations, they said. Your entire community went on believing you were all hometown heroes. I couldn't resist starting out our little party with a present to make sure all that blew up in your face."

If it'd gone as planned, Sophie would've gone up along with the car. The man probably thought he'd been clever. Even better if he'd succeeded.

Anger burned low in Forte's belly. He banked the emotion, leveraged it to keep his thought process sharp. Keeping his joints loose, his posture relaxed, he had his finger off the trigger but ready for the split second he could acquire his target.

There'd be a window of opportunity. He needed to wait for it. "No. I didn't know anyone was impressed."

Always interesting when you could give the truth to the person who hated you for it.

"They wanted to bring you on as an asset. You and your mutt trainers were supposed to be valuable additions. Fucking eliminate my friend and they want to offer you fuckers a position, serving with me? I don't think so." The man tightened his hold on Sophie's hair and brought his gun to her skull.

Her eyes glistened, but she kept them open and on Forte, watching him for any cue. The calm faith in her gaze split his heart. His brave, beautiful, smart Sophie.

"I did receive an offer. I didn't accept." He only wanted to antagonize the idiot to the edge of reason. He didn't want to push the man into enough of a rage to finally kill her.

"No? You mean not yet." The man ground out the words. "But I had a better idea, especially when this contract came in. I volunteered for it. You know, there were assassin organizations back in the old days."

Did the man actually know some history? Could be.

"Define old days." Forte invited him to keep talking, hoping the man would get tired of holding Sophie so tight.

"More than decades, centuries ago." The idiot tossed his head. "Exact time doesn't matter. What matters was those organizations had an initiation system."

This was sounding more like the backstory of a video game than an actual history lesson. There could be some valid history in there somewhere, but it was lost in this guy's interpretation.

"Back then, the final rite of passage was for one initiate to kill another." An ugly grin split the man's face. "I like it. I came out here figuring I'd get paid to kill this bitch and I'd take the opportunity to make sure to take you out, too. Man of your reputation? It'd be worth a raise for me to prove I'm that much more of an asset."

Well, that explained why Sophie hadn't died outright. She'd been smart to keep the man talking. The idiot wanted to talk, wanted the validation of revealing to everyone how clever he was. But there were only so many words inside the man's head, and he was running down the clock now.

"Okay." Forte smiled in return, taunting him. "So kill me."

It'd be a Wild West quick draw. And he only had one chance.

"Oh no." The man shook his head, his gaze sharp. "You can watch her die first. You can go to hell knowing you weren't better than me."

Sophie's arm swung up in an arc, and she twisted to add more momentum to her backswing. The thing in her hand contacted hard with the side of the man's head. The gun came away from her head, and he lost his grip on her hair as he stumbled a step to one side.

Forte raised his arms, took aim, and fired.

CHAPTER TWENTY-TWO

Sophie curled around Haydn, covering him with her body as well as she could. She imagined how painful it would be to be shot in the back or the head. And she tried to brace herself for it. At this close range, even if Brandon had managed to shoot her attacker, she was going to be hurt.

Or at least, she refused to be stupid enough to assume she wouldn't be.

Tremors shook her body, and she clutched Haydn's prosthetic leg in her right hand. It'd worked to get her loose from the man, give Brandon the opening he needed. But she might need to use it again. Or maybe she couldn't make herself let it go. She wasn't sure.

There'd been a gun to her head. The whole logical thought process thing was limited at the moment.

"Sophie." Brandon's voice came to her low, soft, warm.

He hadn't sounded human a few moments ago. She'd never heard him that way. He'd been cold, sarcastic. His words had cut the air, devoid of any caring. He'd told her once, after he'd come back into her life, that he'd become good at compartmentalizing.

What he'd meant was that he'd taken everything human, everything that made him Brandon, and shut it away.

She'd seen him, heard him, and desperately looked for some hint of the Brandon she knew in the man who'd stood facing her. And she hadn't been able to see him. Instead, she'd had to believe he was still in there somewhere.

"Sophie. Are you hurt?" Leaves crunched as he kneeled next to her. He still hadn't touched her.

She was relieved he didn't. Not because she didn't want him to, but because she couldn't stop shaking. "You're back."

A pause. "I wouldn't have left you."

Funny. It was as if they'd gone right back to the conversation they'd been having before guns and fire and people had interrupted them.

She shook her head. "I'm not bleeding. Haydn is. He needs help."

"Let me see." Brandon took hold of her shoulder then, and gently eased her away from the big dog. She moved, but she kept her left hand pressed against the spot where she could feel hot blood seeping out. "Keep a look out ahead of us. Don't look over your shoulder."

The man behind them might be dead then. She'd never seen a fresh corpse. Hadn't ever thought about Brandon as a man who'd killed someone. The idea of a man defending his country had been a lot easier to hold in her mind than the reality a few feet away from her.

She was grateful. She was also still trying to grasp what was going on around her while it all happened too fast.

Haydn was still breathing. When Brandon pressed against the GSD's shoulder, Haydn whined. "We're going to need light to see how bad this is. You've got pressure on the one spot, but I can't tell if the bullet exited somewhere. He could be bleeding from an exit wound."

Her heart dropped into her stomach and both of them churned. "We need to get him to an animal hospital."

Brandon turned his face to her, meeting her gaze. His hazel eyes were still hard and fierce. "There are two more men out there. I can't carry him and keep you safe."

He was making a decision. Just like that. This might not be the first time he'd had to leave someone behind to save someone else.

It was the right thing to do. But it shouldn't be for her.

"I'll hide here." She could do that. It was a valid alternative. She could stay out of the way. "You can take him to get help and come back for me."

"No." Brandon reached for her.

She leaned away. She wouldn't leave Haydn here. "He's dying. Don't let him die . . . for me."

The last words came out whispered, and she hated herself for crying, for wasting time arguing with him. She'd become somebody she didn't recognize anymore. She could not remember a time when she had ever endangered them by questioning Brandon's judgment when urgent matters were at hand. When it came to emergencies, she'd always believed a person should listen to authorities and firemen and Brandon. They were trained, had the expertise and the skills to make a difference.

But right now, this was happening because of her. She was going to have to live with the sight of Haydn burned into her mind. The warmth of his blood was always going to be against her palms.

"Don't let him die for nothing." Brandon's rebuke stung.

He wasn't wrong.

She didn't fight more as he cupped his hand under her

elbow and helped her to her feet. Her ankle hurt, but she gritted her teeth and put weight on it anyway. If he couldn't carry Haydn, he couldn't carry her.

He waited until she was steady, then he stepped in front of her. "Stay with me. Be ready to find cover if I tell you to."

"I'll do my best." She pitched her voice low, quiet, like his.

This was what it took. She wanted to live through this. And she didn't want him hurt, too, because of her. She couldn't make him safe, didn't have a gun to help provide cover for him or whatever a real partner could do. Even if he'd given her a weapon, she didn't know how to shoot it.

They scrambled down the bank. She had to sit and scoot forward on her butt because her ankle wouldn't hold her, and she didn't want to risk falling all the way down. Brandon hadn't said anything, hadn't shown any sign of being upset with her. He'd only kept scanning the area around them as he waited for her to stand and be ready to continue.

He pointed to her left, along the dry creek bed, and she breathed a sigh of relief. This was easier footing, less for her to trip over. She could do this.

"Down!" Brandon's urgent command struck her like a physical blow.

Her knees collapsed almost without thought, and she fell forward on her hands as he pressed her forward, against the incline of the steep embankment. He was shielding her with his body.

She didn't try to get out from under him or run. She only curled up as small as she could and tried to listen to what was going on around them. She kept her eyes open wide, trying to see what was going on.

If a moment came to help or to move, if Brandon needed her to do something, she'd be ready.

"Friendly." A voice came out of the darkness. "Forte, is that you? We're friendlies."

The tension eased in Brandon's posture. "Sa."

There were friends here. Relief flooded through her again, and she wondered how many times her muscles could go from tense to limp in the space of a few minutes.

"Affirmative."

"I've got a dog down." Brandon didn't put away his gun. Instead, he let the other man approach. A black-and-tan shadow approached, the cold nose passing swiftly over her cheek.

"H-Haydn." The tears were falling again, and she wiped them off her cheeks, angry with herself. Crying was useless, and she still needed to be able to see where she was going.

"We neutralized two threats just inside the tree line." Raul Sa directed his words to Brandon. Which was just as well because Sophie wasn't sure what she would've done with the information.

Brandon nodded and holstered his gun in a harness under his T-shirt. "That's it, then. I took out two here in the woods. Both are still alive and unconscious. One has a minor bullet wound. It'll take hours for him to bleed out. We need immediate transport."

"On it." Sa touched his hand to his throat and issued a few terse comments to no one in general.

Sophie stared hard at his throat. He had some sort of equipment at his throat. A communication device. Brandon didn't look surprised.

Instead, he seemed to be softening, his posture relaxing. When he turned to her, the look in his eyes was thawing. "We're safe now. We're going to take you out of here."

Safe.

She breathed slow and gathered up all of those trembling

nerves. Swallowing hard, she shoved away the helplessness and fear. One step at a time. Every moment wasn't a life-or-death decision anymore for her or for Brandon. She could face all that later and be grateful she'd managed to come through it all somehow.

Straightening, she looked from Brandon to Raul Sa and back to Brandon again. "Then we're going to make sure Haydn gets help. Right now."

Brandon smiled. It was a new smile, one she'd never seen before. Fierce and friendly at the same time. "Yes, ma'am."

CHAPTER TWENTY-THREE

There was an animal hospital with full emergency surgery facilities within twenty minutes of the bed-and-breakfast where they'd been staying. It was a lucky thing for Haydn.

If there'd been one thing Forte hadn't thought to check out when he'd decided to bring Sophie to this area for hiding, it'd been the proximity of a veterinarian.

The staff had reacted with admirable calm when they'd come rushing in. The nurse on duty had called in the veterinarian on call and they'd taken Haydn into a back room to prep him for immediate surgery. They'd taken one look at Forte and Sa and hustled them into a private area to keep them out of the way.

Sa, for his part, opted to head back outside to watch the perimeter with his team. His dog, formerly one of Forte's own trainees, had accompanied him outside.

So here Forte sat, in a tiny office, waiting to hear about Haydn.

Sophie had curled up in the corner chair with her feet

tucked under her. She'd leaned into the corner of the room, staring at the wall, until her eyelids had drooped. For the time being, rest was the best thing for her. He didn't want to disturb her, even to get her injured ankle out from under her.

It was still in the medical boot so it had proper support. And Ky would be there in the next couple of hours to help work things out with the local law enforcement. Time enough to get her to elevate the leg and ice the ankle. When there was someone else around to nudge her. She'd hit her tolerance point of following directions from him for the night.

And she'd done wonderfully.

She was a strong, brave woman, whether she realized it or not. And she'd been pushed hard over the past week leading into tonight. Anyone else could've broken down into screaming hysterics. But not his Sophie. No. Once the imminent danger had passed, she'd pulled herself together and insisted on seeing to the well-being of his dog.

She'd looked around as they'd left, but she hadn't complicated things by asking about her cat.

Always sensible, even when she didn't want to be, Sophie'd made the choice not to distract anyone by looking for Tesseract. Not when Haydn needed immediate help.

If he had to, Forte would go out and look for Tesseract as soon as he knew for sure what the outcome would be for Haydn. It didn't matter what the surgery would cost. The dog had taken a bullet for Sophie. They'd take care of him first and worry about the financial logistics later.

Of course, Forte was going to be up to his eyeballs in debt paying off the damage to the cabin, but hopefully they had enough information from the four attackers captured on site to split the costs into something reasonable. Those men were going to jail, so it wasn't as if they'd need those wages in the meantime.

Cold comfort and not any sort of line of thought to cheer him up.

Sophie had seen a part of him she hadn't understood tonight. Oh, intellectually, she'd known he'd deployed and had acknowledged he'd been through things. She was aware of the definition of post-traumatic stress disorder, and she'd seen it manifest in various ways for different people. Her intelligence and incredible empathy had taken her a long way in understanding not only him but Rojas and Cruz better than anyone in the community around Hope's Crossing Kennels.

But until tonight, she hadn't met the cold stranger he'd turned into when he'd gone overseas. He'd told her about the compartmentalization he'd done with his personality. He'd done it to protect himself. The process of going through boot camp and technical training, of the various programs in the military, wasn't just to provide him with skills and technique. The training had had the dual purpose of educating and unmaking an individual's personality. He'd been rebuilt into someone much more capable of surviving life as a soldier during his deployments, and he didn't regret it at all. But he'd learned to take the piece of him that'd grown up in middle-class suburbia and tuck that boy away to protect him from the reshaping that'd been required.

Through those deployments, running mission after mission, he'd become further detached from his old personality. It had to happen. For some, they turned so completely away from who they used to be, they never did go back to civilian life. And that wasn't a bad thing.

He'd simply had a single person in his life he'd wanted to get back to.

She stirred in the chair, her feet slipping out from under her as she turned. Amazingly, she managed to shift her position before she fell out of the seat completely. He kept expecting her to end up like one of those hamster videos online where the fuzzy thing fell asleep and sort of...rolled off its perch.

He was going to hell for waiting to see if it would happen instead of moving to secure her position. He'd have lunged to catch her before she hit the hard floor, though.

Ah, Sophie. He'd wanted to hide the truth of himself from her, shelter her from the monstrous part of him he'd developed while he'd been away. He couldn't call it anything else, because what else could any person become when it was safer to excise the humanity and tuck it away?

She hadn't been afraid of him. And she hadn't fought him, not really. She'd snapped out of fear and she'd gotten stubborn out of concern for an individual she'd cared about. She'd come through it, and held her shit together through it for the most part.

There were a lot of people, men and women both, who'd broken under similar circumstances. Even with training, a person didn't really know what they could survive until they were forced into the real circumstances.

His Sophie was a survivor.

And she'd been a match for him. She'd looked into his eyes and faced the truth he'd hidden since he'd come back to establish Hope's Crossing Kennels. She'd taken a look at every demon he had inside him. And here she was, sleeping in his presence, like she hadn't figured he might have killed someone not a few feet away from her.

It'd been her acceptance he'd come home for, he thought. But he'd been too much of a coward to try to show her in the years since he'd started the kennels. He couldn't find the right time, the right place, and didn't know how to bring his demons out for her to see.

He'd come close to asking her to come with him to therapy sessions so maybe she could get a glimpse there. But she disliked psychologists almost as much as he did. So he'd held off on that last resort.

There was no way he'd have ever wanted the events of the last week or so to have happened to her, but the result wasn't something he was going to regret. She'd seen the person he could become in life-threatening situations.

He wasn't sure where their relationship was going to go after tonight, but at least he knew she wouldn't turn away from him out of fear. She hadn't hated what she saw.

He stood silently and stretched his arms toward the ceiling. Muscles in his back protested, and he breathed in and out, willing oxygen to those abused muscle fibers. He was going to be sore as hell tomorrow and so would Sophie. Best to stretch and keep from getting stiff to give himself a better chance to heal from the bruising and soreness quickly.

Rolling his shoulders, he turned to look at her. He'd relished the chances to watch her sleep over the past couple of days. Maybe it made him a creeper, but it didn't stop fascinating him, the way she was beautiful in any light. It didn't matter if she was curled up in a chair or sprawled out taking up an entire king-size bed.

Years. It'd been years since he'd bought the acres for Hope's Crossing Kennels and broken ground for the buildings. She'd sought him out once she'd heard he was back in town. She'd offered him her friendship like he'd never left.

Then, he'd thought it was the start at rebuilding a life for himself that he'd been looking for. He'd been happy for it and promised himself her friendship would be good enough.

Her father hadn't ever brought up their conversation again, but Forte had been aware of the old man's scrutiny. The wariness had remained. And he'd maintained his distance, preserved his cherished friendship, and told himself it was enough.

But Sophie had been right. He'd betrayed her. He'd taken away her choice in the matter.

In a lot of ways, he'd rebuilt his life all right. He'd built it right from the place they'd left off, thinking that was what he needed to be happy.

The past few days had taught him differently. He hadn't needed to go back to where he'd started. He'd only wanted it.

Truth was, he needed a hard reset. Now that he knew what to do, he wasn't sure Sophie's friendship would be there for him to build from here.

*　*　*

"Mr. Forte?"

Sophie woke with a start at the quiet words. Within seconds, she processed the cool greens of the small office at the veterinarian's.

Brandon stood within reach, facing the nurse at the door. "Yes?"

The nurse glanced at Sophie. "I'm sorry, dear. I didn't mean to frighten you."

"Oh no. Don't worry about it." Seriously. Compared to the rest of the night—hell, the whole week—this was peanuts. "How's Haydn?"

The nurse pressed her lips together, then smiled. "The doctor is just washing up and then he'll be ready to talk to you. Haydn is in recovery."

Tension seeped out of Brandon's shoulders, and emotion welled up in Sophie, spilling over as a happy tear. With all of the damned crying she'd been doing that day, this was one moment when tears were welcome. Happy tears.

Recovery meant Haydn was alive.

Sophie settled back into the chair to wait and give Brandon space. He was a man with a lot of emotion, and he didn't like to admit it, even to her.

He surprised her by turning and kneeling next to her. "I know you might not be inclined, but I'd really appreciate a hug right now."

She stared at him. She'd never, ever deny him comfort. The thought froze in her head as she remembered their argument.

Her words had stuck with him and he wasn't sure where they stood anymore.

Neither was she.

He closed his eyes. He never did that around anyone, not out in public. "I broke your trust. I don't know if I can build it back. I'll understand if you decide not to give me the chance."

As she continued to stare at him, the compartmentalization was happening. The Brandon she knew was withdrawing in minute changes of expression. His posture was becoming stiffer. The humanity was leaching away from his face, turning his formerly neutral expression to a frightening blankness.

She sobbed. No, no, this wasn't what she wanted. It was like her Brandon was leaving even if he was kneeling there in front of her. No.

She threw her arms around his shoulders, almost losing her balance and falling out of the chair.

His arms came around her and he lifted her back onto the

chair. Then he lifted her again and set her so her legs were
stretched out and elevated.

"We need to get you a bag of ice." His voice was gruff,
full of emotion again. This was her Brandon. "I'll be right
back."

He stepped outside and left the door open a crack so she
could hear him out in the hallway.

She wrapped her arms around herself and considered
what'd just happened.

The idea of him withdrawing, losing the part of him she'd
come to associate with her friend, was out of the question.
But how could they go back to being friends?

It was confusing.

She almost laughed at herself. She'd been coasting for the
past day or two, hanging in limbo. Whether she wanted to
admit it or not, she'd been confused the whole time, with no
idea of what she was going to do next.

It'd been easy to let him tell her what each step would be.
Sure, there'd been good reasons for it. He was keeping her
safe. She'd run from her hometown. She'd gone into hiding
with him. And she'd come through almost dying multiple
times without truly facing the reality of it all.

She could have died.

And before that? She'd done everything she was supposed to do according to her parents and elders and everyone
else in her life. There were always sensible, logical, practical
reasons for doing what people told her to do. And she reassured herself that she was a strong, independent, self-
sufficient woman because she carefully thought out each
action and decided to do what they said.

But that'd still been the easy way out, the path of least re-
sistance.

It'd been like taking a multiple-choice test all her life.

Choices were presented to her and she got to pick the best of the options. She'd fooled herself into thinking she'd accomplished so much, built a career for herself. But multiple-choice tests required less thinking, less effort, than coming up with the answers from scratch.

Maybe she should start challenging herself.

She didn't know what the next step would be, but she shouldn't wait for Brandon to come back into the room and tell her what her options were. She needed...no, she wanted to think for herself and decide based on that.

No more going with choice C just because it had the highest percent chance of being the right answer. No more choosing the longest answer of the choices available because that had the highest potential to be the right one.

No more pretending life was a standardized multiple-choice exam.

Brandon returned then with an ice pack.

She reached out and accepted it from him. "Thank you."

He stood, hovering, while she loosened her medical boot and arranged the pack on it. "Maybe we should take it off."

"No." She didn't want to get snappy, but she tried to keep her tone firm. "I think it'll swell if we do. Better to ice it while it still has some compression for now and I'll get it looked at by a doctor for humans when we get the chance to go to a human emergency room."

His eyebrows rose but he didn't argue.

Instead, an awkward silence hung in the air. She was tempted to ask him what needed to happen next. After all, he was the expert in dealing with people who tried to kill other people.

No. That wasn't fair. Okay, maybe it was accurate, but it was unnecessarily snarky and frightening. When it came to what she wanted to do with her life, she didn't need her answers right away, and she didn't need to get pissy about them. She just had to break the habits she'd identified.

"You're thinking hard." He moved to lean against the wall next to her, facing her with his arms loosely crossed over his chest. His biceps and forearms were criss-crossed with tiny scratches.

"I have a lot of questions piling up." Yes, that felt right. She did want to know what to do next, but the old her would've just asked him for next steps. The new her needed information in order to form her own ideas. "I guess I'm wondering if we need to talk to police after this or if we can go to a human emergency room."

Unfortunately, sleep seemed a long way away and there was no actual bed anymore.

Brandon continued to study her, and she thought she caught the ghost of a smile playing over his lips. "The police are probably going to want to talk to us, but if we manage it correctly, I think they'll talk to us while we're at the emergency room."

The thought of those lips sweeping over her skin heated her most intimate parts. Imagining him hovering over her with that ghost of a smile just before he dipped his head to… only she had real-life experience to enhance the imagination and now was so not the time to be indulging in the fantasy.

It took effort to drag her very naughty mind back to the present. She nodded. "Are we likely to get arrested?"

Her stomach did a flip-flop as she considered the possibility. She'd just managed to survive with actual professionals trying to kill her. Getting in trouble with the law, and potentially going to jail, was a horrible way to end this. It seemed insanely unfair. Or just insane. Maybe she was finally losing her sanity under the strain. She wasn't sure.

"Not likely." He definitely sounded amused.

"Okay." She drew in air and blew it out slowly. "How long before we can go back to the cabin and look for Tesseract?"

There was a long pause and Brandon slid his back against the wall until he was sitting on his heels, his arms balanced on his knees. "Hours."

"I want to go look for her." The decision settled in her mind and felt right. Then another question popped in her head. "Is she...is it possible that she died in the cabin?"

Brandon sighed. "She had a lot of escape routes. But I don't want to get your hopes up. There's a chance she might not have made it."

Her throat closed. Ah, she felt awful. She'd only known Tesseract for a couple of days. And she obviously hadn't been a better forever home for the cat than the cat café. As signs went, it seemed relatively obvious she wasn't fit to provide for any other life but her own.

Or, more truthfully, she couldn't even take care of her own life, much less be responsible for another.

"I'm sorry." Brandon touched her shoulder briefly, then the warmth of his fingertips disappeared. "We'll go look for her, but even if she did get out we might not find her."

The woods were a dangerous place for a domesticated cat. Sure, Tesseract had her full set of claws intact, but she could come up against a raccoon or possum. Worse, Tesseract could run into a larger predator.

Sophie nodded. "We'll look, but I won't have false hope, okay? I just need to go and at least look."

"Okay," Brandon acquiesced readily.

"Okay." She stared at the door. Step one had gone well, she thought. Tough question, a decision, and somebody to support her in the decision. "Thank you."

"It's not a thing." He said the words lightly.

She pressed her lips together. "It is. It's a lot of things, actually. Too much to list. But mostly, thank you for letting me decide what we're going to do next instead of telling me what to do."

There. Even if he tended to look like he could read minds whenever he stared at her with those startling hazel-green eyes, he couldn't. She wasn't going to go through her entire thought process from the past several minutes, but he wasn't going to make her, either.

And this, she thought, was something she could settle for. Or she'd have to, because friendship, or whatever their relationship had been turning into, wasn't something they could go back to.

A sharp knock at the door brought Brandon to his feet and they both stared as Raul poked his head in the door. "Hey. The doctor is coming down the hallway."

Brandon dragged his hand through his hair. "Copy."

Raul hesitated, his brow wrinkled with a quirky expression.

"Something else?" Sophie decided to prompt him because maybe the whole ex-military habit of less is more when it came to words wasn't the best approach at the moment.

Raul met her gaze, somewhat relieved. "Something snuck into my vehicle. Taz doesn't know what to do with it but it's definitely not afraid of him and doesn't look like a random stray from the woods around that cabin."

The man stepped all the way into the room, gesturing to a cream-colored puff of fur attached to his shoulders. Her claws were hooked firmly into his weapons harness and her bright blue eyes scanned the room.

Sophie straightened. "Tesseract!"

Her cat uttered an imperious *meow* and leaped from Sa's shoulder to the chairs, then daintily picked her way over to Sophie. By the time her cat had climbed up to her chest, Tesseract's fur had smoothed down and she curled up with a happy purr.

Sophie buried her face in Tesseract's side, reveling in the silky softness of her cat. She smelled of smoke and maybe gunpowder? But she was here and safe.

Raul was talking to Brandon. "It was just sitting in the back of the car where Taz rides. Didn't know what to make of it. Figured I'd bring it in and drop it off here for adoption if you two didn't know where it came from. Does it always freak out like that?"

Brandon chuckled. "Yeah. Yeah, she does."

CHAPTER TWENTY-FOUR

This apartment is a comfort-food-only zone. It's a carb overload. Everything tastes good, and the word 'diet' is banned until every room is cleaned and either set back to rights or redone." Sophie stood in the doorway leading to her apartment, holding off Lyn and Elisa until each of them grinned and nodded in acknowledgment.

There hadn't been any doubt, really. But this way, they couldn't say she hadn't warned them.

"You've been back for a morning. How did you have time to cook?" Lyn picked her way into the living room area and set down bags of cleaning supplies. "And why is Brandon holed up in his office like a bear going into hibernation?"

"Brandon said there were a few more things he needed to take care of," Sophie said slowly. The men who'd attacked them in Virginia were all in custody. But those men worked for an organization, and Brandon had said he had enough to be sure which it was.

"I'm not surprised." Lyn dropped her hands to her sides.

"It'd be weird for you to be back here if Ky or any of the guys thought there was a continued threat."

Sophie sighed. "Mrs. Seong saw us come in before dawn. She was here before noon with enough food to feed an army. Said I shouldn't worry about groceries the first day I'm back from the dead."

Elisa raised her eyebrows, then glanced around the wreck of Sophie's apartment. "To be fair, if one hadn't known what was going on and caught a look at this a couple of nights ago, thinking you must've died is a plausible conclusion."

"I wish I'd been able to tell her I was going, but there wasn't time." And it hadn't been safe. Anyone in contact with Sophie had been in danger and Mrs. Seong didn't live within the protective influence of David Cruz or Alex Rojas or the police. "I don't know how I'll make it up to her. She might never trust me again."

"I'd say she was happy to see you home." Elisa wandered into the kitchen area and surveyed the array of casserole dishes across the counter and on the stovetop. "What *is* all this?"

"Why don't we eat first, then we'll pick a room to start cleaning?" Sophie waved her hand toward the breakfast table, still sitting in the living room by the sofa. It was the only relatively uncluttered surface in the place. "Dishes are clean in the dishwasher. I ran it as soon as I got in this morning."

"Okay, come tell me what all this is. It smells like heaven." Elisa had a plate out and was peering under covers at the contents of the dishes.

Lyn joined Sophie as she gimped her way over to the kitchen area.

"Here, you'll need a rice bowl and a soup bowl, too. Trust me." Sophie snagged the appropriate items out of the dishwasher and handed them to Elisa. "The pot on the stove has *tteokguk.* It's a Korean rice cake soup usually made for New Year. It's simple and tasty with bits of beef brisket and savory seaweed. Just be careful and only take a small amount. The rice cakes are super filling, and I swear they expand in your stomach. I love it, though, and make it when no one is around to judge me for having it in the middle of the year. I guess Mrs. Seong figured it'd be a nice treat."

Lyn shrugged. "Or maybe she meant it as a new beginning. That woman is deeper than she wants to let on. I've only run into her once or twice, but I've always thought she uses her absent-minded chatter with a level of shrewdness bordering on masterful."

Sophie stopped to consider. "You're not wrong, and I kind of want to be her when I grow up."

Assent all around.

"So what are these?" Elisa waved a skewer loaded with long cylinders coated in a brilliant orange-red, spicy-looking sauce.

Sophie smiled. "*Tteok-pokki.* More rice cakes, different shape, spicy sauce. I like mine super spicy. The rice cakes have a sort of bounce to their chewiness."

Elisa's eyebrows rose. "A bounce? Okay. Should be interesting."

She set the skewer on her plate and lifted the lid to another huge casserole. Sophie inhaled the flavorful, spicy, sour scent and sighed happily. "Kimchi fried rice."

Lyn chuckled. "You weren't kidding when you said it was going to be a carb-loading kind of day. Move along, I want to try all of this, too."

The three of them dished up their portions and juggled their way to the breakfast table. After the first few bites in silence, Lyn rolled her eyes up to the ceiling. "Oh, this is good. All of it."

"Mmm," Elisa agreed, waving a long-handled spoon.

"Told you so." Sophie managed to actually form words around a mouthful of kimchi fried rice. "None of it is technically served together, but this makes me so happy."

They all nodded.

Lyn swallowed and tapped her spoon against her plate. "I'm guessing we should dive into your bedroom first. You need a place to sleep."

Elisa was watching Sophie intently. "Unless you plan to sleep at the kennels."

Ah. Sophie shook her head. "No."

"Did things not work out?" Elisa's voice was gentle, sympathetic.

"They did, actually." Sophie took a huge spoonful of her *tteokguk* and chewed slowly, savoring the beef and burst of salty seaweed in contrast to the soft and chewy rice cake. "The T-shirts came in handy. And we were good together. Really good."

Lyn and Elisa waited.

"But I've wanted us to break the friendship barrier for so long, I didn't stop to think about what it would mean when we started talking about the things I'd been wondering all these years. The stuff friends don't need to talk about."

Lyn nodded then. "The things lovers need out in the open to figure out where their relationship is going."

Sophie nodded. Now it seemed so obvious. But then, Elisa and Lyn had been through the hard part of starting a serious relationship. And theirs hadn't failed to launch. "It was me. I needed to know why he left town right after high school. And I couldn't accept his reason."

Neither Elisa nor Lyn asked what Brandon's reason had been. They respected that privacy.

Elisa nibbled on the end of a *tteok-pokki*. "What do you want to do now?"

Sophie smiled, trembling a little. Oh, she'd been afraid her friends would dig too deep or question her decision. She'd worried they'd judge. After all, Brandon was their friend, too. This, though, was friendship.

If she'd decided to go into hiding, to let everyone think she'd died, she'd have left these people behind. And she couldn't imagine life without them.

"I want to get this apartment organized." Sophie focused on her soup. "Once I'm not looking at the wreckage, maybe I can deal with the way someone decided to destroy my life. They didn't succeed. And, actually, it was a kick in the pants I needed. I'll make some big changes."

"Yeah?" Lyn smiled, approving. "Are the big changes the kind you're ready to talk about?"

"I'm not going to look for another full-time job as an accountant." Sophie pressed her lips together. "I'm more than capable of establishing a small individual business and doing accounting locally. That'll provide me with a solid income to live here and save money up for what I really want to do."

Elisa gasped. "The bed-and-breakfast."

Sophie nodded.

Elisa squealed.

Lyn put her spoon down and gave her a slow clap. "Excellent. So is this a six-month plan or a one-year plan?"

Sophie considered. "It's more of a three-year plan, possibly five. But I think it could be a three-year if I'm really careful with my budgeting and very smart about the property I buy."

She'd dreamt about it for as long as she could remember. She'd researched the establishment and management. She'd visited more B&Bs than she could count. She knew the business.

"I'm not sure where yet, but I'm going to make it happen." She smiled at her friends. "Until then, this is going to be my home office, and I'm going to go independent."

Lyn gathered up empty plates. "Well, then, we'll get started with the cleaning. We can snack again in a few hours."

"Let's get to it." Sophie stood and limped toward the kitchen. She had a plan. Her life was going to be happier, especially because she was going to follow her dreams and really do things because they were her aspirations and not what somebody else thought they should be. These were good things, and she was looking forward to having her friends nearby as she built her life for herself.

Mostly.

Tesseract emerged from the bedroom and decided to climb onto Sophie's medical boot for a ride.

"Sophie." Lyn's voice was calm. "There's a feline attached to your leg."

"This is Tesseract. I adopted her."

Elisa giggled. "And you named a cat that why?"

"It was a random line of thought."

* * *

His office needed cleaning. Forte considered getting up to go get a broom and some supplies, but that would require climbing over Haydn, currently parked on the floor by his feet and not actually in the dog bed thoughtfully provided. The vet in Virginia had released Haydn over to the care of the vet they kept on retainer at Hope's Crossing Kennels, so Haydn was being monitored carefully right there on premises.

"You know, that bed is there for you. I don't plan to

take a nap in it come mid-afternoon." Though now that he'd thought of it, it didn't sound like a bad idea.

He was exhausted. Haydn was wiped out. Sophie was... not here. And if texts from Lyn and Elisa were to be believed, all three women were doing some massive cleaning of their own. He had no idea where Sophie was finding the energy.

Or maybe his initiative had fizzled out once he'd gotten home. Instead of catching up on the status of the kennels, he'd been in his office, brooding.

His phone rang and he came to his feet. "Forte."

"It's Beckhorn." The voice on the other end was brisk with a hint of a drawl. "Got news. First part is quick. It's an update on the adoption process for Haydn. Figured I'd call you direct instead of e-mail."

"Ah." Forte did step over Haydn as he decided he wanted to be out from behind his desk for this news.

"Family of Haydn's former handler doesn't have the means to provide a stable environment for him. No one has the time to spend on his physical therapy or even maintaining his training." Beckhorn paused. "If he were older, calmer, it might be a reasonable fit, but Haydn is still active and ready to work."

And had proved he could. Forte didn't argue the point, though. He'd given Beckhorn a report on Haydn's activities, including the altercation last night. He'd had to. Technically, Haydn didn't belong to Hope's Crossing Kennels. He belonged to the US government, and Beckhorn was responsible. Getting Haydn shot hadn't been something he could hide and still expect a relationship with the Air Force dog training program at Lackland.

"Not going to lie. No one is going to praise your work with Haydn, considering recent events. But your history with dogs is to be considered. And these were extenuating circumstances." Beckhorn cleared his throat. "The situation being what it was, an exemplary working relationship was demonstrated despite the injury sustained by Haydn. Final decision is to allow you to adopt him, on the condition of regular health checks and reports on his well-being."

Forte tilted his face toward the ceiling, glad not to have to fight to keep his dog. "I appreciate the trust."

Beckhorn chuckled. "You're a good dog man, Forte. You, Rojas, and Cruz provide quality training. We had to conduct a serious investigation into your most recent report but, as I said, extenuating circumstances."

Forte grunted. "Sa was a solid referral. Thank you for sending him our way, too."

Sa had been a huge help in recent events, and all things considered, Forte planned to maintain a positive working relationship with Sa's squad. Forte still didn't plan to take on any private contracts, but he felt the need to build up his network. Even though the immediate danger had passed for Sophie and the contract for her life was no longer out there, the company that'd taken the contract was aware of its failure. Never a good way to end a situation.

But he and Cruz and Rojas had plans to mitigate the issue. They were going to make sure Sophie could build her life the way she wanted it, and the rest of their loved ones could go on living theirs.

"Glad the referral worked out." Beckhorn let out a gusty sigh. "Actually, are you planning on expanding your operations any?"

Forte turned to look at Haydn, who'd rolled onto his back and started snoring. "How many military working dogs do you need?"

"Actually, I've got some experienced handlers coming

out of active duty looking for work. Some of them would make good trainers, but I can only hire so many directly." Beckhorn headed up the dog training program at Lackland Air Force Base. He tended to keep in touch with his students.

Ah. Forte considered the concept. "I've got room to expand conservatively. Depends on the demand for well-trained dogs from year to year. I'd be open to meeting with a few."

"Good. Would want to see these handlers become trainers with your kind of professionalism."

Haydn yawned in his sleep. His jaws remained partially open and his tongue hung out one side of his mouth. The big dog passed gas. Yeah. Hope's Crossing Kennels. Professional polish and dignity all around the place.

Forte stepped out of his office. Rather, he'd been literally gassed out. "I might expand the training we do here."

"Yeah?"

"There's a need for military working dogs, for sure. I plan to extend into search and rescue training, too." Forte had been considering it over the past year, actually. "And there's also a need for service dogs to work with soldiers after they've come home. We've got at least three examples now of dogs who're doing veterans a hell of a lot of good in life after active duty."

Beckhorn made a sound of approval. "You considering training up service dogs for PTSD?"

"PTSD, yeah." Forte had more in mind, though. "And wounded veterans in need of a service dog to help with a physical disability. There's a lot of room to evolve over time. I'm thinking that kind of work would require more handlers staying here at the kennels for a certain amount of time to meet the dogs. I'll be developing specialized training for each pair based on the need and the dog personality."

There was a lot to define in his idea. It was a broad scope and there'd be research to do into the financial aspect. He would be looking for grants for the project, most likely.

"Sounds like you've got big plans for the future." Beckhorn laughed. "Just make sure you maintain your current work, too. It's hard to find trainers of your caliber to work with, and we'll continue to need dogs from your facility."

Forte chuckled. "We're not changing direction. This is definitely an expansion."

"Good. Sounds like things are going well for you and yours."

"Maybe." Forte sobered.

There was still a shady feeling nagging at him when it came to Sophie. He'd been poking at it all day, chewing on his thoughts about her. He could be bitter. He didn't want to be the man who couldn't take no for an answer. And he was fairly certain her answer to him and their relationship had been a solid "no."

But his gut kept twisting, and he kept looking out the window. There was still an issue. He needed to tie up the loose ends or Sophie wouldn't have the chance to live her life.

Without him.

Didn't matter if he was there as her lover or as her friend. He wasn't even sure he'd be welcome as the latter. But he'd be there on the sidelines, making sure she was okay.

Right now, she wasn't.

It was time to see to it that she and anyone else close to Hope's Crossing Kennels now or in the future would be safe from this particular threat.

Plans in place.

Go time.

CHAPTER TWENTY-FIVE

Forte had been waiting for exactly twenty minutes. In a suit. He'd opted not to sit because every chair in the reception area was the soft kind that swallowed a person if they sat back into it. And he was not in the mood to relax into any kind of comfort at the moment.

Of course, the trendy, modern decor of this office building wasn't meant to put a person at ease. It was a lure, intended to draw people inside and intimidate them once they were stuck waiting.

"Mr. Forte, what brings you to our offices?"

Forte smiled. The man facing him had the voice he'd spoken to over the phone. But this wasn't the man in charge. "Mr. Zerta. Do you do all the recruiting for your organization, or do you divvy up the duties with others?"

His host tugged on the edge of his suit jacket. "This is still a relatively small private organization. I'm solely responsible for the recruiting at the current time."

"Ah." Forte nodded, then waited. He let the silence settle around them with an awkward weight. He could be a patient man.

Zerta cleared his throat. "I do apologize for the security procedures, but I'm sure you must be used to being searched for weapons."

It'd been a thorough pat down in addition to walking through a weapons-detection unit. They'd been looking for surveillance equipment on his person. They hadn't found any.

"I can understand the need for precautions." Forte kept his expression amiable. He was there to deliver a message and see what the reaction might be.

This wasn't the man he needed the reaction from, though.

"Why don't we step into my office and we can discuss our offer?" Zerta gestured to a room completely walled in glass.

It was a fish bowl, basically. Forte made a mental note again to be happy he didn't have an office job requiring him to come to work day in and day out in this sort of environment. Hell, wearing a suit today was irritating enough, and he wasn't even strapped with uncomfortable surveillance equipment underneath his dress shirt.

Keeping pace next to him, Haydn didn't seem to be bothered by his surroundings. Then again, the dog didn't have to wear a suit.

The man offered him a seat with his back to the main portion of the office and the entrance. Forte took the indicated seat but set it so he could be positioned at an angle to have a better view of who might be approaching from behind. Haydn's presence sitting next to him helped ease the tension of being vulnerable with nothing but glass at his back.

"As you know, Mr. Forte, we'd be very interested to add

you to our team here at Labs-Anders Corporation." Zerta sat
behind his desk and began typing at a Bluetooth keyboard.
After a moment, he turned a monitor to face Forte. "We've a
proposal assembled for you, including a structured compen-
sation package to use as a basis for each contract you accept
as part of our organization."

Forte only half listened. There were people walking past
in the hallways. Some turned and glanced his way with the
same curiosity anyone might have working in the same environment day in and day out. Those people just wanted to
catch a glimpse of the new face. But there were a few, no
more than two or three, who walked by at a measured pace
and looked him up and down. They weren't surprised, and
their interest was sharper than idle curiosity. Those were the
men and woman he was there to get a look at. Or more
specifically, when he looked at them, so did Haydn.

"I think it's obvious we've put together an attractive offer." Zerta was finishing up his pitch. "A man of your skill
sets and experience is valuable and we hope you'll agree
working with us is equally of benefit for you."

Forte tipped his head to one side, pretending to consider.
"Perhaps."

Zerta's face flushed red. "This offer is extended without
room for negotiation."

Forte raised his eyebrows. "Is that so? I find that hard to
believe."

"We've already expended significant resources in our in-
teractions with you." Zerta snapped his mouth shut.

Temper, temper. This man had a short fuse. How fun.

Forte shrugged.

A vein began to literally pop out on Zerta's forehead. The
man had to have some insanely high blood pressure. "If you
aren't enticed by our offer, I've been authorized to inform

you that our organization is prepared to apply pressure on certain persons of interest in order to assure your cooperation."

"Already threatening me. *Tch*." Forte shook his head slowly. "I don't respond well to threats."

"There was a contract out on a young woman named Sophie Kim." Zerta ground out the revelation as if Forte didn't know.

"Tell me something I don't know," Forte shot back. But he had what he wanted. All they'd needed to do was acknowledge the existence of it.

"We—"

Forte stood. "Threatening me and mine isn't the way to gain our cooperation. This is not the kind of team I want to work with and you all know it. I shouldn't have to say more, but just to be sure, I'll say this clearly: Leave Sophie Kim alone. We're done here."

He walked out of the office, leaving Zerta sputtering in his wake. Haydn kept pace with him as he found his way back to the front entrance. He'd visually confirmed the presence of each of the three individuals he'd noted previously, spread out around the office as he left.

He walked out into the parking lot and wondered how quickly he was going to find himself in hell. A spot between his shoulder blades itched. They weren't likely to shoot him down right in their own parking lot, but there were eyes on him. He didn't like it, even if it was exactly what he'd planned.

Getting Haydn safely in the back of his SUV and pulling out of their parking lot took patience. He pulled out on the highway and made a call.

"Kymani."

"I'm out." Forte scanned the road as he drove with the

flow of traffic. There were a couple of potential vehicles behind him. They could be following him or they could've pulled onto the highway at the same time as him out of co-incidence.

"We've got you."

Forte ended the call. He considered calling Sophie. He hadn't told her he was coming here to do this. In fact, only Kymani, Rojas, and Cruz knew. None of them had liked leaving the ladies out of this but what one of them knew, they all knew. It was a part of the way their friendship worked. Considering how tough it must be to be partnered with veterans like them, neither he nor Rojas nor Cruz minded the way they shared with one another. They were a support network.

The scary part was that they were all going to be mad at him if he got through this.

A dark SUV pulled up next to his. Forte glanced to his left and caught the impression of a familiar face from the Labs-Anders Corporation offices. Then his right tire blew.

Gripping the wheel, he fought to control his vehicle as the other SUV swiped him, sending him into a spin across the highway.

* * *

"This hospital room is more familiar than it should be." Forte groaned.

Cruz leaned against the far wall. "This is the first time you've been the one in the hospital bed."

The sound of a stampede grew loud in the hallway.

Forte swallowed hard and looked at the door apprehensively. "Save me."

Cruz laughed. "Uh-uh. I'm in enough trouble just knowing about this crazy plan in the first place. You get to have all of them fuss over you."

"Shit." Forte watched as Sophie, Lyn, and Elisa piled into the hospital room. Rojas followed at a slower pace and shut the door behind him to give them all some privacy.

Sophie skidded as she came in, still wearing her medical boot from her stay in the same room. "Are you okay?"

"I'm awake," he responded cautiously.

She stopped at his bedside, staring at him intently. She was pale, tired looking, with bruises under her eyes.

Guilt crushed his chest. "I'm sorry."

She didn't respond, instead crouching to look under his hospital bed. "Haydn, he's lucky you came out of this without any new injuries. You could've been seriously hurt."

Oh great, she was more concerned about the dog than him.

There was a perfunctory knock on the door, then it opened to admit three more people. Forte would've called it a party, but none of them had particularly party-type expressions.

The doctor was probably irritated with their entire group. They were all becoming too familiar in these hallways. Kymani was in law-enforcement mode, there in his capacity as a police officer rather than as a friend. Captain Jones rarely smiled, if ever, as far as Forte knew.

Sophie straightened and studied each of them. Then she crossed her arms over her chest.

Forte wasn't the only one to tense.

"Someone please explain." There was an element of command in her quiet tone worthy of the highest-ranking officer in any of the armed forces.

Or maybe it was just that what she said mattered so much to him.

Captain Jones took note of everyone in the room and sighed. "I'd like to allow the good doctor to complete his checks first, then answer your question."

Sophie considered, then stood back.

Forte thought he saw sweat on the doctor's forehead as the examination moved along.

"Concussion. Bruises and minor cuts. I'd recommend a day or two of rest, but all in all, the vehicle took the brunt of the damage. He should be ready for release in the morning after a night of observation." The doctor looked at Sophie to give his diagnosis, and Forte mildly resented not being included in his own results.

"It could've been worse." Forte didn't know why he was so defensive. Especially since he was actually damned happy Sophie had come.

"Much worse." The doctor shook his head. "Each of you is here far more often than this quiet hospital can handle. I suggest all of you take stock of what it is about your lives and take steps to live healthier."

"As if you can fix car bombs or assault and battery with regular exercise and a balanced diet," Sophie muttered.

Forte choked back a laugh as the doctor gathered his dignity and departed.

"Sophie." Lyn's reproof triggered a release of tension in the entire room.

"Okay, I'll go apologize later." Sophie sounded genuinely repentant. "It's weird being back here."

"I know what you mean." Elisa sighed, and Rojas wrapped his arm around her shoulders.

Forte leaned back in the hospital bed and ignored the twinge of pain in his back. Bruises would probably be showing up for days. "Captain Jones, I think the number of people in the room is going to remain steady at this point."

Captain Jones exchanged a glance with Lyn and rolled his shoulders. "The intel you gathered by investigating Labs-Anders Corporation turned out to be valuable."

Sophie turned and stared at Forte. He studiously kept his gaze on Captain Jones. "I'm relieved."

"The video capture allowed us to confirm several operatives we've been investigating and looking to tie to unresolved cases. The connection to Labs-Anders is extremely helpful."

Ky pushed away from the wall to stand next to Captain Jones. "The files Sophie audited were account records for at least one executive of Labs-Anders Corporations. There were transactions between private accounts and organizations also under investigation by the federal government."

The odds had definitely not been in their favor there. Not only had the mercenary group Captain Jones had been investigating held a grudge with Cruz and Hope's Crossing Kennels, but Sophie had stumbled across valuable proof of their activities.

"The account records Sophie audited, those will help build your case?" Forte waited until Captain Jones nodded. "And the video I captured?"

"Allows us to go after those individuals directly." Captain Jones looked pleased, actually. "We wanted to go to the root of this issue, but it'll be good to clean up the stragglers, too. This gives us key evidence to ensure this specific group is shut down permanently."

Which meant Sophie was safe. Forte leaned his head back and allowed himself a moment of satisfaction. There were others who'd experience a similar moment out there, maybe more than they knew about. The people involved with Labs-Anders Corporation had joined either because they'd been warped individuals attracted to the company or because they'd been coerced. Hell, Zerta had attempted to threaten Forte, too. When a person had family, friends, loved ones, those people were points of leverage.

Labs-Anders Corporation had to be eliminated.

"You went in there with a camera on you?" Sophie asked him quietly.

He opened his eyes, drank in the sight of her beautiful face. "No, I didn't."

Her gracefully arched brows drew together. "Then how?"

Cruz cut in before Forte could answer. "We all got involved with Labs-Anders Corporation because Atlas's camera had been on and capturing video feed during an unsanctioned interrogation. Seemed fitting to send Haydn in with a camera installed in the harness that holds his prosthetic on him. The dogs captured the video. The handlers were just providing escort."

Captain Jones nodded.

"We're done now." At least, as far as Forte was concerned. They were all safe now and free of the shadow of this organization and the investigation.

"Your collaboration has been appreciated." Captain Jones stepped toward the door. "It'll take some time for the prosecution to complete, but we have the right people in custody. It's only a matter of time, and for now, all of you can get back to your individual lives."

The captain opened the door and exited. Lyn exchanged glances with Cruz and followed her stepfather, probably to have an extra word with him. Their familial relationship had been strengthening incrementally.

Kymani nodded to Forte and exited, too. They'd touch base once Forte was out of the hospital. With Captain Jones taking over the investigation, Ky had probably handed over all of his findings. They'd wrap up any last questions Ky needed answering.

Rojas sighed. "You know, I'm thinking we're going to go find some coffee."

He and Elisa took themselves out of the room.

No. Not obvious or anything.

It was several long seconds before he dared to look at Sophie. He'd been half afraid she'd find a reason to leave, too. He'd deserve it if she did.

She was staring down at the sheets, fussing with wrinkles. "You did this for me, didn't you?"

If he said no, he'd be lying. If he told her what she expected to hear, she'd wallow in guilt. "It needed to be done, for a lot of people."

"I wouldn't have wanted any of you to go in there." A tear fell and hit the sheet. Followed by another and another. "You couldn't have been sure you'd come back home alive."

"No. But then again, I wasn't sure I'd come back in one piece when I left to join the military, either." As soon as he said it, he cursed himself.

She shook her head. "This is why I didn't want to forgive you. Because you did it again. You would do it again. It's who you are. You are going to keep leaving and there'll be no way to know if you'll come back safe. Healthy. Whole."

It was the challenge faced by every military family. There wasn't any getting around it. Some tried to pretend. Others fought emotional battles to keep the soldier from deploying again. But the truth was, every relationship faced it and the way to weather through it varied for every individual.

"I can't promise I won't do something like this again." His throat constricted as he forced out the words. He could lose her with his honesty.

But she wouldn't be his friend anymore if he wasn't honest. It was who Sophie was. He waited, his mouth going dry. A cold weight settled deep inside his chest. He wanted to brace himself for the worst possible answer, but he didn't have it in him.

"I wouldn't ask you to," she said finally. "I wanted to be angry with you. It was easier. Because I had no control over my own life. You let me know I'd lost control way back when you left, not just in the last week. It wasn't a car bomb that took my life away from me. I never really built it for myself. And I wanted to be angry at you for taking a major decision from me."

He'd left. He hadn't let her decide if she wanted to challenge her father over him. "Your ties to your family were more important."

"So you decided." She glared at him. "I am mad at you for still thinking it was okay to decide it by yourself. You had a family, too. Parents, siblings. They still love you even if they aren't as much a part of your life as my family is involved in mine."

She was right about that. But he'd admired the way her heart could expand and give so generously to so many. She had a big family, a circle of friends, and she'd wrapped him in her joy effortlessly.

"I didn't fit." He mumbled it because she'd have a quick retort for that. "You deserved better and I decided to go make myself into someone I could respect."

She opened her mouth, then closed it.

"You asked why I left." He reached out and slipped his finger under her chin. "Ask me why I came back."

She blinked. "You were building a new life for yourself."

"Yes." He kept her gaze locked through sheer power of will. Their friendship was in pieces anyway. So this, at least this, needed to be out in the open. It was time for her to understand. "Why?"

"Because you needed to come back home." It seemed so

simple to her. And it was, but not for the reason she thought it was.

"Did I? I could've gone to where my parents decided to move, or one of my siblings. Why do you think I came and settled here?"

C'mon, Sophie, quit hiding from it.

"Because this is home for you, where you grew up."

"No."

She jerked her head back angrily. "Yes. This is home. Don't you see? Maybe you don't even know why. But I was here, and I saw you. You came back. You built Hope's Crossing Kennels here because this is home."

He shook his head. "No. If you'd have moved somewhere else, made someplace else yours, I'd have built Hope's Crossing Kennels there. Where didn't matter. *You* are home for me, Sophie."

She froze.

"I left and remade myself. When I was ready, I'd have followed you wherever you were to see if you'd have me. And here, now, if you don't want me, that's your choice. I'll respect it." It'd kill him, but there it was. "It's up to you, Sophie. This is me and I'll be a friend if that's what you want. But I want more. I want to build our lives together from here on out, and I don't know how else to say I love you."

She stood, staring at him, without moving. Hell, she was barely breathing.

He didn't know what to do, so he held his empty hands out to her.

She placed her hands in his. "This."

"What?" He spoke carefully, out of words and not sure if the next thing he said would ruin everything he'd managed to tell her.

"You went through hell and came back. It hurt my heart

to see how many ways you'd been broken and scarred. I watched you work with your dogs and heal day by day, and I wanted so much for you to be happy. I wasn't sure when you would be. But I was so determined to be there the whole way." She traced the inside of his palms until he closed his hands over hers. Her gaze met his again, finally. "I thought this week was my own personal hell. I wondered how you survived these things. And now, I'd go back and do it again if you were with me."

It was his turn to hold still, hoping he didn't break this moment. "With you."

"In the middle of hell, I've never been happier," she whispered. "I've always loved you, Brandon. And the minute you gave in and let me into your arms, I was in heaven. Even with people trying to kill me. Because I've always trusted you to keep me safe."

He tugged her hands until she leaned over him, then he wrapped his arms around her. "I always will."

"No more leaving without warning." She whispered it into his neck. Her warm lips pressed against his pulse. "If you have to, I'll understand. Just tell me."

He adjusted his grip and hoisted her up and over, until she landed next to him on the hospital bed with an incredibly cute squeak. "If I go anywhere from here on out, it'll be with you. I'm not leaving you, Sophie. Not ever again."

"Promise?" she whispered.

"Promise."

LOVE IS AN
ACT OF BRAVERY

See the next page for an excerpt from
ULTIMATE COURAGE, the second
book in the True Heroes series.

Available now.

CHAPTER ONE

You've got to be insane."

Elisa Hall took a prudent step—or two—back as she observed the standoff brewing in front of her. A tall man stood between her and the emergency room reception desk, glaring at the woman in scrubs behind it. He stood at an angle to Elisa, so he could see the reception desk to his right and the entirety of the waiting area in front of him.

He clenched his fists.

Elisa retreated farther back toward the entrance, releasing her throbbing wrist and letting her hands fall to her sides. Harmless. Nothing to see here.

"I'm sorry, sir, but ambulances take precedence over walk-ins," the nurse repeated. She was braver than Elisa would've been in the face of rage on a level with the man's at the counter.

He was dressed in loose fitness shorts and a close-fitting black tee. His hands were wrapped in some cross between tape and fabric.

"Fighter" might as well have been printed across his very broad, muscular shoulders.

Actually, now that she was looking, his tee said Revolution Mixed Martial Arts Academy.

Well, then. Maybe she should just take more ibuprofen and forget about seeing a doctor for her swollen wrist after all. Getting her injury examined wasn't worth staying anywhere near this guy.

The nurse glanced quickly at Elisa then returned her attention to the man, her expression softening with sympathy. "As soon as an examination room opens up, we'll get you in to see the doctor. Please, wait right here and fill out these forms while I help this young lady."

Wait, what? The man's face, and his focus, turned toward her. *Oh, great.*

Usually she envied nurses their ability to sympathize with so many patients and make such a difference in their lives. Now was not one of those times.

Elisa squashed the urge to bolt. Never ended well when she tried it. Better to hold very still, wait until the anger in front of her burned itself out, and pull herself together afterward.

Instead, she fastened her gaze on the floor and tried to keep her body from tensing visibly. Silently, she sang herself an inane nursery rhyme to take her mind off the weight of the man's intense glare. *Please, please, let him walk away.* They were in public, and even though the emergency room waiting area wasn't packed, it still had a dozen people scattered around the seats.

But the expected explosion, shouting, other things… never happened. Instead, the man had quieted. All of the frustrated aggression seemed to have been stuffed away somewhere.

She swallowed hard. Relief eased her constricted throat,

and she breathed slowly for the time being. Leaving remained the best idea she had at the moment.

But he stepped away from the counter and farther to her right, motioning with a wrapped hand for her to step forward. As she forced her feet to take herself closer to the reception desk—and past him—he gave her room.

Belatedly, she realized his movement also happened to block her escape route toward the doors. He couldn't have done it on purpose, could he? But Elisa took a step up to the reception counter and away from him anyway.

"Yes, dear?" The nurse's gentle prompt made Elisa jump. *Damn it.* Elisa's heart beat loud in her ears.

The nurse gave her an encouraging smile. "Don't mind him. He's been here before. I've already asked another nurse to bring ice packs as fast as possible. I don't mind if he blows off some hot air in my direction in the meantime. I would be upset, too, considering today's situation."

Elisa bit her lip. She could still feel the man standing behind her, his presence looming at her back. He couldn't possibly appreciate the nurse sharing some of his private information. And he didn't seem to need ice packs or any other medical attention. He appeared very able-bodied. "It's none of my business."

The nurse placed a clipboard on the counter and wrinkled her nose. "Oh, trust me, the entire waiting room knows what his concern is. Tell me what brought you here."

This might be the most personable emergency room reception area Elisa had been to in years, not counting the extremely angry man standing behind her. They were either not very busy—not likely if all the examination rooms were full up—or extremely efficient.

Efficiency meant she could get in and out and decide what her next steps would be.

"My wrist." Elisa held out her left arm, her wrist obviously swollen. "I thought it was just a bad sprain, but it's been more than a few days and has only gotten worse. I can barely move it now."

And if she could have avoided it, she definitely wouldn't have stopped in to get it treated. An emergency room visit, even with the help of her soon-to-be nonexistent insurance, was still an expense she didn't need. It'd been six months or so since her last significant paycheck, and she could not afford to extend her insurance much longer. Plus, it might be better not to. One less way to track her.

"Is that your dominant arm, dear?" The nurse held up a pen. Elisa shook her head.

"Oh, good. Leave your ID and insurance card with me so I can make copies. Take a seat over there to fill out this form and bring it back to me."

Okay, then. Elisa took the items and made her way toward the seating area, thankful the nurse hadn't asked her to give her name and pertinent information verbally. It was always a risk to share those things out loud.

She'd learned over and over again. There was a chance a slip of information in the unlikeliest of places would find its way to exactly the person she didn't want to have it. No matter how careful she'd been over the last several months, it hadn't been enough yet.

But it would be. This time. She was learning, and she was free. Every day was a new chance.

Nodding to herself, Elisa looked for a seat. It might not be crowded, but just about everyone in the room had decided to sit with at least a chair or two buffer between them and the next person. The buffer seats were all that were left, and most of the other people waiting to be seen were either men, or women sitting with men.

Then she caught sight of a young girl sitting with her legs crossed in the seat next to the big planter in the corner. Slender but long limbed, the girl had a sweet face and the gangly look of a growing kid. Elisa guessed the girl was maybe eight or nine, could even be ten. Hard to pin down age when the kid had such an innocent look to her. The seat next to her was open, and she was waiting quietly, hugging a big, blue, plush...round thing. Whatever it was.

Elisa walked quickly over, and when the girl looked up at her with big, blue eyes, Elisa gave her the friendliest smile she could dig up. "Mind if I sit next to you?"

The girl looked around, her gaze lingering on the reception area behind Elisa for a moment before saying, "Sure."

Elisa took a seat.

After a few silent moments, the little girl stirred next to her. "Are you sick?"

Well, paperwork didn't take much of her attention, and it'd been a while since Elisa had been outside of her own head in a lot of ways. Conversation would be a welcome change and a good distraction from the constant worry running in the back of her mind. "Not sick so much as hurt. I won't give you the plague."

A soft, strained laugh. "Same here."

Elisa took a harder look at the big, plush toy. It wasn't for comfort as Elisa'd first assumed. It was supporting the girl's slender left arm, which was bent at an impossible angle.

"Oh my god." *Why was she sitting here alone?*

"Don't worry." The girl gave her a quick thumbs-up with her right hand. "The doctors are really good here, and I'm in *all* the time."

Such a brave face. She had to be in an insane amount of pain. And here she was encouraging Elisa.

"Is there someone you should talk to about how often you

get hurt?" Elisa struggled for the right tone. It was one she'd heard more than once when people had been concerned for her. Some places had safeguards in place for...

Blue eyes widened. "Oh, it's not what you're thinking. Trust me, people ask my dad. And it's not like that *at all*. I study mixed martial arts. I get bruised and bumped all the time, and usually it's nothing, but Dad always makes me come in to get checked."

It was hard not to believe in the earnest tone. But monsters were everywhere.

The girl gave her a rueful smile, still amazing considering how much pain she had to be in. "This time it wasn't just a bump."

"Which is why they're going to see you as soon as they can, Boom."

Elisa hadn't heard the man approach. He was just there. He kneeled down in front of the girl then gently tucked an ice pack around her arm while moving it as little as possible. For her part, the girl hissed in pain but otherwise held up with amazing fortitude.

Elisa would've been in tears. The forearm had to be broken. Both bones. It didn't take a doctor to figure that out. No wonder the man had been mad earlier. She'd want this girl to be seen as soon as possible, too. She dropped her gaze, unable to watch.

"Here." An ice pack appeared in her view. "Your wrist should be iced, too. Take down the swelling while you wait."

Speechless, Elisa looked up.

The man's words were gruff, awkward. His expression was blank. But his eyes—a softness around his eyes—and a...quiet in the way he watched her made her swallow and relax a fraction. Her heartbeat stuttered in a fluttery kind of way. A completely different reaction from what she should be experiencing if she were wise. She didn't know this man and he was probably married. The girl had a mother somewhere. Where? Maybe on her way. This man was just being nice. Maybe.

Learn from your mistakes. You never know who a person really is.

"You should listen to Dad." The little girl had regained her earnest tone. "He's usually right. Even when I think he's crazy, it turns out he's right and I wish I'd listened to him. Besides, he gets hurt even more than I do. He says ice is his best friend."

"So is ibuprofen." Elisa snapped her mouth shut, not even sure why she'd let the comment pop out.

The little girl gave her a brighter smile. "Yeah. He says that, too."

The dad in question stood, his knees creaking a bit as he rose up and took a step back.

Elisa was grateful for the space even though he probably wanted to be near his daughter. His presence was intense even if his movements were all steady and smooth. No sudden or frenetic motion. Nothing to freak her out.

"Have you ever had self-defense?" the girl continued. "Dad says every person should take at least one class or seminar. It's what got me started in mixed martial arts. I liked it so much I started taking classes."

Where is your mother? Elisa wanted to ask, but kept it to herself. A thoughtlessly asked question could put a person in a worse than awkward position. Better to just stay in the conversation at hand.

"I haven't, no." Elisa wasn't sure if the man minded the line of chatter, but it did seem to keep her mind off her own wrist, so maybe it was a distraction for the girl, too. If it was, the least she could do was help a girl this sweet. "But it sounds like good advice. Will you be worried about mixed martial arts now?"

The girl gave a slight shake of her head, grimacing as she unintentionally shifted her arm. "I want to go back as soon as this is fixed. I've got a belt test at the end of the year, and I want to make black belt before I get to middle school."

"We'll let the doctor take a look and get some X-rays," the man interjected, his voice low and maybe amused. "Then we're going to follow doctor's orders to let you heal up correctly."

"*Then* I'll go back to class." The little girl was not to be deterred.

Elisa couldn't help but smile. Dauntless. So much conviction in such a young package.

"Rojas?" A new nurse stood in the double doors leading from the waiting room back into the emergency room area.

The girl's father straightened. "Here."

The nurse nodded and motioned for a young man in scrubs pushing a wheelchair.

In moments, the girl was eased into the wheelchair, big, round, plushy support and all. She gave Elisa a wave as she was wheeled away to see the doctor.

Elisa waved back.

Wow. Just wow. Elisa took a deep breath. There was one heck of a personality. Someday that little girl was going to grow into a powerful, confident woman.

Someone cleared his throat near her.

She jumped.

For the second time in the space of a few minutes, the man had snuck right up on her. This time, he was holding out a cup of coffee and a card. "Revolution Mixed Martial Arts. It's local, if you're staying in the area. There's a women's self-defense workshop coming up in the next couple of weeks. Boom made me promise to come give this to you."

Words stuck in her throat as she stared at the proffered card. The hand that held it was strong, the fingertips callused, and the nails trimmed back out of practicality rather than aesthetics. Even wrapped in tape as his hands were, she took note of those details. She imagined they were a sign of honest, hard work. The hands of a good person.

If she could believe she knew how to recognize good anymore.

This man had been very gentle with his daughter and with Elisa. And here he was, being kind again. Her chest tightened, and she savored it, this small act.

It took a long minute for her to pull her wits together enough to take it from him—and the coffee, too. His hands remained steady until she had both in her own. He didn't give any sign of impatience, didn't try to shove either cup or card at her to make her hurry despite probably wanting to get back to his daughter.

Oh no, she shouldn't keep him.

As she gingerly took the offerings, he didn't extend his fingers to touch her the way some men would.

Warm brown eyes the color of dark chocolate studied her, saw straight through her, and left her feeling exposed. "The workshop takes it slow and easy. It's assumed everyone is a beginner. If you mention my name, you'll get a discount. Rojas."

She blinked. "Oh, but that's not nec—"

"You distracted Boom for a while. I appreciate the help." His tone had gone back to gruff. "And she's right. You'd benefit from the workshop."

He turned on his heel and headed back to the ER.

Okay, then. Elisa studied the card for a minute. She was

too new to the area to recognize the address, but if she could get a hotel room with Wi-Fi, she could map it pretty easily.

Exhaustion rolled over her in a wave. *If* she decided to get a hotel room tonight. Everything she owned was stuffed into her car, not that there was much. Just as easy to sleep in her car if she could find a safe place to park, tucked away and secure. She could find an out-of-the-way rest stop and catch a little sleep before trying to find a job tomorrow morning. It'd be cheaper and not as easy to find her.

The thought of stretching out in a king-size bed—hell, a queen-size bed, even—tempted her to be reckless. She shook her head and took a cautious sip of hot coffee. This was comfort. Splurging on a hotel room was ill-advised at best.

Even trying not to think of the worst-case scenario, her heart rate kicked up and she glanced at the entryway. No one was there. Not yet. Hopefully, no one would come in looking for her.

Once upon a time, she'd had a steady salary in a corporate environment and an expense budget for travel. A king-size bed was a given. Now, she'd be glad to get an hourly job with some sort of benefits. Even fast food restaurants had full-time positions if it came down to it. But she'd try bookstores or maybe a nearby mall first. Anything fast to get an income going while she looked for a more stable position. Practicality first, bruised pride later. Better than other bruises that took months to heal.

She'd think more on it. Later, when her thought processes weren't skipping around between what she ought to do and what might come through the door at any minute. After she had her wrist examined. One step at a time.

As she worked through her jumbled thoughts, realization washed over her in a wave of caffeine. She'd completely misjudged the man at first. He'd done one nice thing after another, and she hadn't thanked him. Not once.

Elisa looked around the waiting room. A few people had entered, but the room seemed emptier somehow, without the girl and her dad. Boom, he'd called her. Had to be her nickname. Elisa could picture the girl kicking butt in a martial arts class. "Boom" was probably appropriate. Imagining what her father could do was something Elisa shied away from, but the thought was tantalizing more than frightening.

Elisa shifted her position in her seat, her hamstrings and backside aching from hours of driving. This time, it'd been too close. She'd driven up Interstate 95 for as long as she'd been able to manage it before stopping. This was about as far away from where she'd started as she could get and stay on the same continent.

Her foot hit something, and she looked down to see a stray glove on the floor, almost under the chair. She bent to pick it up and found a tag on the inside wrist of the glove.

Boom.
Hope's Crossing Kennels.

Elisa rose and wondered if she could ask the nurse to return the glove to Boom and her father. After all, they'd be here awhile.

But as she approached the desk, the nurse took the clipboard from her without looking at her. "Thank you, dear. They'll be calling you any minute now to take you back. Have a seat."

Before Elisa could say anything about the glove, the nurse had turned her attention to another person who'd just entered. Elisa jumped, then silently cursed herself. And there were two more people coming through the doors. The night was getting busier.

Heart pounding, Elisa returned to her seat and struggled

to remain watchful without letting fear get the best of her. Hopefully, she'd either catch sight of Boom in the ER area or ask a nurse to find the girl and her father to return the glove.

She really wanted to manage to thank him if she saw him again.

Acknowledgments

Thank you to Caroline Acebo for working with me to make Brandon and Sophie's story shine.

Thank you to Police Lt. Dan Pang for answering my questions regarding police investigation and to Christopher Baity, Executive Director of Semper K9 Assistance Dogs, for your insight into service dogs and the considerations to be taken for a dog fitted with a prosthetic limb. Any exaggerations or errors are my own—because sometimes we writers need to stretch a few truths to make things work—but hopefully the story is plausible thanks to you.

I've said writing can be an isolated profession in many ways. I've also given the advice to surround yourself with nifty people, people who can inspire you. Katee Robert, Philippa Ballantine, Tee Morris, Allison Pang, and Linnea Sinclair have continually been there. The ideas and energy we give one another are invaluable, and I very much hope we'll continue to support one another for a long time to come.

Those who wander are not always lost, but eventually the wanderer finds a way back home for a while. My day job takes me traveling often, and I've said before that home isn't always a building or a place. Thank you to Matthew for being the heart in which mine finds home.

And finally, thanks to my readers. There wouldn't be a True Heroes series without you, and I hope you'll continue with me for more to come.

ABOUT THE AUTHOR

Piper J. Drake began her writing career as PJ Schnyder, writing sci-fi and paranormal romance and steampunk, for which she won the FF&P PRISM Award as well as the NJRW Golden Leaf Award and Parsec Award.

Now Piper writes romantic suspense, incorporating her interests in mixed martial arts and the military into her writing.

Play Find the Piper around the Internet for insight into her frequent travels and inspiration for her stories.

PiperJDrake.com
Facebook.com/AuthorPiperJDrake
Twitter.com/PiperJDrake
Instagram.com/PiperJDrake
YouTube.com/PiperJDrake

Fall in Love with Forever Romance

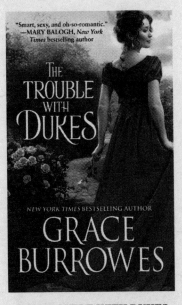

THE TROUBLE WITH DUKES
By Grace Burrowes

USA Today bestselling author Grace Burrowes brings us the first book in her new Windham Brides series! The gossips whisper that Hamish MacHugh, the new Duke of Murdoch, is a brute, a murderer, and even worse—a Scot. But Megan Windham sees something different, someone different. She isn't the least bit intimidated by his dark reputation, but Hamish senses that she's fighting battles of her own. For her, he'll become the warrior once more, and for her, he might just lose his heart...

Fall in Love with Forever Romance

ABSOLUTE TRUST
By Piper J. Drake

When Brandon Forte left to serve his country without saying good-bye, Sophie Kim tried to move on. Now he's back, and she can't forget what they shared. When her life is threatened, Brandon uses his specialized skills to protect her.

Fall in Love with Forever Romance

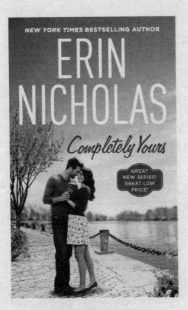

COMPLETELY YOURS
By Erin Nicholas

New York Times bestselling author Erin Nicholas kicks off her new Opposites Attract series! Zach Ashley is an EMT who lives to save people, while Kiera Connelly is a graphic designer who prefers to hide behind her computer. When disaster strikes and Zach must rescue Kiera, there's an instant attraction. The two don't agree on much, but despite their differences, they have one very important thing in common: They are crazy about each other.

Fall in Love with Forever Romance

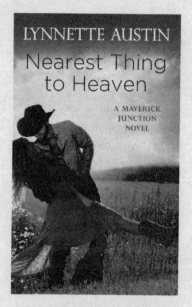

NEAREST THING TO HEAVEN
By Lynnette Austin

Ty Rawlins had a soul mate—and lost her. Now, the young widower refuses to love again. But when he meets Sophie, the cowboy suddenly finds it difficult to control his desire to wrangle the gorgeous city girl.